I Want to Be
Left Behind

Ted Noel

Copyright © 2002 by Ted Noel

Library of Congress Cataloging-in-Publication Data

ISBN 0-9725996-0-6 15.95

Library of Congress Control Number

2002095643

CONTENTS

ACKNOWLEDGMENTS

No book is possible without assistance, and this book is no exception. Its genesis can be traced to my childhood, where my parents taught me critical thinking and analytical skills. It has been said that conversation in the Noel household was a competitive exercise in which the person who spoke last was declared the victor. But this somewhat flippant description hides the fact that facts were at stake. The accuracy and relevancy of the material presented was always key.

The next thanks must go to Wil Horton, assistant pastor of Calvary Church of the Nazarene in Apopka, Florida, who listened to the Holy Spirit at the right moment to lead me over the threshold into the presence of the Savior. The Holy Spirit then lit a fire in me. I can never learn enough about our Lord's goodness.

My search led me to the true doctrine of the second coming of Christ. After seeing stacks of *Left Behind* books one too many times, I dashed off a brief essay listing Futurism's major errors titled *I Want to be Left Behind*. When my brother Dick saw it, he immediately called me and said, "You have to write the book." That simple statement had the force of a direct command from God. I suddenly became unable to work on the other writing projects I had underway. Dick has continued to help throughout the process of writing with his expertise in biblical Greek. His insights and application of the manly art of conversation has refined my presentation of biblical arguments.

I cannot leave out my lovely wife Nancy. The time invested in this project has been in large measure taken from our time together. She has endured this for months, recognizing the importance of the message. She has also served as eyes to help choose a readable typeface to be used in printing.

Kevin Shull composed both the explanatory graphics and the cover art. He put up with numerous revisions after I told him that each was the "final" form. His ability to translate poorly defined visual ideas to final art has made this book a far better tool for teaching scriptural truth.

Finally, I must thank my good friend and editor, Ed Christian. Even though he is seriously overworked, he agreed to review and edit my work for publication. The first time he e-mailed an edited chapter to me, I thought it was all my original writing, for it was a perfect match for my style. But when I saw the hand-marked draft, I realized Ed was a writer's editor. Literally hundreds of changes were made with total transparency. Later, as a major problem in interpretation reared its ugly head, Ed pointed me to material that helped me resolve it properly. No better editor could be requested. In some ways he is more a co-author than an editor.

I cannot end without thanking the Lord for his gracious gift of salvation and the prophecies that tell us of the manner in which it will be delivered. The Lord truly blesses the study of his word.

–Ted Noel

INTRODUCTION

Tim LaHaye and Jerry Jenkins have written the most popular set of "religious" books in memory. In virtually every religious store, the *Left Behind* series occupies large amounts of shelf space, with prominent displays set aside for it. Even secular stores such as Costco and Borders have large spaces reserved for these books. While they are obviously fiction, as Tim LaHaye says regarding these books, "The amazing response to our *Left Behind* series of prophetic novels . . . proves that laymen who take the Bible literally want to believe what it says . . . "[1]

Such a statement substantially understates the nature of the phenomenon. Many of these books are being read by non-believers who, through compelling storytelling, are brought to a point where they are ready to believe not only in the return of Christ, but in the specifics of the prophetic outline espoused by LaHaye and Jenkins. That outline is presented as if it were biblical truth, and as Hamlet said, "Aye, there's the rub."

We can agree fully with LaHaye that the specific sequence of end-times events is far less important than the overwhelming importance of conversion of sinners into servants of Christ. If nothing more were known than the availability of ultimate salvation through the blood of Christ for those who want it, it would be enough. As LaHaye says, "*agreeing on the fact that* He IS *coming is more crucial than agreeing on* WHEN He *is coming*" (97; emphasis in the original). But prophecy serves a far greater purpose. Amos 3:7 tells us prophecy is given to reveal God's purposes to men. And much revelation has indeed been given. About a quarter of Scrip-

---

[1] Tim LaHaye, *Rapture Under Attack* (Sisters, OR: Multnomah, 1998), 11.

ture is prophetic in nature. Much is classical prophecy, dealing with such issues as the exile of Judah in Babylon. But a substantial amount tells of the great spiritual conflict leading to the end of time. That apocalyptic material must be useful to God's people, since 2 Timothy 3:16 says that *all* Scripture is useful.

So what is the point of investigating end-time prophecies? We should first note that the very promise of future salvation is prophecy. Thus, the hope of all Christians is based on prophecy. And this hope is based on a faith reinforced by the evidence of prophecies already fulfilled. In other words, as Jesus said in John 14:29, prophecy is given to build our belief. When prophecy is fulfilled, it bolsters our faith. The fulfillment of past prophecy shows us God is able to fulfill the prophecies that are still future.

Next, when we look at the details of prophecy, we see not only the victory of God over Satan, but also many key battles of the war. These give us insight into the nature of the acts of the deceiver, thus allowing us to avoid falling into his traps. Many of these are subtle deceptions to which, without prophetic help, we might yield. Prophecy is a guide in our walk with God.

Certainly we should expect that some prophetic interpretations will be incorrect, for two reasons. First, Christ tells us in the Olivet discourse that there will be false prophets (Matt 24:24). They will be very convincing and will deceive many. Some may even prophesy with the best of intentions, sure that God is guiding them. Beyond that, because so many conflicting interpretations exist, most must be wrong. If we place our faith in an incorrect interpretation, when it fails to come true our faith in redemption will be shaken. On the other hand, if this interpretation tells us to look for something in the future, while the true interpretation tells of events *prior* to the expected but mistaken schema[2], the believer will be looking for the wrong things and so be unprepared for the real events.

In concrete terms, if the secret rapture doctrine is false, it will lead people to expect events that will not occur. Nominal Christians lulled by the *Left Behind* scenario may be expecting an obvi-

---

[2] A "schema" is an outline of events. The secret rapture is one such outline. This is not to be confused with a "scheme," which may in some cases be thought of as a nefarious plot.

ous prophetic event followed by a seven-year second chance when they will make their decision to belong fully to God. If there is no pre-tribulation rapture, however, and the second coming comes *after* the last chance for this earth, these wavering individuals could lose faith and be lost eternally because they were influenced by a false message (1 Thes 5:3). Believers in the rapture preparing for one set of events may find their faith tested when events progress toward a tribulation where they are present on earth rather than being absent in heaven as they expected. They may assume God can't be trusted, when it is actually wrong interpretations of the Bible that lead to disappointment. Many may be unready for Christ's return and so lost because of an incorrect view of prophecy. It won't be the failure to solve the puzzle that destroys them. It will be the failure of faith brought on by belief in "cunningly devised fables" (2 Pet 1:16, KJV).

With so much at stake, we should carefully consider the elements of the interpretation presented by LaHaye and Jenkins before we trust our eternal destiny to it. Fortunately for our analysis, Tim LaHaye has written *Rapture Under Attack* and Tim LaHaye and Jerry B. Jenkins have written *Are We Living in the End Times?* [3] as technical discussions of issues pertinent to the question. We will use these books as our primary sources for discussion, although other authorities favorable to this position, such as Sir Robert Anderson, John Walvoord, and J. Dwight Pentecost, will be cited when appropriate.

One area we will not discuss in detail is the origin of the rapture doctrine. Tim LaHaye has asserted that although the doctrine was considered in print as early as 372 AD, its modern roots are found in the biblical studies of John N. Darby around 1830. Various accusations that he borrowed his doctrine from the work of the Jesuit priest Manuel Lacunza or learned of it from a vision of erstwhile prophet Margaret MacDonald are *ad hominem* [4] attacks unworthy of our time. We must consider the doctrine on its own merits.

---

[3] Tim LaHaye & Jerry B. Jenkins, *Are We Living in the End Times?* (Wheaton, IL:Tyndale House, 2000).

[4] An *ad hominem* attack is an attack on the person, generally in avoidance of the argument put forward by that person.

LaHaye lays out the key issues neatly. Each will be considered in turn, based on biblical data. While we may not be able to exhaust any of them, we will study deeply enough to gain an adequate understanding of what the Bible says. This will help us assess the weight that should be given each point he proposes. We will then be able to assemble a correct understanding of the grand outline of the great controversy between God and Satan and its implications for us.

Two difficulties present themselves to us here. Our first problem is to find a short name for the position LaHaye presents. Those who believe in it often refer to it simply as "the Rapture" or "the Pre-Tribulation Rapture." It is closely associated with what is technically known as Dispensationalism. Since it speaks of a future fulfillment of the seventieth week of Daniel 9:24–27 and a future fulfillment of most of Revelation, scholars generally call it the Futurist position. Thus, the proper term is Dispensationalist/Futurist. This mouthful is further compounded by the fact that it is a Pre-Tribulation Rapture view, yielding the formal title of "Pre-Tribulation Rapture Dispensationalist/Futurist."[5] This awkward title is simply too much for either the reader or the writer to encounter repeatedly, so we will generally call it the Futurist position.

This should not be taken to mean that if one is not a Futurist one believes the second coming has already happened. Historicists and Partial Preterists believe the second coming is future, but the seventieth week of Daniel 9 is past. Our use of the term is strictly with regard to the seventieth week of Daniel, since it is the singular prophetic element on which the entire Futurist schema rests.

Our second difficulty is a result of the intertwining of many threads of discussion in the Futurist outline. If we simply present an argument that one piece of the prophecy is misinterpreted, Futurists can readily point to another thread in the tapestry. Such

---

[5] There are Mid-Tribulation and Post-Tribulation rapture positions as well. These are technical variants. In most respects (the distinction between church and Israel, a millennial kingdom on earth, the displacement of the seventieth week of Daniel 9 into the future, literal hermeneutic, etc.) they are the same as the Pre-Tribulation position, so they will not be dealt with separately to any great extent.

a discussion would be doomed to failure. No one would see the forest for the trees.

Instead, we must isolate the foundational elements of the outline and discuss them independently. It may seem at times that this discussion is moving away from the central issue, but in fact, when all is done it will provide a firm foundation upon which to form an assessment of the Futurist position. If the reader will be patient, the threads will be tied together.

The title for the *Left Behind* series is drawn from the Olivet discourse. There we find the following passage.

> "But of that day and hour no one knows, not even the angels of heaven, nor the Son, but the Father alone. For the coming of the Son of Man will be just like the days of Noah. For as in those days which were before the flood they were eating and drinking, they were marrying and giving in marriage, until the day that Noah entered the ark, and they did not understand until the flood came and took them all away; so shall the coming of the Son of Man be. *Then there shall be two men in the field; one will be taken, and one will be left. Two women will be grinding at the mill; one will be taken, and one will be left.* Therefore be on the alert, for you do not know which day your Lord is coming." (Matt 24:36–42; italics added)[6]

The italicized lines describing one taken and another left allow a ready literary device to be used. This image in modern view seems to show God taking the saints with him while leaving the wicked behind. This yields a title: *Left Behind.* Unfortunately, this is exactly the opposite of what Jesus says. He states that the time of the end will be like the time of Noah, where the flood took away the wicked, leaving the saintly Noah and his family behind, the only ones still alive. And since Jesus puts it that way, *I want to be left behind!* [7] But if this is only a literary device, we can allow a

---

[6] Unless otherwise noted, all scriptural quotations in this book are from the New American Standard Bible (1977).

[7] A Greek scholar might point out that in the Greek New Testament, the word "took," referring to those killed by the flood, and the word "taken," referring to the men in the field and the women grinding, have different roots, even though "took" and "taken" in English are forms of the same verb. This is true, but the two Greek words are synonyms. Furthermore, the "took" verse is the immediate antecedent of the "taken" verses. Jesus gives the flood example to explain the end-time scenario. To ignore the flood example and impose our own speculations on the "taken" verses is not sound interpretation.

bit of poetic license. So we must consider more substantive issues as LaHaye sets them out.

- John Darby claimed he got the inspiration for the pre-Tribulation rapture of Christ in 1828 after he saw the distinction between Israel and the church in his study of the Book of Ephesians. Few scholars who do not make that distinction see a pre-Tribulation rapture of the church. In fact, separating Israel and the church is one of the major keys to rightly understanding Bible prophecy. (*Rapture*, 43–44)

- The second key is taking the prophetic Scriptures literally whenever possible. (44) [The only exception he allows is if] the immediate context indicates otherwise. (11) Frankly, once a person starts to spiritualize Scripture, any conclusion at all can be reached. (195)

- The Hebrew prophet Daniel predicted that the Tribulation would last seven years. Seventy *heptads* or seven-year periods were determined upon the people of God, the nation Israel (*see* 9:24–27), meaning seventy times seven (or 490) years. They fell into three divisions: seven *heptads* or forty-nine years to restore the wall of Jerusalem; sixty-two *heptads* or 434 years until "Messiah shall be cut off" (Christ's crucifixion); and seven years that have not yet been fulfilled. Israel has been on prophetic "hold" for almost two thousand years, but someday it will fulfill the final seven-year period. (56)

There are several secondary issues that flow from the tribulation theory. It will not be possible to discuss them all, but some key elements can be studied. They include:

- . . . the faithful church . . . will be kept out of the hour of trial (the Great Tribulation) that shall try the whole earth. The guarantee of rapture before Tribulation could hardly be more powerful. (50) Plainly, if the church were to go through the Tribulation, she would not survive it. (62)

In this schema, the church will be removed from the earth prior to the Great Tribulation. During that seven year period, the Jews and remaining Gentiles will be subject to terrible troubles, during which they have a chance to repent. Then, at the end of the seven years, God will return with the church to set up his kingdom on earth for a thousand years. In this kingdom of peace most will be saved, but some will be lost and will be judged in the Great White Throne judgment of Revelation 20.

- Down through the centuries millions of Christians have lived out their hours and days and years . . . (in) an Expectation . . . that in the next breath, the next blink of an eye, the next tick of the clock . . . the Lord Jesus would descend from heaven with a shout and call them home. (19)

The second coming is divided into two sections. The first is the Rapture, in which the church is removed from the earth. This is a "sudden" event, such that no one left behind on earth actually sees their departure. Then, seven years later, the church returns to earth with Christ in his glorious appearing to begin the millennial kingdom on earth. As LaHaye states,

- "The Blessed Hope is definitely a reference to the Rapture of the church . . . The Glorious Appearing is quite a different matter. (77, 79) I see no contradiction in viewing the Second Coming as a single event in two phases. These two episodes, the Rapture and the Second Coming, are so different that it is impossible to combine them. One involves His coming for His church; the other concerns His appearance in power and judgment to the earth. (38)

Certainly there are other issues that can and will be considered, but this is enough for us to evaluate the reasonableness of the Futurist doctrine. If as we study these issues we find them consistent with Scripture, then we may be assured that the smaller points are likely to be correct as well. On the other hand, if we find that the foundational concepts are unscriptural, then conclusions based upon them are like a house built on the sand and cannot stand. It will not be necessary to deal with every point in the process of coming to a conclusion.

It is our fervent hope that this book not be considered merely as an attempt to prove a point. While we may end up doing just that, our purpose is to allow God's children to build their hope on the guarantees of Scripture, not on cleverly designed fables. Nor are we interested in saying that any particular person is not a good Christian because he holds to an incorrect understanding of prophecy. If we find that LaHaye and Jenkins have presented a wrong understanding of end-times prophecy, we will not say they are servants of the devil. It is legitimate to infer that the devil will use well-intentioned but incorrect interpretations to shake the faith of otherwise good Christians. But this does not mean the interpreter is consciously serving Satan. It does mean Satan is a master at misdirection, and good people can be unwittingly misled.

In this voyage of discovery, we must acknowledge those who have gone before. None of this book would be possible without their work. Perhaps John of Salisbury said it best, back in the twelfth century.

> We are like dwarves sitting on the shoulders of giants. We see more, and things that are more distant, than they did, not because our sight is superior or because we are taller than they, but because they raise us up, and by their great stature add to ours.

And now, without further ado, it is time to bring our court into session and begin the presentation of evidence.

–Ted Noel

CHAPTER ONE:

HOW DOES SCRIPTURE SPEAK TO US?

A text without its context is a pretext. –Anonymous

Bible prophecies are written in a language so different from modern speech that modern readers may readily throw up their hands in frustration. We might expect that a prophet would speak directly and clearly, in such simple terms that no misunderstanding would be possible. But God did not tell his prophets to say that in the year 2000 AD the election for President of the United States would be ultimately settled by the courts. Nor should He have done so. The details of politics are not God's primary concern in Scripture, although in some prophecies political details are included because they aid our understanding. Jesus told us that throughout Scripture the prophecies speak of Him (John 5:39; Luke 24:27, 44). The book of Revelation specifically states that it is "the Revelation of Jesus Christ" (Rev 1:1). Even though the ostensible reason for most Old Testament prophecy may be to admonish Israel and the nations around it or to reveal God's plans for them, beneath this is another, more important level, though it is less obvious. Prophecy is written first and foremost to help us know God and the ultimate victory of righteousness over evil.

The pictures painted by the prophets were a product of their time. The earliest were written about 3,400 years ago, and the most modern about 1,500 years later. They were written in ancient Hebrew, Aramaic, and Greek—languages that have no native speakers today (modern Hebrew, Syrian, and Greek are quite different). And the cultures of the writers are very foreign to our modern technology-focused world. They had none of our modern conveniences. Their life was agrarian to the core. And their daily worship centered on a sacrificial system that would repulse a post-modern world.

The politics of the ancient Israelites were directed in large measure by the prophetic voice. Their social structure and rules were established by divine fiat in the wilderness, and they modified them little thereafter. The people frequently strayed from God's instructions—apparently even lost them for decades at a time (see 2 Kings 22:8)—and eventually were taken from Palestine because of divine judgments against them. After the Babylonian exile, however, the voices of the prophets from the sacred writings remained the authoritative voice of God in the daily life of the Hebrews.

This culture and history was the fabric on which prophetic pictures were painted. Each prophet recorded the oracles given to him by God in the language of his day. "As is always the case in the Bible, the end is described in language of the prophet's past."[1] This gives us our first clue as to how we should read prophecy in the Bible. We must put ourselves in the prophet's shoes. We need to see his world through his eyes. Then the images he presents will come into sharper focus. We need to consider his figures of speech and patterns of thought in order to understand the way his ideas are presented. To illustrate this, let us consider Psalm 91.

> He who dwells in the shelter of the Most High
> Will abide in the shadow of the Almighty.
> I will say to the LORD, "My refuge and my fortress,
> My God, in whom I trust!"
> For it is He who delivers you from the snare of the trapper,
> And from the deadly pestilence.
> He will cover you with His pinions,
> And under His wings you may seek refuge;
> His faithfulness is a shield and bulwark. Ps 91:1–4

In this famous passage the Psalmist draws the picture of a mother bird covering its chicks with its feathers (pinions) to pro-

---

[1] Jon Paulien, *What the Bible Says About the End-Time* (Hagerstown, MD: Review and Herald, 1998), 135.

tect them.[2] They will be safe under the bird's wings. Of course, God is not really a bird, and we needn't believe that he has wings. This is what is called "metaphor." Metaphorical language is omnipresent in Hebrew poetry and prophecy. If we ignore that fact and expect prophetic language to be basically literal, we will seriously misinterpret the Bible. The "snare of the trapper" is also metaphorical—even in Bible times people were not very worried about being trapped by snares. To what does the metaphor refer? Small animals were often snared, but given the references to wings in the passage, it seems likely that this snare metaphor refers to the snaring of birds. We might expect the "deadly pestilence" to be literal, but given that so much of the passage is metaphorical, probably this is, too. What about "'My refuge and my fortress'"? Is God literally a mighty fortress? No, of course not. Again we are dealing with a metaphor. But is it really a metaphor of being protected by God as if one were in a fortress? It might be, but on the other hand, later in the verse God's "wings" provide the "refuge." So it may be that the "fortress" is not a metaphor for God, but for God's wings, which are in turn a metaphor for God's protection. This may seem complicated, but it's also a lot of fun, and if we read the Bible this way we can meditate on God's word day and night. We have in this passage, thus, what is sometimes called an "extended metaphor," because we have several metaphors pointing to the same idea from different angles.

This brings us to a second bit of context. Notice the way in which this blessing is expressed.

> He will cover you with His pinions,
> And under His wings you may seek refuge.

The same thought has been stated twice in different words. This is called *parallelism*, because the two lines express *parallel* ideas. This is a very common Jewish way of emphasizing an idea. Here we find repetition of the metaphor of security for chicks applied to those who are loyal to God. But let's look deeper.

---

[2] See Matt 23:37; Luke 13:34

A I will say to the LORD, "My refuge and my fortress, My God, in whom I trust!"

> **B** For it is He who delivers you from the snare of the trapper, And from the deadly pestilence.
>
> **B´** He will cover you with His pinions, And under His wings you may seek refuge;

A´ His faithfulness is a shield and bulwark.

These are the same words in the same order as before, but we have rearranged where the line breaks are found. Line B´ is the one we just reviewed. It has parallelism inside it. But when we compare line B´ with line B, we find that the two lines are parallel with each other. In fact, as we extend our view further, line A´ is parallel with line A. This is extended inverted parallelism, and is a simple example of the *chiasm*.[3] This is very common in Hebrew writing, as we see here in the opening of Psalm 91.

Why have we devoted so much time to parallelism? We will see it again and will use it to interpret one of the texts used to support the secret rapture doctrine. Because it is an intrinsic part of Hebrew thought, we may use it to help us understand the way an idea is presented. It will give us a deeper view of the statement.

This passage uses figurative language to paint a word picture of a literal truth that might otherwise be difficult to describe. This truth is expressed in words having definite real-life meanings and presenting real-life images. Their ability to present these truths depends on the reality of the words and images used figuratively and symbolically.

All of the features of Hebrew life come into view when we examine Hebrew writing. The writers of the Bible could not remove themselves from the fabric of their social, political, linguistic, and religious situation. It is the tapestry upon which Scripture was written and permeates the way ideas were expressed. When we understand these elements, we will be able to leave the flat picture painted by bare words and walk into the three-dimensional world of the writer to see his intent more clearly.

---

[3] A chiasm is a literary structure named for the Greek letter Chi (X). In the simple example we used, it can be seen that when diagrammed in this way, it looks like the left hand side of the letter. An example with more steps would make this more obvious.

2) Next we must consider the thread of his discussion. Each prophecy presents a specific train of thought. If we take one part of it in isolation, or out of context, the meaning may be lost or distorted. This would have the potential to lead us astray in our interpretive efforts.

3) Finally, we must consider what other scriptural writers have said on the same subject. Since all Scripture is inspired by God (2 Tim 3:16), who cannot lie (Titus 1:2) and does not change (Mal 3:6), all scriptural statements on a single subject, properly understood, will agree in essence. Further, earlier writers are part of the cultural, religious, and linguistic heritage of later writers, even though the Israelite culture, religion, and language developed over the centuries. Thus, we may rightly expect to see significant use of the images recorded by prior inspired authors in a later prophet's work. In fact, such repetition of thought patterns and symbols is the rule in Scripture. New Testament writers quote Old Testament writers directly over a thousand times and allude to them or echo them many more times.

When we direct our attention to the book of Revelation, it is impossible to separate the prophecy from its Hebrew heritage, since the apocalypse drips with the culture of the Israelite sanctuary in almost every line. This will require us to investigate the Hebrew roots of the images John recorded. When we do this, we will become confident that we are beginning to properly understand the message prepared for us so long ago.

Proper scriptural interpretation relies on the foundation of the inspiration of the writers by God. Behind every statement is a revelation of reality, not a nebulous wisp of aromatic aura. It is authoritative, not just inspirational. As students, our task is to ascertain the meaning of Scripture by seeing each statement within its original social, linguistic, religious, and political setting. We must then consider other statements on the same subject, thus bringing all of Scripture into an interpretive unity. And it will not matter whether we study the end times from Matthew 24, Ezekiel, Daniel, or Revelation. If we understand any one of them correctly, all the others will tell the same story, although perhaps from a slightly different perspective.

It is possible to understand the messages God has placed in Scripture. We don't have to be scholars to make sense of them. All is available for each of us to understand. But if at any time we find that some part of our understanding is contradicted by a new passage on the subject, we must reconsider our conclusions.

> "To whom would He teach knowledge?
> And to whom would He interpret the message?
> Those just weaned from milk?
> Those just taken from the breast?
> "For He says,
> 'Order on order, order on order,
> Line on line, line on line,
> A little here, a little there.'" (Isa 28:9–10)[4]

---

[4] The final three lines in this passage are confusing in Hebrew. Many scholars think they refer to the baby talk of those not yet weaned, or the way the Assyrian language sounded like babble to Hebrew speakers (the Hebrew reads *sav lasav sav lasav kav lakav kav lakav*). In the good company of the translators of the King James Version, the New American Standard Bible, and others, however, the passage reminds us of the way God's message is revealed as we carefully compare verse with verse, chapter with chapter, author with author, even though this may not be exactly what Isaiah meant.

CHAPTER TWO:

WHO, BY THE WAY, IS ISRAEL?

[S]eparating Israel and the Church is one of the major keys to
rightly understanding Bible prophecy. (LaHaye, 44)

Perhaps the most important pillar of Futurist eschatology[1] is
the radical separation of ethnic Jews and the Church. This derives
in large measure from a literalistic reading of Old Testament
prophecies couched in language promising a future for "Israel."
These prophecies certainly seem at first glance to be targeted toward the Jews. Since the Church is, on the face of it, different
from the Jews, the last two thousand years, during which the
Church has obviously been the object of New Testament teaching and exhortation, has to be accounted for. Futurists argue that
this two thousand year era of Christian influence is merely a "parenthesis" between eras where the Jews are the focus. God is
seen as having a set of different plans for the Jews and the
Church. These plans are known as "dispensations" and give the
Futurist school its formal name of Dispensationalism.

The Problem:

As Futurists read prophecy, they automatically assume that
"Israel" refers to ethnic Jews. Since the Bible was written in large
part by Jews and the Old Testament is clearly a "Jewish" history,
this assumption has a natural appeal. But any student of Scripture
can readily come up with more than one biblical definition for
"Israel." It can be:

---

[1] Eschatology is the study of end-times.

1. Jacob, who was renamed Israel by God.
2. Jacob's descendants.
3. The congregation in Egypt and the wilderness, including the "mixed multitude" not descended from Jacob.
4. The united monarchy.
5. The northern kingdom during the divided monarchy.
6. The name of the nation of Jews after the return from Babylonian exile.
7. The Church (accepted by most Christians, but disputed by Futurists).

Other definitions are certainly possible. Since there are enough legitimate definitions available to confound any interpretation of prophecy, it is helpful to identify the root meaning of the name.

History of the Name

On the way to meet his brother Esau, Jacob wrestled with God by the brook Jabbok. When Jacob persisted in this fight until dawn, God gave him the new name Israel, "for you have striven with God and with men and have prevailed" (Gen 32:28). The name itself means "God persists or "God perseveres" or "Let God persist,"[2] reminding us of Jacob's tortured cry, "'I will not let you go unless you bless me'" (v. 26). Jacob recognized the great favor granted him by God and named the place Peniel, which means "the face of God," in recognition that he had been allowed to see God's face, yet live.

The religious significance of the name cannot be overlooked. Whenever God gives someone a new name in the Bible, it serves a specific purpose. In this case the name was to direct the attention of Jacob and his descendants to their dependence on God. When they took the message of deliverance to the people around them (cf. Gen 12:3), the name would remind them of the power of the God Israel served. When they won battles under the direction of God, the name would carry the message of Yahweh to

---

[2] Francis Brown, S. R. Driver, Charles A. Briggs, *Hebrew and English Lexicon*, (Peabody, MA: Hendrickson, 1999), 975.

other peoples. The very name "Israel" would become a message to the world.[3]

This name was evidence of a line of faith already established. The promises of God to Abraham had been conveyed onward to Isaac, not because of a father-son relationship, but because Abraham had been faithful (Gen 26:4–5). Isaac and Jacob were "fellow heirs of the same promise" (Heb 11:9), implying that their heritage was not that of blood but of belief. It may be significant that the promise was not that Abraham would be the father of a bloodline (Hebrew *'am*), but of a "nation" (Hebrew *goy*).[4]

When Jacob and his family went to Egypt, the name came with them, in the forms "Israel" and "sons of Israel."[5] God led Pharaoh to allow them to settle in the richest grazing land, in large measure because they were relatives of Joseph. Egypt had been saved from the catastrophe of famine through God's grace, and Pharaoh was in God's debt. The name Israel was a herald of the Almighty at this point. Before Jacob died, his blessing of Joseph's sons Ephraim and Manasseh included the desire that his God-given name should live on in them (Gen 48:5). The honor of the name would require obedience to God which would convey the power of Yahweh to all around, just as Israel had done during his life.

A later Pharaoh did not know of Joseph or Yahweh (Exod 1:8). The passage of four hundred years had dimmed societal memories.[6] Also, the descendants of Jacob had multiplied greatly

---

[3] It is interesting to note that when the Hebrew people failed in their allegiance to God, they lost their battles. In Egypt there are stone inscriptions which describe Egypt's victories. One such inscription on the Merneptah Stele tells of taking "Habiru" (Hebrew) people captive. The name Israel is absent in defeat due to the failure of the Israelites to remain faithful to God and carry out His mission to the nations.

[4] The Hebrew word *'am* generally means a "people," but it originally meant "kinsmen," pointing to consanguinity or common parentage, which might be the expected promise if Abraham was to become the father of an ethnic group. (This usage is seen in the phrase, referring to death, "gathered to his people," found in Gen 25:8 and other places. See Brown, Driver, and Briggs, 769.) Instead, he is promised a *goy*, a "nation," which refers to an identifiable people with common boundaries, not necessarily related by blood. This word has become the modern Yiddish term for a Gentile.

[5] The phrase "children of Israel" often used in English Bibles is literally "sons of Israel" in Hebrew, though "children" is the better translation when it clearly refers to both men and women.

[6] In only two centuries, Americans have pretty much forgotten the factors that led to the War of Independence. A mere sixty years have removed most appreciation for

(1:7). They intermarried with Egyptians and took on their customs. Unfaithfulness led God to allow them to become enslaved (1:11). When Moses returned to Egypt to lead them from slavery, God had to deal with this rebellion.

> "On the day when I chose Israel and swore to the descendants of the house of Jacob and made Myself known to them in the land of Egypt, when I swore to them, saying, I am the LORD your God, on that day I swore to them, to bring them out from the land of Egypt into a land that I had selected for them, flowing with milk and honey, which is the glory of all lands. And I said to them, 'Cast away, each of you, the detestable things of his eyes, and do not defile yourselves with the idols of Egypt; I am the LORD your God." (Ezek 20:5b–7)

Unfortunately, as soon as Pharaoh increased the workload on the Israelites, they again rebelled against God, thinking their temporary allegiance with Him was the reason for troubles. God maintained His resolve in the face of rebellion.

> "But I acted for the sake of My name, that it should not be profaned in the sight of the nations among whom they lived, in whose sight I made Myself known to them by bringing them out of the land of Egypt." (Ezek 20:9)

God's *name* was the key issue. As Daniel notes in his prayer (Dan 9:19), the sons of Israel carried God's name with them. If God allowed the rebellious people to be destroyed, that destruction would act as an insult to his name. After all, they were his "firstborn" (Exod 4:22). This status could not describe their literal origin, since Adam was God's firstborn in the earthly sense. Rather, it described the fact that God had bestowed on them the birthright blessing.

This blessing was of great importance. The Israelites were blessed with the presence of God in supernatural ways. He led them out of Egypt. His presence filled the tabernacle. His prophets directly conveyed His messages to them. And His miracles showed all the peoples around them the power of God. In a

---

the sacrifices of our soldiers in World War II. For a pharaoh four hundred years after Joseph to remember him would be surprising.

sense, the children of Israel were God's name to the world. They *carried* God's name with them. Though they were generally in rebellion, God kept trying to train them and use them. "God persists" was not just a name; it was the root meaning of the name in every way. His people were meant to be an acted out daily example of the name.

The phrase "for the sake of my name," like "for his name's sake" in Psalm 23, seems on the surface to mean that though the children of Israel were often naughty children, God had to preserve his reputation This sounds rather selfish, as if God were more concerned about his reputation than his people.

There is a deeper and more important meaning, though. God planned that his "only-begotten son" would become flesh and live as a real person among the people of the world (John 1:14). For the promised Messiah's message to spread around the world, he needed to be born within a people that knew about God and could fit the Messiah's teachings into the context of what God had revealed in the Old Testament. In a sense, God chose Abraham and guided Israel so Jesus would have a metaphorical nest in which to be born.

Thus, "for the sake of my name" means, "because I'm using Israel to teach the world about me, to prepare the world for the Messiah who will more accurately represent my name to the world, to work out my plan to destroy evil and rescue whoever is willing to be rescued."

Early Hebrew Heritage

Israel (Jacob) was not a Jew. In fact, neither were any of his sons, or their sons, for many generations. The identity of a Jew was eventually conferred by the fact that his mother was a Jew, and there were no people known as Jews until the time of the Babylonian captivity. Then the name was derived from Judah, the name of one of the two remaining tribes and the name of the southern kingdom destroyed by King Nebuchadnezzar of Babylon, long after the nation of Israel was destroyed by the Assyrians. So, if we wish to be technical, there were no Jews for about twelve centuries after Israel. If we consider the genesis of the Hebrew lineage as Jewish, then we can be a bit more expansive.[7]

Abraham was not a Jew. God called him out of a heathen society. Abraham's wife Sarah was also his half-sister,[8] and Isaac and Jacob both married their cousins descended from Abraham's father. For several generations after this time, however, most of the wives came from outside Abraham's line. Therefore there could not be any Jews as Jews are reckoned today, even if the name had existed. God's chosen messengers to the world were of mixed heritage. Joseph's sons were half Egyptian, yet they were clearly part of God's people and were blessed by Israel before he died.

The people who were to carry God's name were winnowed before the exodus. Exodus 12 begins with God instructing the "congregation of Israel" regarding the Passover. This term shows that the primary meaning of Israel was religious.[9] When the first Passover took place, the sons of Israel placed the blood of the sacrifice on the doorposts and the destroying angel passed them by, but the Israelites were not the only ones who obeyed God and observed the rite. We find that "a mixed multitude also went up with them, along with flocks and herds, a very large number of livestock" (12:38). While every Egyptian household suffered loss (12:30), many of the other foreigners who had been living among the Egyptians heeded God's command.

No direct reference to this large group of mixed heritage is ever again made in the account of the exodus. But a few verses later we find that if a foreigner was circumcised and celebrated the Passover "he shall be like a native" (12:48). In other words,

---

[7] We will generally use the term "Jew" or "ethnic Jew" in the discussion to refer to the physical descendants of Jacob. However, the reader will discover that this is not totally consistent or exclusive, due to the subject under discussion.

[8] Gen 20:12, though the Hebrew word *bat* can also mean granddaughter (2 Kgs 8:26), in which case Sarah was Abraham's niece. In the NIV, Gen 11:29 reads, "Abram and Nahor both married. The name of Abram's wife was Sarai, and the name of Nahor's wife was Milcah; she was the daughter of Haran, the father of both Milcah and Iscah." In this verse "she" probably means "Milcah," but it may mean "Sarai," in which case Sarah was the daughter of Haran, granddaughter of Terah, sister of Lot, and the wife and niece and sister of Abraham (because his father's "daughter" would be classified as his sister, even if actually his father's granddaughter).

[9] Every use of the term in Scripture denotes a religious assembly. Stephen specifically uses it in Acts 7:38 to refer to the people of the exodus as a church.

the believing foreigner was assimilated and became a son of Israel. Direct blood descent was not essential to the claim of being a son of Abraham, Isaac, and Jacob, even though most Israelites had that blood descent and perhaps assumed its necessity. Belief was everything.

The term translated "native" is based on a Hebrew verb meaning "arise" or "come forth" and related to the noun meaning "seed." It is based on the idea that one who "sprouts" from the land belongs there, is planted there. This is used several times in Scripture. It can also be used with a secular meaning. For example, Leviticus 19:34 indicates that a stranger is to be treated with the hospitality due to the native-born.

The religious use of the term actually begins in Exodus 12:19, where anyone—whether alien or "the native of the land"—who does not observe the Passover will be "cut off from the congregation of Israel." Numbers 9:14 directs that there should be "one law" for both the alien who observes the Passover "and for the native of the land."[10] This is repeated in Numbers 15:11–16. While the alien is not described as a native in these passages, he is to be treated "like the native of the land" (literal translation of Exod 12:48) and subject to the same rules. Since Exodus 12:48 declares that the alien is to become "like" a native, effectively by adoption, the separation between the two groups was destined to disappear.[11]

By New Testament times, these converts to Judaism were known as proselytes (Matt 23:15, Acts 2:10; 6:5; 13:43). As soon

---

[10] The Hebrew for this idiom, *'ezrach ha'arets*, is translated slightly differently in different places. In Numbers 15:13 and Ezekiel 47:22 it appears only as *'ezrach* (native), with *ha'arets* ("the land") implied in the construction.

[11] It is tempting to extend this analogy. If one is not "born in the land" but then becomes "born in the land," this could be considered a "new birth." Could this be the origin of Jesus' statement to Nicodemus that he must be "born again" (John 3:3)? After all, if Nicodemus were to be "born of the spirit" (John 3:5), he would become a native of the heavenly country (Heb 11:16). The idea of adoption can also be expanded. Throughout the New Testament, when one accepts Christ, one is "adopted" as a son of God (John 1:12–13). Thus the incorporation of the convert to Judaism may be seen as a type of the transformation of a sinner from alienation to sonship in the family of God. Scholars have found that "born again" was indeed a term used in Jesus' day of the new convert to Judaism. Nicodemus asks, "'Can a man enter his mother's womb a second time?'" because he has already been born as a Jew, so he can't be reborn as a Jew, as well. He is puzzled—and perhaps a bit insulted—to have Jesus suggest that he needs to convert and become a Jew. Jesus, however, reveals a new meaning of rebirth.

as a proselyte completed his circumcision and baptism in the mikva, "he was in full standing in the religious community, having all the legal rights and powers and being subject to all the obligations of the Jew by birth."[12]

Ezekiel 47 figuratively describes the eschatological (i.e., last-day) land inheritance of Israel. In it the various tribes are granted specific blocks of land. The lot of the alien is also described.

> "So you shall divide this land among yourselves according to the tribes of Israel. And it will come about that you shall divide it by lot for an inheritance among yourselves and among the aliens who stay in your midst, who bring forth sons in your midst. **And they shall be to you as the native-born among the sons of Israel;** they shall be allotted an inheritance with you among the tribes of Israel. And it will come about that in the tribe with which the alien stays, there you shall give him his inheritance," declares the Lord GOD. (Ezek 47:21–23; emphasis added)

In other words, the alien who resides in eschatological Israel will not be any different from a native. He is to be "as the native-born" and will share in the inheritance of Israel.

This identical status of native and "adopted" members of the congregation of Israel is confirmed when the Day of Atonement is considered.

> On exactly the tenth day of this seventh month is the day of atonement; it shall be a holy convocation for you, and you shall humble your souls and present an offering by fire to the LORD. Neither shall you do any work on this same day, for it is a day of atonement, to make atonement on your behalf before the LORD your God. If there is any person who will not humble himself on this same day, he shall be cut off from his people. (Lev 23:27–29)

This was the most important of the ceremonial sabbaths given to the Israelites. Each year, they were to bring every sin to the Lord. Great effort was to be given to soul-searching so that no sin was missed. The KJV refers to this effort as "afflicting

---

[12] George Foot Moore, *Judaism in the First Centuries of the Christian Era.* 3 vols. (Cambridge: Harvard University Press, 1927-30), 1:332. Quoted in J. Julius Scott Jr., *Jewish Backgrounds of the New Testament* (Grand Rapids: Baker, 1995), 344.

their souls," indicating the extreme level to which this introspection was to be taken. Any person who declined to fully participate in the atonement was to be "cut off" from the people. This judicial term shows that such a person was no longer part of Israel. His heritage was lost.[13] Genetics was unimportant. Only belief and obedience mattered. Thus, a foreigner who believed became part of Israel, while a Hebrew who disbelieved ceased to be part of Israel. If this sounds like the pruning and grafting of Romans 11, it should, for it is exactly what Paul discusses there.

The language of Leviticus 16 makes this point even more directly. The goat of the sin offering (16:15) was offered for "the people." Its blood was used to make atonement "because of the impurities of the sons of Israel" (16:16). Since the only sins brought to the tabernacle were those that were confessed, "the sons of Israel" is identical to "those who were obedient to God's command to afflict their souls and confess their sins." In other words, the name only applied to believers. This is repeated virtually word for word in the ceremony of the scapegoat (16:20–22). The high priest was to confess over the head of the goat "all of the iniquities of the sons of Israel." Again, these were only the sins that had been brought to the tabernacle.

In this highest of sabbaths, the day of judgment on earth, the definition of Israel was exclusively limited to believers. The Day of Atonement continued to be valid until Jesus died on the cross. Therefore, in the central defining ritual of the Jewish religion, genetics was excluded and any believer was included. No allowance was present for a hereditary definition of Israel.

The story of Ruth again illustrates this fact. It was established law that no Israelite should marry a woman of a heathen nation (Deut 7:3). In fact, God had commanded, through Moses, that no

---

[13] Scholars still argue about the Hebrew word *karet*, translated "cut off." In some circumstances it clearly means death. To be "cut off" from Israel because of a refusal to repent and be forgiven, however, might possibly mean execution or exile, but it may refer to a *spiritual* cutting off, something God himself does without the knowledge of other people. A man could cherish some secret sin, believing in his heart that no one sees, believing God doesn't really care, and so refuse to repent before the Day of Atonement. He might then be "cut off" from salvation by God without his even realizing it! To his neighbors he may seem like a true son of Abraham and Israel, while in God's eyes he has been pruned off and is no longer part of Israel (though he can be grafted back in if he ceases his rebellion against God).

Moabite was to ever be permitted to enter the assembly of Israel (Deut 23:3). Yet the sons of Naomi took Moabite women as wives (Ruth 1:4). When the men died, Naomi returned to Judah (Ruth 1:5, 7). Ruth accompanied her, stating,

> "Do not urge me to leave you or turn back from following you; for where you go, I will go, and where you lodge, I will lodge. Your people shall be my people, and your God, my God. Where you die, I will die, and there I will be buried." (Ruth 1:16–17)

This statement identifies the fact that Ruth had accepted Yahweh. According to the Law of Moses, she was now "like a native." She had become a Jew. This allowed Boaz to claim her "in order to raise up the name of the deceased on his inheritance" (Ruth 4:10). Had she not been Jewish, Boaz could not have invoked the Law of Moses (cf. Deut 25:5–6) to take her as his wife. If the children of Israel were faithfully following God—though the evidence suggests that they weren't—she could not even have come with Naomi from Moab to Israel!

Ruth appears again in Matthew's genealogy of Christ. There (Matt 1:5) he identifies Ruth as the grandmother of King David, who was an ancestor of Christ and prefigured him typologically.[14] But perhaps more interesting yet is the inclusion of Rahab. This ancestor of David was a Canaanite from Jericho. Her presence in the genealogy tells us she became a daughter of Israel and Abraham by faith in God. Like Ruth, her conversion was required before any Jew could legally marry her, according to the Torah. Unless these two women who were not Jews by blood were truly part of Israel, the greatest king of the monarchy and the incarnate king of the universe were not "of Israel" (Rom 9:6).

---

[14] A "type" is a person, animal, or thing having characteristics later identified as having "typological" significance in helping people understand the work or purpose of some later person or thing or event. For example, the early Israelites probably had no idea that both the Passover lamb and the Lord's goat on the Day of Atonement were acted-out prophecies of aspects of the Messiah's future sacrifice, but John the Baptist identified the relationship and, later, so did the New Testament authors. With a symbol, the people using it recognize the significance, or at least could if they noticed. With a type, they may not see it, but they are being prepared to see it someday.

Prophetic Use of the Name

It is not possible here to cover all the uses of the name Israel in prophecy. But since the prophet Daniel is the focus of much Futurist attention, it will be helpful to consider the way he uses the name. Daniel 1:3 describes how some of the "sons of Israel" were taken to Babylon in 605 BC by Nebuchadnezzar. Sargon II of Assyria deported "the people of Israel" in 721 BC and resettled the country with foreigners (see 2 Kgs 17:23–24), so by the time of the events of Daniel 1 over a century had passed since "Israel" had existed. The northern kingdom had been so wicked for so long that God passed judgment on it by "cutting it off from the camp" (Lev 23:29). The natural way for Daniel to record this event would have been to describe these captives as only coming from Judah. Instead he calls them "sons of Israel." Such an unusual usage suggests a purpose.

Only four names of captives are mentioned in the book: Daniel, Hananiah, Mishael, and Azariah. These four immediately demonstrated their loyalty to God by refusing to eat from the king's table (Dan 1), even though this could have resulted in their deaths. Later on, Daniel refused to pray to Cyrus (Dan 6), and the other three refused to worship the image (Dan 3). In both cases, the penalty was death, but God delivered them. These examples of radical faith strongly suggest that Daniel's intent in using the term was to indicate that the captives were not just Jews, but at least potentially faithful servants of God.

When we get to the prayer of chapter 9, we find this identification confirmed. Daniel begins his prayer by calling on God to honor his covenant with those who "love Him and keep His commandments" (Dan 9:4). He pleads for "the men of Judah, the inhabitants of Jerusalem, and all Israel, those who are nearby and those who are far away in all the countries to which Thou hast driven them, because of their unfaithful deeds which they have committed against Thee" (Dan 9:7).

Daniel specifically includes three groups of people. We may be certain that this list is not parallelism because "the men of Judah" is a large group including "the inhabitants of Jerusalem." Therefore "all Israel" is a third group. But then this list is placed in parallel with "those nearby and those far away." Finally, Daniel notes that those far away have been sent there by judgments of God. It would be possible to suggest that this terminology includes the sum of the northern and southern kingdoms. But as we look further, that premise breaks down.

Daniel continues with a litany of the sins of his people and the righteousness of God in punishing them. He includes himself in the group on which "open shame" (Dan 9:7) falls. Finally, he calls on God to act for the sake of His name (Dan 9:16) because "Thy city and Thy people are called by Thy name" (Dan 9:19). God's reputation was at stake. It was not irretrievably wicked Jews who were causing this problem. Those people were blending into the cultures of their captors and becoming "like natives." In a sense they were invisible. It was those who claimed God's name who stood out. Their continued presence in captivity was interpreted by their captors as evidence of Yahweh's impotence and the power of their pagan gods. This put God to open shame in the person of his faithful people.

Daniel's plea is therefore for the ultimate benefit of those who love God. The captive people about whom he prays were from the tribes of Judah and Benjamin, and the country was called Judah. None of those names include God's name. But the name Israel *does* contain God's name, as does Jerusalem.[15] Therefore, Daniel is calling himself part of Israel. National origin is not at issue, faith is. His plea recalls the fact that God has brought the faithful out of Egypt (Dan 9:15) and has promised to do the same again (Dan 9:16).

Years had passed since any physical group of people or political entity identified by the secular world as "Israel" had existed— 184 years. Jacob died many centuries earlier. His descendants had ceased to be known as a group by that name since the division of the monarchy. The congregation in the wilderness was long dead, and the northern kingdom had been dispersed by Assyria's conquest. In other words, by secular, genetic, or social designation,

---

[15] Jerusalem, originally *yᵉrushalem* (and now *yᵉrushalayim*), probably meant "foundation of peace" in King David's day, but some hold that the first two letters refer to the name of God, *Yahweh*, leading to the meaning "God is peace." See the article on "Jerusalem" in the *New Bible Dictionary*, second ed., ed. J. D. Douglas, F. F. Bruce, J. I. Packer, N. Hillyer, D. Guthrie, A. R. Millard, and D. J. Wiseman (Downers Grove, Ill: InterVarsity, 1982), 567.

Israel did not exist. Daniel's use of the name identifies the name Israel with faith in God, independent of national heritage. He echoes what we have already discovered about the root meaning of the name.

It is tempting to take the time to explore every prophetic use of Israel, but space does not allow this.[16] We can, however, take a moment to consider one variant on the theme. Israel was the new name for Jacob, and occasionally in prophecy Jacob is used as a synonym for Israel.

> "Then I will draw near to you for judgment; and I will be a swift witness against the sorcerers and against the adulterers and against those who swear falsely, and against those who oppress the wage earner in his wages, the widow and the orphan, and those who turn aside the alien, and do not fear Me," says the LORD of hosts. "For I, the LORD, do not change; therefore you, O sons of Jacob, are not consumed." (Mal 3:5–6)

Here God discusses the final judgment of mankind and states that those who do not fear Him will be destroyed in the judgment. But because the sons of Jacob do fear the Lord, they will survive. The language used here is functionally identical to "all Israel will be saved" (Rom 11:26). As before, "sons of Jacob" is primarily defined by belief in Yahweh. Bloodline is not central to identity.[17]

This very brief survey of prophetic uses of "Israel" has obviously left many questions unanswered. Related discussions of sacrificial and temple language deserve full books of their own. But because we are now aware of the root meaning of the name, we can use that knowledge to assist us in the interpretation of other

---

[16] For those who wish to explore the prophetic use of the name in detail, we can highly recommend Hans K. LaRondelle, *The Israel of God in Prophecy*, (Berrien Springs, MI: Andrews University Press, 1983).

[17] The Hebrew words translated "therefore" in "'therefore you, O sons of Jacob, are not consumed'" can also be translated "this is why." Essentially, God is saying, through the prophet Malachi, "I'm going to come and bear witness against everyone who has done evil without repentance and so been cut off from Israel. I warned them these things would lead to judgment, and I haven't changed my mind about that. However, my unchanging and consistent justice and mercy is also why *you*, who are *true* sons of Jacob because you walk in my ways, are *not* consumed." The background of this prophecy is the covenant blessings and curses of Deut 28.

language we may encounter in prophecy. It is particularly important—indeed crucial to accurate interpretation—to realize that prophecies using the name "Israel" cannot be casually interpreted as referring to the entire ethnic group generally known as Jews. It is tempting to jump on the "literal interpretation" bandwagon, but doing so here will inevitably lead to errors in interpretation.

To *a priori*[18] apply "Israel" specifically to all genetic descendants of Abraham assumes as fact what the Bible itself disclaims. It would be just as (il)logical to declare that the term should apply to the descendants of the northern kingdom only, for example. But if we understand the term to mean the body of believers, regardless of the time period, we have a consistent definition in accord with the usage of the prophets. This gives us a useful key to unlock the intent of each prophecy.

We have not ignored the fact that there are other uses of the name. The common secular use for the political entities of the united kingdom first and the northern kingdom later is just that—common. But as with all Hebrew words, the name expresses a range of meanings drawn from a root. And that root is the literal meaning of the name.[19]

Israel and the Church in the Septuagint

The Septuagint is a translation of the Hebrew Old Testament into Greek done in the third or second century BC. It was well known to Jesus and the apostles and is the source of most of the quotations of Old Testament scripture found in the New Testament. One particular word used in the Septuagint is of particular interest: *ekklesia*. *Ekklesia* is the Greek word commonly translated "church" in the New Testament. If the Futurist idea that the church was a mystery undisclosed in the Old Testament is cor-

---

[18] An *a priori* assumption is one that presumes a conclusion without any consideration of alternate possibilities.

[19] This is not to say the etymology of the name was constantly in mind, but neither was it entirely forgotten. There are too many clearly meaningful names in Scripture to think parents named a son Joshua ("Yahweh saves") merely because they liked the sound of it. Similarly, the citizens of Philadelphia have not forgotten the name means "City of Brotherly Love" in Greek, even though they may not think of that every time they say the name.

rect, we should expect not to see this word in the Septuagint. Instead, it appears forty-one times. In at least thirty-eight of those instances, *ekklesia* is used in the context of a religious assembly.[20]

The translators of the Septuagint were Jewish scholars steeped in Jewish traditions. It is unlikely that they were unaware of the consequences of their word choices. They used a term describing the "called out" nature of Israel,[21] and this would become the chosen word for the religious assemblies of the apostolic era. This word is first used in the New Testament era by Christ, who, in Matthew 16:18, said the "gates of hell" would not prevail against his *ekklesia*. Thus, our Savior identifies the New Testament body of believers as being identical to the Old Testament body of believers. This is confirmed in Stephen's covenant lawsuit, when he describes Israel in the wilderness as the "church" (*ekklesia*, Acts 7:38, KJV).

In the New Testament, when a single word is used to describe the body of believers, it is usually *ekklesia*, after our Lord's statement in Matthew. Thus, when the two testaments are allowed to speak together, we find a continuity of language. Israel, from its earliest days, had all the characteristics of the church. And the New Testament writers, acting as inspired commentators on the Old Testament,[22] adopted the Septuagint description of the believers called Israel to identify believers in Christ. They saw no difference between the two groups.

---

[20] Our English word "church" is related to the Scottish "kirk" and the German "Kirche." We generally translate *ekklesia* as church, but it really means an "assembly," a "gathering together of people." The word "synagogue" comes not from Hebrew but from the Greek word *synagoge*, which also means an "assembly." Thus, these two "technical terms," church and synagogue, simply mean "a get-together," generally for worship. They are synonyms, though in the New Testament an assembly of Christians is only once called a synagogue—that name was generally associated with Jews. In the New Testament, by the way, the church is never a building but a people.

[21] See Hosea 11:1, "out of Egypt I called my son," referring to Israel, with reference to Exodus 4:22.

[22] New Testament writers quote the Old Testament over a thousand times in making their points. It is not overstating the case to suggest that the bulk of the New Testament is nothing more than an inspired commentary on the Old Testament, making clear various points that were poorly understood or explained in the Old Testament.

Use of Israel in the New Testament

Paul's use of Israel in Romans 9–11 stands out as the most prominent discussion in the New Testament of how the name should be understood. He actually begins this discussion in the introduction to the epistle. There Paul points out that all people of all ages have had the opportunity to be saved because God made the truth evident to all through nature (Rom 1:19–20). Thus, all have had the opportunity to be saved by their faith (Rom 1:17). The theme of salvation by faith regardless of ethnic heritage is the central issue of the entire epistle. Various discussions of related topics take up considerable space, but Paul always finds his way back to this central truth. It is within this framework that the natural descendants of Israel are discussed.

Paul begins by pointing out that there is no difference between Jews and Greeks[23] in God's eyes.

> *There will be* tribulation and distress for every soul of man who does evil, of the Jew first and also of the Greek, but glory and honor and peace to every man who does good, to the Jew first and also to the Greek. For there is no partiality with God. (Rom 2:9–11)

Tribulation will befall anyone who persists in evil, regardless of genetic background. Similarly, salvation comes to all without partiality. This would have been Paul's golden opportunity to point out a different plan for the Jews, but instead, he emphatically equates Jews and Gentiles. His mission made no distinction between them, since in his daily ministry he actively evangelized both Jews and Greeks without prejudice.

Paul's next example is circumcision.

> For indeed circumcision is of value, if you practice the Law; but if you are a transgressor of the Law, your circumcision has become uncircumcision. If therefore the uncircumcised man keeps the requirements of the Law, will not his uncircumcision be regarded as circumcision? And will not he who is physically uncircumcised, if he keeps the Law, will he not judge you who though having the letter *of the Law* and circumcision are a transgressor of the Law? For he is not a Jew

---

[23] "Greeks" is used in this setting to refer to all Gentiles, because of the audience to whom the epistle was written.

who is one outwardly; neither is circumcision that which is outward in the flesh. But he is a Jew who is one inwardly; and circumcision is that which is of the heart, by the Spirit, not by the letter; and his praise is not from men, but from God. (Rom 2:25–29)

The church was considered by its own leaders to be a reformation and revitalization of the Jewish faith as God had long meant it to be. As Jesus pointed out throughout his ministry, the gospel was not new. It was taught throughout the "Law of Moses and the Prophets and the Psalms" (Luke 24:44). The church was even considered to be a sect of the Jews (Acts 24:14). Jews had always been "sealed" by circumcision, as reiterated when the mixed multitude who left Egypt became Israelites through circumcision and profession of faith (Exod 12:48). This led some evangelists to feel that circumcision was an essential part of conversion.

While the Jerusalem council (Acts 15) terminated that approach, Paul here takes the time to explain just why circumcision is not needed. One becomes a true Jew by the circumcision of the heart, not by a physical act. It is the Holy Spirit within a person that marks one as a servant of God.

Paul has made his position clear here. The external differences thought to distinguish between God's people and others are of no value. God's people are all alike. They "do good" and have the "circumcision of the heart." That said, Paul points out that the ethnic Jews have a great advantage over the Gentiles in that they have the "oracles of God" (Rom 3:2). They have had the benefit of both the live ministry of the prophets and the written record of past prophets. These direct testimonies of God should have been of great help to the Jews in understanding salvation, unlike the Gentiles, who did not generally have this opportunity.

As he continues, Paul discusses Abraham, "our forefather according to the flesh" (Rom 4:1). In doing so, he is making absolutely certain that all his readers understand that there is a distinction between physical and spiritual heritage. And his first justification for this is to quote Genesis 15:6, pointing out that Abraham's inheritance came through faith. This echoes his other comment in Hebrews 11:9, where Isaac and Jacob are heirs through faith.[24] This is nothing new being taught by Paul, but the same gospel that had always been taught. And Abraham's blessing through faith came *before* circumcision. The outward sign was a seal making no actual contribution to the blessing.

> and he received the sign of circumcision, a seal of the righteousness of the faith which he had while uncircumcised, **that he might be the father of all who believe without being circumcised**, that righteousness might be reckoned to them, and the father of circumcision to those who not only are of the circumcision, but who also follow in the steps of the faith of our father Abraham which he had while uncircumcised. For the promise to Abraham or to his descendants that he would be heir of the world was not through the Law, but through the righteousness of faith. (Rom 4:11–13; emphasis added)

Abraham is to be the father of all who believe and walk with God by faith, whether natural Jews or not! Obviously he cannot become the physical father of the believers, but he can be the spiritual father. Isaac and Jacob were both the physical and spiritual heirs of Abraham, as testified by both Genesis and Hebrews. And the mixed multitude which left Egypt with the Israelites and became "like natives" were his spiritual heirs.

A bit later Paul makes what might be seen as a bold statement. Speaking directly to the Jews (Rom 7:1), he discusses the marriage statutes laid out in the Law of Moses (Rom 7:2–3). But the Jews were made to "die to the law" through Christ's death on the cross in order to be "joined to Christ" through his resurrection (Rom 7:4). In other words, the Jews are, through faith, betrothed to Christ. This means they are to take part in the marriage supper of the Lamb (Rev 19:7–10).

In chapter 9 Paul begins his detailed discussion of Israel. Beginning with a great lament, he points out the advantages the Jews have had (Rom 9:1–5). Even with those advantages, they have failed *en masse.* Then comes a difficult sentence.

---

[24] This discussion assumes that Paul wrote Hebrews, although many scholars doubt this. There are many typically Pauline turns of phrase in Hebrews. The differences in language should be attributed to the different audiences—Hebrews instead of Greeks—and probably to a talented secretary given a free hand in polishing into excellent Greek Paul's often obtuse language, which he generally dictated rather than writing himself.

> For they are not all Israel who are *descended* from Israel; neither are they all children because they are Abraham's descendants, but: "through Isaac your descendants will be named." (Rom 9:6b–7)

The problem comes first from the question of "Who is the 'Israel' Paul is talking about?" Since that is the fundamental question we are investigating, we cannot assume anything.

If we take "Israel" as identifying ethnic Jews, then we have Paul saying that not all are ethnic Jews whose parents are ethnic Jews. That is utter nonsense, since the ethnic Jewish status of a child depends on the Jewishness of his mother. If we take "Israel" as intending the body of believers, then we have the possibility that the offspring of believers might be unbelievers. That is surely possible, and Paul's statement can make sense in that fashion. If we assume the first "Israel" means believers and the second means ethnic Jews or "Jacob," that also can be true. The original root meaning of "Israel" is the only one which is consistently true here. Paul has to be referring to "true Israel" as those who believe in God, in accordance with both the original meaning in Exodus 12 and his own usage earlier in Romans.

The second statement, "Through Isaac your descendants will be named," quotes Genesis 21:12. There Abraham is reassuring Sarah that her son would be the true heir, rather than the son of Hagar. Paul goes on to explain:

> That is, it is not the children of the flesh who are children of God, but the children of the promise are regarded as descendants. (Rom 9:8)

In other words, Isaac will be faithful, and will receive the promises as a result.[25] This is once again the intent of his comment in Hebrews 11:9. And the argument is again made, using the same quote found in Hebrews 11:17–21. Only a definition of Israel based on faithfulness makes sense here.

Moving from Moses to the prophets, Paul recasts the argument. Quoting Hosea (Rom 9:25–26), he points out that it had

---

[25] Of course, Isaac's son Jacob became Israel, whose name the descendants and believers carry.

been prophesied that Gentiles would become the people of God. And Isaiah is quoted (9:27–29) to point out that only the remnant, a small minority of ethnic Jews, would be saved. Most would be lost. But there would still be both Jews and Gentiles saved. Yahweh is not a god who plays favorites.

> For there is no distinction between Jew and Greek; for the same Lord is *Lord* of all, abounding in riches for all who call upon Him; for "Whoever will call upon the name of the Lord will be saved." (Rom 10:12–13)

This statement should conclude the matter. Paul explicitly states here that as far as God's favor is concerned, there is "no distinction between Jew and Greek." His argument has been couched in detailed references to the Old Testament pointing out that the true Israel of God, the people of the promises, are those who are faithful to him. He is preaching nothing new here. All of the definitions are straight from Moses and the prophets. To be a true Jew, one must be faithful. Failure to maintain that faith is legitimate cause to be removed from the camp. But Paul is not done. The most famous illustration comes next.

Romans 11 tells of the parabolic olive tree of Israel. Paul begins (11:1) by denying God has rejected his people. After a couple of illustrations, Paul says:

> What then? That which Israel is seeking for, it has not obtained, but those who were chosen obtained it, and the rest were hardened. (Rom 11:7)

Paul could have used "the Jews" to make the point that a specific body of people had not obtained salvation, but that would deny that many Jews were believers. The same difficulty arises if he uses "Israelites," as he does in describing himself in 11:1, or "the circumcision," as in 4:12. His prior use of "Israel" would seem to indicate that believers had not obtained salvation, but that would be contradictory. In fact, no easy choice of words is available. So Paul instead uses the common designation for the bulk of ethnic Jews, and contrasts them with the chosen of God. He is not trying to tell us his primary meaning for "Israel" is the

Jewish nation. Instead, he is making the best of a bad set of choices in the available vocabulary.

Verse 16 begins the olive tree illustration. Of this, LaHaye states, "Romans 11:19 teaches that Israel was broken out of the covenant stock so that we could be grafted in and that Israel would one day be grafted in nationally [vv. 23–26]" (108). This echoes other Futurists. John F. Walvoord writes, "As Paul has brought out, Gentiles have been grafted into the place of blessing, the olive tree. The Jews, on the other hand, have been temporarily cut off as a nation."[26]

Futurists unanimously define "Israel" as being the nation of Israel. Thus, the secular state established in 1948 in Palestine is seen by them in this illustration as the logical continuation of "Israel." As we have already seen, such a definition is not consistent with the root meaning of the word.[27] But we cannot simply dismiss that view without carefully examining just what Paul says.

> But I am speaking to you who are Gentiles. Inasmuch then as I am an apostle of Gentiles, I magnify my ministry, if somehow I might move to jealousy my fellow countrymen and save some of them. (Rom 11:13–14)

As an apostle, Paul is seeking the salvation of all men. And as a Jew, he has a special burden for his own people. But he recognizes that he will not be able to save very many of them. This does not sound as if he expects that the Jews would be "grafted in nationally."

> And if the first piece of dough be holy, the lump is also; and if the root be holy, the branches are too. But if some of the branches were broken off, and you, being a wild olive, were grafted in among them and became partaker with them of the rich root of the olive tree, do not be arrogant toward the branches; but if you are arrogant, remember that it is not you who supports the root, but the root supports you. (Rom 11:16–18)

---

[26] John F. Walvoord, *The Prophecy Knowledge Handbook* (Colorado Springs, CO: Chariot Victor, 1990), 452.

[27] We should also note that in the entire 2,300 plus years from Abraham to Paul, there existed a unified nation called by that name for only 120 years. This is only one year in twenty of the span.

We must first consider the nature of the illustration. Paul is extending an illustration Jesus used by adding it to the prophecy of the olive tree in Hosea 14:6.

> "I am the true vine, and My Father is the vinedresser. Every branch in Me that does not bear fruit, He takes away; and every branch that bears fruit, He prunes it, that it may bear more fruit. You are already clean because of the word which I have spoken to you. Abide in Me, and I in you. As the branch cannot bear fruit of itself, unless it abides in the vine, so neither can you, unless you abide in Me. I am the vine, you are the branches; he who abides in Me, and I in him, he bears much fruit; for apart from Me you can do nothing. If anyone does not abide in Me, he is thrown away as a branch, and dries up; and they gather them, and cast them into the fire, and they are burned." (John 15:1–6)

Jesus identifies himself as the true vine without whom no one bears fruit. The Father prunes the branches to make them more fruitful. Anyone who is unfruitful will be cut off and burned. When applied to the illustration Paul uses, the root that supports the branches is seen to be Jesus.[28]

Paul, like Jesus, states that there will be some branches broken off or pruned. If the Jewish nation were the root, it could not be broken off. Paul is quite explicit in stating that *some* of the branches were broken off, not all. Branches are only pruned off for unbelief (Rom 11:20).[29] If the Jews were *all* pruned off, then all the apostles would have been pruned off, since they were all Jews. Also, the thousands of converts because of the ministry between the cross and Peter's vision of Acts 10 would have been pruned off. The implausibility of this indicates that another explanation must be sought.

Since *some* of the branches were pruned off for unbelief or lack of faith, believing Jews were *not* pruned off. Thus, the Futur-

---

[28] Note that Jesus is described as the "Root of David" (Rev 5:5; 22:16), and the "Root of Jesse" (Isa 11:10). It appears that Paul's choice of illustration is designed to point out that we are rooted in Jesus Christ. This must stand in opposition to any interpretation that the root is the Jewish people.

[29] "Unbelief" is a common translation of the Greek word *apistia*, but because it is the opposite of the word "faith" (*pistei*) in the same verse, it's worth noticing that "lack of faith" is synonymous with "unbelief."

ist assertion that the Jews were "pruned off as a nation" is incorrect. The future of any person is determined only by faith, not by genetics. But those initially pruned off *were* Jews, since Paul describes them as the "natural branches" in verse 21. Without grafting, the only branches left would be believing Jews, the same group that is described by the root meaning of Israel.

Paul has already pointed out in verse 13 that he is speaking to Gentiles. So when he speaks of "you" being grafted in, he is speaking of Gentiles becoming part of the olive tree rooted in Christ. In other words, Gentiles have become part of the body of believers. They have been circumcised in the heart and are following God. In the root sense of the word they have become part of Israel.

Paul next recites a litany of caution that the new believers should remain steadfast or they will be pruned off just as unbelieving Jews were. Then come the verses which seem to give a foundation to the Futurists.

> And they also, if they do not continue in their unbelief, will be grafted in; for God is able to graft them in again. For if you were cut off from what is by nature a wild olive tree, and were grafted contrary to nature into a cultivated olive tree, how much more shall these who are the natural branches be grafted into their own olive tree? (Rom 11:23–24)

This statement demonstrates that fallen Jews can be grafted back in. This is taken by Futurists to mean that the entire nation of Israel *definitely will* be re-grafted during the seven-year Great Tribulation. But that is not what Paul says. Verse 23 is quite explicit in noting that those who do not continue in unbelief can be re-grafted. That is, those who accept Christ can then be rejoined to Him. Just as they were individually separated from Christ, they can individually become whole again. Unbelievers are left as dead branches to be burned. Why then does Paul comment on the ease of re-grafting? The Jews were already in possession of the oracles of God (Rom 3:2) and did not need instruction in the basics (Heb 5:12). Since practicing Jews of all succeeding ages have had instruction in Torah, they also have this advantage.

> For I do not want you, brethren, to be uninformed of this mystery,
> lest you be wise in your own estimation, that a partial hardening has
> happened to Israel until the fulness of the Gentiles has come in; and
> thus all Israel will be saved; just as it is written,
> "The Deliverer will come from Zion,
> He will remove ungodliness from Jacob." (Rom 11:25–26)

Futurists take "partial" (*apo merous*) to imply a period of time.
Verse 25 is then read as "For *a while* hardening has happened to
Israel until the fullness of Gentiles has come in." This allows an
interpretation which indicates that when that period of time is
over, the hardening will end and all ethnic Jews will receive
Christ. Unfortunately for that view, there is not even one other
use of that phrase in the New Testament that clearly allows this
translation, so it should not be accepted. Further, the word "until" does not imply that there will be events following the end of
the time that the process of grafting Gentiles lasts "until."

> "The phrase rendered 'until' (*achris hou*) is essentially terminative. . . .
> The phrase brings matters 'up to' a certain point or 'until' a certain
> goal is reached. It does not itself determine the state of affairs after
> the termination. . . . For example, Acts 22:4 states that Paul perse-
> cuted Christians 'up to' or 'until' death. The point of 'until' is not that
> Paul's activity of persecution ceased after the Christians died. Instead,
> the point is that he persecuted Christians 'up to' the ultimate point,
> the point of finalization. . . . In 1 Cor 15:25, Paul declares that Christ
> must reign 'until' he has put all his enemies under his feet. The point
> is not that a day will come in which Christ will no longer reign. In-
> stead, the point is that he must continue reigning until the last enemy
> is subdued. . . . In the same manner, Romans 11:25 speaks of
> eschatological termination. Throughout the present age, until the
> final return of Christ, hardening will continue among part of Israel."[30]

Paul's argument here simply does not discuss events after the
fullness of the Gentiles has come in.

Next, "*thus* all Israel will be saved" is read as "*then* all Israel
will be saved."[31] This would seem to be an explicit promise of

---

[30] O. Palmer Robertson, *The Israel of God* (Philipsburg, NJ: P & R, 2000), 179–180.

[31] F. F. Bruce, *The Epistle of Paul to the Romans: An Introduction and Commentary* (Grand Rapids: Eerdmans, 1963), 222. The two changes in translation would have the key parts of verses 25 and 26 to read, "for a while hardness has happened to Israel until

Jewish salvation. But the Greek *kai houtos* means "in this manner," or "and so," not "at that time."[32] "All Israel will be saved" is the result of the pruning and grafting, not a new event at the end of it.

Futurists would have both uses of "Israel" in these verses mean "ethnic Jews" to imply that after the time of the Gentiles all ethnic Jews will be saved.[33] But if this is true, it means that every Jew of every age will be saved. This would include such obviously wicked people as Ahab, Saul, Judas Iscariot, and the various groups that were punished from time to time. In fact, when the kingdom known as Israel was dispersed by the Assyrians, God was very thorough about reversing the process of assimilation. They were so wicked that God dispersed them back into the nations from which they were called so completely that no trace of them exists today. They were made *Lo-ammi*, "not my people" (Hos 1:9–10).

To get around the word "all" Futurists find various verbal excuses.

> "Paul has previously declared (Rom 9:6) that God is not numbering all the physical seed of Abraham as descendants, but that the promises are to those who are in faith. Thus we understand the "all Israel" in Romans 11:26 to refer to this believing remnant, the believing Jews at the second advent of Christ."[34]

Pentecost avoids the inclusion of the wild olive branches in his definition of Israel. Yet this was precisely Paul's point. The grafting in of ethnic non-Jews to Israel is the means by which "all Israel will be saved." By their own rules of interpretation the language must have direct application to the real world. Thus, "all" means "all." Paul did not say "some." The inclusion of people

---

the fulness of the Gentiles has come in, and then all Israel will be saved." If this were correct, the Futurist approach could easily be seen.

[32] William F. Arndt, F. Wilbur Gingrich, *A Greek-English Lexicon of the New Testament and Other Early Christian Literature* (Chicago: University of Chicago Press, 1957), 602.

[33] It is true that v. 25 does refer to ethnic Jews as Israel, since Paul has placed Israel in contrast to the Gentiles there. He is faced with the same language problem discussed earlier and has a restricted choice of words.

[34] J. Dwight Pentecost, *Things to Come* (Grand Rapids, MI: Zondervan, 1958) 294.

from "all nations" (Matt 28:19) completes the olive tree identified as Israel, so "all Israel" can be saved. In the above quote Pentecost admits that the definition of Israel is related to belief. Yet in his other discussions he identifies in the Old Testament prophecies a guarantee of restoration for the nation of ethnic Jews. It can't be both ways. It is not possible that every Jew of all time will be saved. Paul is saying that even though there are some Jews who will not accept the gospel (a "partial hardening"), some will. And this process will continue until the last Gentile who will be saved has accepted Christ. By this time, the last Jew to accept Christ will have also done so. Paul does not say, as the Futurists suggest, that at that point the Jews will no longer be resistant. Rather, he follows by saying that as a result of the pruning and grafting "all Israel will be saved." Since Israel in this sentence *cannot* be the Jewish nation, the only definition fitting here is the original one we developed. All those who believe in Christ are guaranteed salvation. What a glorious hope! Our bloodline is unimportant. All we need do is keep our eyes fixed on our savior and walk in His way. Every person of faith throughout history is part of Israel, and *all Israel* will be saved.[35]

We cannot leave without a brief look into the last book of the Bible.[36] While the entire apocalypse is permeated with Hebrew imagery and thought, two specific examples will be examined. In Revelation 4, which is supposed to be the first scene after the

---

[35] This discussion invites a glance at the logical absurdity of the Futurist position. Two issues come to mind. First, how much "Jewish" heritage is required for a person to be a "Jew"? Jacob's descendants lived in Egypt for 430 years, during which intermarriage with Egyptians was a virtual certainty, spreading "Jewish" genes throughout the Egyptian populace. Similarly, the ten Northern tribes were thoroughly dispersed, spreading their gene pool throughout what became the peoples of Europe and Central Asia. Are all Egyptians and Northern peoples "Jews" because they have an element of "Jewish" ancestry? Second, "seed of Abraham" (Ps 105:6; cf. Gal 3:29) is a common expression describing a person's status as a Jew. Ishmael was Abraham's son and father of the Arab peoples. By this definition the Arabs are "Jews." If this definition is rigorously applied, then the Futurist Armageddon scenarios that have the Arab/Israeli conflict at their center are actually "Jew" against "Jew." The allegedly evil Arab hordes are actually righteous Jews! It's enough to make even a rabbi's head spin!

[36] The book of Revelation is quite likely the last book written, as well as the last in publishing sequence.

rapture of the church,[37] we find twenty-four elders seated on thrones, wearing victor's crowns (*stephanoi*) and white robes. While the text does not explicitly identify these persons, a probable identity may be established. The position of the elders surrounding the throne suggests that they represent the church (cf. Matt 19:28; Rev 3:21). They are wearing white, as promised to the saints (Rev 3:4–5; 19:8). The *stephanoi* they wear are the award given to the victor in a conflict, not the *diademata* of royalty (cf. Rev 3:11). Curiously, they are twenty-four in number. This number has no corresponding reference in church structure or history. But it is the number of courses of priests in the Levitical priesthood (1 Chron 24:1–4, 19). This suggests that the elders are performing a priestly function. On the basis of 1 Peter 2:5, 9, which points out that the church is called to a holy priesthood, Pentecost identifies the elders as church-era saints (253–258). But the fact that this is actually a recapitulation of the call to ancient Israel (Exod 19:6) indicates that both the church and ancient believers are in view. No distinction between them can be identified.

At the very end of the apocalypse the New Jerusalem descends. This city is the bride of the Lamb (Rev 21:9). Since the bride of the Lamb has made herself ready (19:7) and her white linen is the righteous acts of the saints (19:8), it is probable that the physical descriptions of the city are at least partially symbolic in nature. The gates are named for the twelve tribes of Israel (21:12), indicating that the way to salvation starts with the cultivated olive tree (Rom 11:24) and its rich heritage. But the foundations bear the names of the apostles (Rev 21:14), indicating that the faith of the saints is also built on the teachings presented by the Holy Spirit in the New Testament. These foundation stones are adorned with twelve varieties of precious stones, evoking the twelve stones on the breastplate of the High Priest. The River of Life parallels the description of the river flowing from the Temple in Ezekiel's vision (Ezek 47:1–12).

---

[37] In this case, the interpretation that the church has already been raptured is exclusively the province of the pre-tribulation camp. The mid-tribulation, post-tribulation, and pre-wrath positions place the rapture later.

The Futurist schema suggests that the marriage supper of the Lamb (Rev 19:7–9) is limited to the New Testament church which has been raptured. Because so much of the physical description of the New Jerusalem is Old Testament Hebrew in character, we must conclude that the bride of Christ is made up of both Old Testament and New Testament saints. New Testament saints enter by way of Old Testament Hebrew heritage. Old Testament saints are supported by New Testament apostolic teaching. In other words, there is only one way into the city which is made up of all the saints.[38] God does not have different programs for different peoples. He has one program for all time, and all parts of it are complementary.

Summary

The earliest "ethnic Jews"[39] were not Jewish by birth. They were called by God out of a heathen world and became God's people. They became Jews by faith and accepted the sign of the covenant, following in Abraham's footsteps. This was the way any person became a true Jew throughout history. The mixed multitude in the Exodus became "like natives" in this manner. And any foreigner who joined himself to the Lord in the years that followed also became a Jew (Isa 56:3; Ezek 44:9). This definition of Israel continued throughout the apostolic era. The church was "called out" in exactly the same manner as Abraham. The congregation in the wilderness (Acts 7:38) was the church in exactly the same way as New Testament believers are the church. Thus, when Jesus spoke of "building" His church (Matt 16:18), he was speaking of *building up* a church that already existed. Israel had always been the church.

Jesus and the Apostles did not preach a new religion, but a revitalization of the only true religion, true Judaism.[40] Membership in the church was achieved by the same method as becoming

---

[38] Revelation uses the word *hagion*, translated "holy ones" or "saints," not in the traditional way but as a synonym for God's people, his church.

[39] Again we are using the term anachronistically to describe Abraham and his physical descendants.

[40] This might more accurately be described as true Yahwism, since the God of true Jews is Yahweh.

a Jew. One had to believe and be circumcised. But as the Jerusalem council realized, the true circumcision was that of the heart (Acts 15, cf. Ezek 44:9). Paul's exposition of righteousness by faith follows the same root definition. Israel is the body of believers. This is why he can say:

> There is neither Jew nor Greek, there is neither slave nor free man, there is neither male nor female; for you are all one in Christ Jesus. And if you belong to Christ, then you are Abraham's offspring, heirs according to promise. (Gal 3:28–29)

The root definition of Israel has nothing to do with genetics. It is only identified with faith. Any interpretation of eschatological prophecy which relies on an ethnic definition of Israel must therefore be questioned. While space will not permit an exploration of all eschatological prophecies using the name, it may be confidently stated that all have contextual material which allows their fulfillment to be properly applied to the Israel of God, not the Israel of Palestine.

Futurists apply the pejorative "substitution theology" to the term "spiritual Israel," often used to describe the church today. This is designed to indicate that interpreters who do not see the ethnic nation of Israel in prophecy are using a liberal spiritualizing method to avoid the plain meaning of Scripture. Unfortunately, most interpreters in both groups are unaware that while the term "church" does not appear until the New Testament, the church and Israel are identical throughout biblical history. Both are "called out" (Hos 11:1; Rev 18:4), both are identified by belief, and both have the sign of circumcision of the heart. Both are based on the holy foundation of Yahweh. In fact, there is no substantive difference which would allow the careful student to distinguish them.

If the term "substitution theology" is to be seriously considered, then the nature of the substitution must be established. Since the church and true Israel have always been identical, the idea that ethnic Jews have a unique place in the redemptive plan of God is substituting ethnicity for faith. Therefore, the Futurists are the ones practicing substitution theology. The first pillar of

Futurist interpretation is based on a false understanding of the nature of Israel. Israel *is* the church.[41]

---

[41] We hope it is clear from this chapter that we are *not* saying the Christian church *alone* is the true Israel, "spiritual Israel." This is *not* "substitution theology." We are saying that "spiritual Israel" includes both truly believing and faithful Jews and truly believing and faithful Christians and anyone else God sees fit to include (see Rom 2:6–16). The true Israel has *always* been those who are faithful. The fact that there are now a million Messianic Jews shows that physical Israel is being grafted back into spiritual Israel *now*.

CHAPTER THREE:

SEVEN YEARS OF TRIBULATION?

Daniel was specific in 9:27 that the Tribulation
would be seven years long. (LaHaye, 194)

Israel has been on prophetic "hold"
for almost two thousand years. (56)

The outline of last-day events proposed by Futurists has the church being removed from the earth in the Rapture, which is the "first phase" of the second coming. Then will come the seventieth week of Daniel 9, which is a seven-year Great Tribulation. Jews will be converted *en masse*, and unrepentant Gentiles will also have a chance to convert. At the end of the Tribulation, Jesus will return to earth in his "Glorious Appearing" to set up the thousand year kingdom of peace on the earth. LaHaye and others discuss numerous other details of this sequence in many technical works.

> In order to understand the time elements in the tribulation period it is necessary to go back to the prophecy of Daniel where the chronology of Israel's future history is outlined in the great prophecy of the seventy weeks (Dan 9:24–27). (Pentecost, 239)

As Pentecost notes, the primary scriptural foundation for the tribulation theory is the seventy weeks prophecy of Daniel 9. Other scriptures fill in various details, but without Daniel 9, no chronology is possible. The sixty-nine are said to have concluded, but a two thousand-year "parenthesis" has been inserted between the sixty-nine weeks and the seventieth week, so that the seventieth week has yet to take place.

The examination of this theory will not be simple. A detailed study of the prophecy will be required. Because of translation issues, it will be necessary to examine the Hebrew. Various idiomatic expressions must be deciphered. When all this is done, Scripture will be able to speak for itself.

The prophecy reads as follows:

> "Seventy weeks have been decreed for your people and your holy city, to finish the transgression, to make an end of sin, to make atonement for iniquity, to bring in everlasting righteousness, to seal up vision and prophecy, and to anoint the most holy *place*. So you are to know and discern *that* from the issuing of a decree to restore and rebuild Jerusalem until Messiah the Prince *there will be* seven weeks and sixty-two weeks; it will be built again, with plaza and moat, even in times of distress. Then after the sixty-two weeks the Messiah will be cut off and have nothing, and the people of the prince who is to come will destroy the city and the sanctuary. And its end *will come* with a flood; even to the end there will be war; desolations are determined. And he will make a firm covenant with the many for one week, but in the middle of the week he will put a stop to sacrifice and grain offering; and on the wing of abominations *will come* one who makes desolate, even until a complete destruction, one that is decreed, is poured out on the one who makes desolate." (Dan 9:24–27)

Sir Robert Anderson comments on this passage as follows.

> "I. It was thus revealed that the full mead of blessing promised to the Jews should be deferred till the close of a period of time, described as 'seventy sevens,' after which Daniel's city and people are to be established in blessing of the fullest kind.
> "II. Another period composed of seven weeks and sixty-two weeks is specified with equal certainty.
> "III. This second era dates from the issuing of an edict to rebuild Jerusalem, – not the temple, but the city; for, to remove all doubt, 'the street and the wall' are emphatically mentioned; and a definite event, described as the cutting off of the Messiah, marks the close of it.
> "III. The beginning of the week required (in addition to the sixty-nine) to complete the seventy, is to be signalized by the making of a covenant or treaty by a personage described as 'the Prince that shall

come,' or 'the coming Prince,' which covenant he will violate in the middle of the week by the suppression of the Jewish religion."[1]

The Prophetic Context of the Seventy Weeks

We need to examine the Scriptures to see just what *God* says, not what any author says. And as LaHaye tells us, we must consider the immediate context (11) found in the verse immediately preceding the prophecy itself. There the archangel Gabriel speaks to Daniel.

"At the beginning of your supplications the command was issued, and I have come to tell you, for you are highly esteemed; so give heed to the message and gain understanding of the vision." (Dan 9:23)

Daniel is going to receive help in understanding a message received in the past. It cannot be the prophecy he is about to receive, since that is not going to be a vision. In fact, Daniel will never receive another vision. His later prophecies will be divine visitations, with prophecies dictated to him rather than shown. In chapter 8 Daniel has not understood part of the vision he has received, and this is the only vision he has not fully understood.

"And the vision of the evenings and mornings
Which has been told is true;
But keep the vision secret,
For it pertains to many days in the future."

---

[1] Anderson, 52–53. The key structure of the Futurist interpretation may be summarized as follows: 1) The seventy weeks begin with a decree to rebuild Jerusalem. It is divided into two blocks: sixty-nine weeks and one week. These two blocks of time are separated by a "parenthesis" of indeterminate length. 2) The faithful members of the church are removed from the earth at the beginning of the seventieth week, leaving Jews and unrepentant Gentiles on the earth to go through the Great Tribulation. 3) The Great Tribulation involving the "Antichrist" figure occurs during this seven-year period, after which Jesus and the saints return to the earth in the Glorious Appearing. 4) The next thousand years are a time of peace on earth with Jesus ruling in person from his new temple. At this time the Jews receive the blessings listed in Daniel 9:24. The key interpretive elements are: 1) Identification of the consent given to Nehemiah by Artaxerxes to rebuild Jerusalem (Neh 2:1–8) as the starting point (444 BC). 2) The use of "prophetic years" of 360 days to calculate the time to the end of the sixty-nine weeks. 3) The identification of the "prince who is to come" (v. 26) as the Roman General Titus. 4) The identification of the desolator (v. 27) as the "Antichrist."

Then I, Daniel, was exhausted and sick for days. Then I got up again and carried on the king's business; but I was astounded at the vision, and there was none to explain it. (Dan 8:26–27)

This is a two-part vision. In the first part he sees beasts. These represent the same kingdoms as the second, third and fourth beasts of the vision of chapter 7, which he clearly has understood, since an angel has explained that vision. Gabriel has explained the beasts of chapter 8. But in 8:13–14 Daniel hears something unlike anything in either vision. There two angels reveal that a prophetic period of 2,300 "evenings/mornings" is coming. At the end Gabriel tells Daniel this discussion is "true," but does not explain it. This so disturbs Daniel that he becomes ill.

The Hebrew used here is of considerable importance. In Daniel 8:26, the "vision of the evenings and mornings" is called a *mar'eh*. The vision he is to keep secret, however, is identified as a *chazon* (v. 13). Daniel does not understand the *mar'eh* (v. 27). The use of two different words by Gabriel suggests that an important distinction is being made. When Gabriel returns to Daniel, he identifies his message as one which will help Daniel understand the *mar'eh*. This explicitly indicates that the prophecy he is about to receive will explain the 2,300-day day prophecy of Daniel 8:14.[2]

Daniel 9:24 declares that "Seventy weeks have been determined." Virtually all commentators recognize that these are not common weeks of seven days, but are rather weeks of years. Immediately this should alert us to the fact that this is covenant language. Weeks of years appear in Leviticus 25, where the Jubilee is defined as a multiple of land sabbaths (sabbatical years—one year in seven—when the land is to lie fallow). These were supposed to occur every seven years, just as the weekly Sabbath comes every seven days. The exile of the Jews resulted in part from failure to observe this part of this covenant law (2 Chron 36:21).

The word translated "determined" is *nechttak*, and it is used nowhere else in the Bible. It means something like "has been cut

---

[2] There are a host of other technical reasons why this conclusion is correct. They are discussed in numerous technical papers and will not be explored in detail here.

off," rather like an amputation. "The usage of this verb emphasizes the unity of the seventy weeks as one piece of uninterrupted
chronological time which is cut off from a larger whole."[3] This
verb reminds us of the act of cutting an animal in two as part of
establishing a covenant, as is seen in Abraham's vision of Genesis
15. In that vision sacrificial animals were cut in two, then God
passed like a smoking oven or a flaming torch between them,
confirming his covenant to make Abraham father of a great nation.

Nechttak is not the usual word for "determined" or "decreed."
That word is *charats*, and Daniel uses a form of it in verses 26 and
27.[4] If God intended for this to be merely the determination that
in a certain amount of time various blessings would occur, he
would have used *charats*. But by saying the time is "cut off,"
Gabriel tells Daniel this is a covenant period. And since this is
intended to explain the 2,300 days, it would be related to the
2,300 days.

The 2,300-day answer (8:14) is given to the question: "How
long will the little horn carry on his evil acts" (8:13)? This actor
would attack the very foundation of the sanctuary. The ram (8:2–
4) and goat (8:5–8) were sacrificial animals, and even the four
horns (8:8) evoke the four horns of the altar. The fabric of the
vision reminds us of God's covenant and sanctuary. Thus, when
Gabriel says, "seventy weeks are cut off," he is actually saying a
seventy-week period of covenantal probation is being "cut."

Since the seventy weeks (the equivalent of 490 days) have
been cut off, the question arises, "From what have they been cut
off?" One doesn't cut "weeks" off a loaf of bread or hair or a
piece of land. Logically, "weeks" must be cut off from some
length of time. To this point, the only other length of time mentioned in Daniel's book has been the 2,300 days of Daniel 8:14.

---

[3] Brempong Owusi-Antwi, *The Chronology of Daniel 9:24–27* (Berrien Springs, MI:
Adventist Theological Society Publications, 1995), 123.

[4] The "ch" in *nechttak* and *charats* is pronounced like the "ch" in German, which is
a hard guttural "h." It is not pronounced like the "ch" in English. That sound does not
exist in Hebrew.

So they must be cut off from the beginning of the 2,300 days.[5] Further, since the seventy weeks are an explanation of the 2,300 days, they must be cut from them. When the seventy weeks are cut off, they are cut off in a single piece. If the plan were for there to be two separate blocks of time, Gabriel would have said, "Sixty-nine weeks and one week are cut off." The seventy weeks was later expressed verbally in smaller pieces for interpretive purposes, not to allow it to be separated into parts that are far apart in time.

Relationship Of 70 Weeks And 2,300 Days

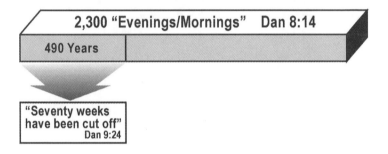

The seventy weeks are cut off for Daniel's "people and holy city." This again reminds us of the "cutting" of a covenant.[6] But more than that, it refers back to Daniel's prayer. This prophecy has not simply appeared at night like the visions preceding it. Gabriel comes in response to a fervent prayer of contrition, confession, and supplication (9:3, 23). In it, Daniel pleads for God to act for the sake of his reputation. The city bearing his name and his sanctuary are desolate and need restoration. Because of the conquest of Jerusalem by Babylon, the sacred vessels of the sanctuary were in pagan hands, the temple was destroyed, and the city sacked. Jerusalem was completely dominated by a power that gave its allegiance to pagan gods. As Petersen translates verse 16,

---

[5] Both the seventy weeks and the 2,300 days thus begin at the same time. Theoretically, the seventy weeks could be cut from the end of the 2,300 days, but that would make no sense, as we will see.

[6] In Old Testament times, a covenant (or treaty) was generally said to have been "cut" rather than "made."

"Jerusalem and your people have become the objects of scorn."[7] If God's honor is to be restored in the world, he must bring his people back so they can properly worship him in His holy mountain. After all, "How shall (Israel) sing the Lord's song in a strange land?" (Ps 137:4).

The first three acts to be accomplished within the seventy weeks are to finish the transgression, make an end of sin, and make atonement for iniquity. This list is found in only two other places. Exodus 34:7 describes God as forgiving iniquity, transgression, and sin. In Leviticus 16:21 the high priest confesses all the iniquities, transgressions, and sins of the people over the head of the scapegoat in the atonement ceremony. This is a covenant act by the people, required by Israel's true ruler, Yahweh, as part of a yearly reaffirmation of the treaty or contract between Yahweh and Israel. The people were to afflict their souls, to confess all sins before the Day of Atonement so the entire camp could be cleansed of sin. God promised blessings to those who followed His statutes, but this cleansing was not one of those blessings. Rather, it was an act required by the statutes. We must therefore differ with Sir Robert Anderson's statement that, "The fulfillment to Judah of the blessings specified in Dan. ix. 24 is all that Scripture states will mark the close of the seventieth week."[8]

Covenant issues permeate the prophecies of Daniel. In particular, the seventy weeks bring the covenant to a climax. The language may be roughly paraphrased to say, "Your people have seventy weeks to bring themselves and the city which bears the name of Yahweh into full compliance with the covenant."[9] This is not the language of promises, but of probation. Implied within this declaration is judgment and condemnation in the event of failure. It's as if Israel is being given one last chance before their contract is terminated.

---

[7] Paul Birch Petersen, *The Theology and Function of the Prayers of Daniel*, (Doctoral Dissertation), 1998, 164.

[8] Anderson, 184.

[9] We have not yet discussed the other three elements listed in 9:24. Those will be covered later.

The Starting Point of the Seventy Weeks

The beginning of the seventy weeks is specified in Daniel 9:25.

> "So you are to know and discern that from the issuing of a decree to restore and rebuild Jerusalem until Messiah the Prince there will be seven weeks and sixty-two weeks; it will be built again, with plaza and moat, even in times of distress."

This verse is probably the most badly translated verse in all of Scripture. Almost all of the difficulties in understanding this prophecy revolve around this problem. Futurists accept the reading of the NASB as accurate in the sense that it refers to the "rebuilding" of the city of Jerusalem. This focus leads Futurists to Nehemiah 2, where Nehemiah seeks permission from Artaxerxes to go to Jerusalem to build the city, since its walls and gates have been burned. Anderson quotes Nehemiah 2:5 to highlight what he considers the structural emphasis of the prophecy.

> "If it please the king, and if thy servant hath found favour in thy sight, that thou wouldest send me unto Judah, unto THE CITY of my fathers' sepulchres, THAT I MAY BUILD IT."[10]

The permission granted to him is the only royal act in the pertinent era involving construction in Jerusalem. As such, it seems to be a good fit with the prophecy. However, it has some serious problems.

First, there is no decree in the text. Nehemiah presents his request (Neh 2:3, 5) and the king consents (2:6). There is no record of a royal pronouncement. Nehemiah has to make a special request for letters of safe passage and provision (2:7–8) that would be unnecessary if a decree had been issued.

Daniel 9:25 states that there will be "seven weeks and sixty-two weeks." It is commonly suggested that forty-nine years was the period of rebuilding Jerusalem. But Nehemiah completed his task of repairing the gates and walls in fifty-two days (Neh 6:15).

---

[10] Ibid, 60. Quotation from the KJV. Emphasis in the original.

Since "(t)here can be no loose reckoning in a Divine chronology" (Anderson, 122), another answer must be sought. The decree is specified in Hebrew with two hiphil infinitives. These two verbs cause an event to take place on their common object: Jerusalem. This creates a major problem for the Futurist view. If Jerusalem is to be rebuilt, Jerusalem must also be restored. This may not seem to be a difficulty to the modern mind, but it is a severe problem in Hebrew. We think of restoration projects involving historical buildings, but in Hebrew, the verb *shuv* has no such uses.[11] In over a thousand biblical cases, *shuv* never applies directly to physical objects. A town or other property may be "restored," but that action refers to restoring ownership and control, not rebuilding structures. Every biblical use of the word revolves around the primary thought of turning, and is an action by or on people. Thus, the restored Jerusalem cannot be the physical city unless the ownership and control of the city is in view.

No decree exists that restores control of the city to the exiles and also directs its rebuilding. But Anderson suggests the rebuilding of the walls and gates under Nehemiah "was nothing less than the restoration of the autonomy of Judah" (62). This is asserted because a city without intact walls was supposedly incapable of autonomous existence. While this may potentially be true, we must reject this idea, since there is no decree in view and the autonomy is inferred, not conferred.

Any candidate decree must first be a decree, and then it must restore Jerusalem, either by explicitly returning its autonomy or returning the people, or both. But more than that, a true restoration must reverse the desolation God inflicted on Jerusalem in the person of Nebuchadnezzar when that king destroyed the temple and removed its sacred vessels to Babylon. Since "the religion of the Jew knows no worship apart from the hill of Zion" (Anderson, 62), it must restore the ability of the Jews to properly

---

11 *Shuv* is usually translated "return" or "turn," depending on the context. It is often used when God pleads with his people to "return" to him. When used in this way, it is synonymous with the word "repent." Similarly, the New Living Translation translates the Greek word usually translated "repent" as "turn away from sin and toward God."

worship in Jerusalem. Preconditions for this include the presence of people in Jerusalem and a rebuilt temple.

The second action which must take place is "building" Jerusalem. We have already found that no candidate decree exists which satisfies the restoration requirement as well as commanding the rebuilding of the city. This suggests that God got the prophecy wrong, but there is another legitimate translation possible for the Hebrew verb *banah*, usually translated "build."

If we accept the perspective on restoration that focuses on the people of Jerusalem, we would have a decree that "builds" people. This is obviously nonsense, but it is possible to "build up" people. And the word used, *banah*, would be the same. This exact usage appears in Jeremiah's prophecy regarding the exile to Babylon.

> Thus says the LORD concerning all My wicked neighbors who strike at the inheritance with which I have endowed My people Israel, "Behold I am about to uproot them from their land and will uproot the house of Judah from among them. And it will come about that after I have uprooted them, I will again have compassion on them; and I will bring them back, each one to his inheritance and each one to his land. Then it will come about that if they will really learn the ways of My people, to swear by My name, 'As the LORD lives,' even as they taught My people to swear by Baal, then they will be **built up** [*banah*] in the midst of My people." (Jer 12:14–16; emphasis added)

Those who would return to God's ways would be "built up." This expression indicates permanence and prominence. Four times in the Old Testament this expression is used regarding individuals to be built (up).[12] This word occurs six times in reference to families.[13] Fourteen times we find that God would *banah* a "house" for someone.[14] These figurative statements speak of dynasties God would establish for the king in question. Since they

---

[12] Different translations render *banah* as either "built" or "built up" in the passages cited. The passages included in this discussion for "built up" are ones that can be translated "built up" and remain consistent to the context. The four verses where *banah* can be taken as "built up" with regard to individuals are Job 22:32, Ps 28:5, Jer 12:16, and Mal 3:15.

[13] Gen 16:2; 30:3; Deut 25:9; Ruth 4:11; Prov 14:1; 24:3.

[14] 1 Sam 2:35; 2 Sam 7:13, 27; 1 Kgs 11:38 (twice); 1 Chron 17:10, 25; Ps 89:4; 127:1; 147:2; Jer 18:9; 33:7; 42:10; 45:4.

did not yet exist, it is appropriate to say that they would be "built" from nothing, but at the same time, since the emphasis is on the enduring nature of the "house," it is also legitimate to translate the word in the passages as "built up," as the translators have done in some cases.[15] On ten occasions *banah* is used eschatologically.[16] In these passages, various expressions are used to describe the ultimate prominence of God's kingdom, from building the temple to building up Judah. Because of the prophetic focus on the greatness and permanence of the "house of God," *banah* can be legitimately understood in the sense of "build up" in these texts.

With this mass of lexical evidence, it is proper to suggest an alternate to the standard translation of "to restore and to build Jerusalem." Remaining completely faithful to the Hebrew we may read this passage as "to restore and to build up Jerusalem." This then identifies Jerusalem as the people, where the name is used *pars pro toto*.[17] The proper decree to fulfill the prophecy will be one which restores the people to Israel with self-government and also restores the house of God with its sacred vessels and worship.

Only three legitimate candidate decrees exist. In the first (Ezra 1), Cyrus frees the exiles to return to Judea, and sends with them a substantial part of the furnishings of the temple taken by Nebuchadnezzar. Instructions are given that the temple should be rebuilt. This decree is the first step in the restoration of Yahweh's good name. The destruction of the temple and removal of sacred vessels have in effect said that Nabu, Bel, and Sin[18] are stronger than Yahweh. But this decree is insufficient to meet the specifications, since it includes no provision for autonomy.

As the returning exiles begin to rebuild, surrounding satraps become upset and prevail on Artaxerxes (Ezra 4) to order that

---

[15] In the NASB, Ps 89:4, 147:2, Jer 18:9, and 42:10 are translated "build up."

[16] Ps 51:18; 69:35; 102:16; Isa 60:10; Jer 24:6; 31:28; Ezek 26:14; Zech 6:12, 13, 15.

[17] *Pars pro toto* literally translates "part for all." It means the use of the name of a single person or city to represent a group. The prototype of this usage is the identification of the people of God as "Israel" or "Jacob," as established in chapter 2. Similarly, in the Bible "Babylon" means not only the city but its people, its empire, or what it symbolizes.

[18] Nabu, Bel, and Sin were pagan Babylonian deities.

work be stopped.[19] When Darius ascends the throne, Zerubbabel leads in the rebuilding of the temple (Ezra 5). There is again opposition, which leads to a search of the archives. Darius then reissues the decree of Cyrus. As with the original decree of Cyrus, Scripture includes considerable detail, but it does not meet the specifications of Daniel 9:25.

The final decree is found in Ezra 7. In the seventh year of Artaxerxes Longimanus, after the temple is completed (6:15), Ezra is granted a decree allowing any Israelite in the Medo-Persian empire to return to Jerusalem (7:13).[20] The king "freely offered to the God of Israel" gold and silver (7:15) as well as the last of the sacred vessels taken by Nebuchadnezzar. Other offerings are included from "all the silver and gold which you shall find in the whole province of Babylon" (7:16).[21] These are to be "offered on the altar of the house of God which is in Jerusalem" (7:17). Other specifics are included which add up to a full restoration of the worship of God in a fully furnished temple. Artaxerxes then continues with a full restoration of civil authority for the returned exiles. Magistrates and judges are to be appointed to apply the law of God in Judea (7:25–26). He even provides for teachers of the law.

This decree fully restores Jerusalem. The autonomy of the city is explicitly re-established under the laws of God. The rebuilt temple can now be properly used for the worship of God, complete with all the sacred vessels. Artaxerxes further indicates his submission to God by providing gifts for the temple from both the royal treasury and the people of the land. Even the treasurers of neighboring provinces (7:21–22) are required to contribute. But most important is the reason stated in the decree.

---

[19] Artaxerxes in this passage should not be confused with Artaxerxes Longimanus, who issued the decree in Ezra 7 and consented for Nehemiah to return and repair the walls. This is likely to have been the throne name of Smerdis, a usurper to the Medo-Persian throne who preceded Darius Hystaspes.

[20] Siegfried H. Horn, Lynn H. Wood, *The Chronology of Ezra 7* (Washington: Review and Herald, 1953), 117. This decree was issued in the fall of 458 BC. It "went forth" from Babylon on the first day of the first month (Ezra 7:9) and arrived in Judea in the fifth month (7:8). Shortly thereafter it was published to the governors around Judea, giving it an effective date of August/September of 457 BC.

[21] This is reminiscent of the plundering of Egypt that occurred when the Israelites left Egypt (Exod 12:35–36).

Whatever is commanded by the God of heaven, let it be done with zeal for the house of the God of heaven, lest there be wrath against the kingdom of the king and his sons. (Ezra 7:23)

Artaxerxes makes it clear that he is submitting his authority to the God of heaven. By all the related actions in the decree he makes it clear that all of his subordinates are to respect Yahweh as well. Ezra confirms this effect (7:28). In this way Jerusalem becomes more prominent in the world. It is "built up." This is a complete and exact match to the specifications given by Gabriel. Artaxerxes has issued the decree "to restore and to build up Jerusalem." As a final note, Ezra identifies this decree as something God has put in the king's heart (7:27), suggesting that Ezra understands its prophetic significance.[22]

Daniel 9:25 says Jerusalem will be "restored and built up." We do not need to revisit the derivation of this language, since it is identical to what we have just covered. But the next phrase does require attention. The KJV says the restoration will be "with streets and a wall." The NASB reads "with plaza and moat." The first word, *rehob*, means a wide place. Since streets were generally narrow, "plaza" or "square" (RSV) is the preferred reading. The second word is one we have seen before: *charats*.

The root meaning of *charats* is "to cut." Thus we find that the NASB and NIV indicate that there will be a moat or trench. But Jerusalem has never had a moat, and the Old Testament only uses *charats* in the concrete sense once.[23] Its primary usage is with regard to decision-making.[24] In Old Testament times civil decisions were carried out in the square near the city gate. If we read this phrase as "square and decision making," then we have encountered an idiom which describes having both the place and power of independent civil authority. This is a perfect description of the civil autonomy granted in the decree of Ezra 7. No further search

---

[22] The entire text of the decree is included in the account in Ezra 7 in its original Aramaic so that it is possible to verify that if fulfills the criteria in Daniel 9:25. The decrees of Cyrus and Darius are only quoted in part.

[23] Lev 22:22 uses *charats* to refer to injured or mutilated animals unfit for sacrifice.

[24] Perhaps the best example of this is Joel 3:14, where the word is used in the repeated phrase "Valley of Decision."

is necessary. When properly translated, the specifications in Daniel 9:25 are matched in exacting detail by the decree given by Artaxerxes in his seventh year.[25]

"Until Messiah the Prince"

The first segment of the decree is seven weeks or forty-nine years. Some have suggested that this was the time required to rebuild Jerusalem. As we have already seen, this was not the intent of the decree. Also, since no city is ever fully completed, we should not expect to find any record of completion, and none exists. Instead, this is the length of the jubilee cycle. In part, the Babylonian captivity was a result of the failure to observe the land sabbaths and jubilees (2 Chron 36:21). The restoration might then be expected to fall on the jubilee, and it does. The returnees with Ezra arrived in Judea in August of 457 BC. They were able then to present the decree to the Babylonian officials in the province just in time to celebrate the fall feasts with the Jews who had returned to Jerusalem before them.[26] This allowed them to announce the freedom from slavery to Babylon as the jubilee, precisely at the time that all slaves should be freed (Lev 25:8–10, 13). Seven weeks of years later would be the next jubilee, and would be a celebration not of rebuilding, but of accomplished restoration and building up.

It is now relatively simple to calculate the time when the Messiah should arrive. At the end of seven weeks of years and sixty-two weeks of years, Daniel is told (483 actual years), "Messiah the Prince" will begin his ministry.[27] Beginning with 457 BC, a period

---

[25] Anderson writes, "The movement of the seventh of Artaxerxes was chiefly a religious revival, sanctioned and subsidized by royal favor; but the event of his twentieth year was nothing less than the restoration of the autonomy of Judah" (62). We must vigorously disagree with this suggestion, since this is only an inference. Daniel 9:25 requires an explicit decree, and the "decree" of Artaxerxes' twentieth year is not even a decree, and does not meet its specifications in any particular.

[26] The religious year began in the first month (on the 14th day of which the Passover was celebrated), about March of our modern calendar. The civil year, beginning from which the jubilee was counted, began in the seventh month, around September. Sabbatical and jubilee years were supposed to begin right after the Feast of Tabernacles, or Booths, the last feast of the religious year.

[27] Why doesn't the prophecy point to the date of Jesus' birth? Because a king is anointed at the time he begins his reign, not at his birth.

of 483 years takes us to 27 AD.[28] Luke supplies the next piece of chronological data by locating Jesus' baptism in the "fifteenth year of Tiberius Caesar" (Luke 3:1). By the Roman calendar, this would be in a twelve month period beginning August 19, 28 AD. But Luke was born in a part of the empire which used the Syrian calendar and royal chronology. He was also a convert to Christianity, which used the Jewish calendar and royal chronology. Both of these methods place the fifteenth year in the twelve months beginning Tishri 1, 27 AD.[29] The other VIPs in Luke's discussion fit this timing. Jesus' baptism was in the fall of 27 AD, precisely as predicted by the prophecy, giving us a firm anchor for the chronology of Jesus' ministry.

As Jesus was baptized, "the Holy Spirit descended upon Him in bodily form like a dove, and a voice came out of heaven, 'Thou art My beloved Son, in Thee I am well-pleased'" (Luke 3:22). With this divine announcement the Messiah was manifested to the world.[30]

Literally translated, the second half of verse 22 reads: "You are my son, the chosen. Today I have brought you forth." We must compare this with Psalm 2:7: "I will surely tell of the decree of the LORD: He said to Me, 'Thou art My Son, Today I have begotten Thee.'"[31] The literal Hebrew of this passage states "today I have brought you forth." Jesus' baptism was a direct, word for word fulfillment of this messianic Psalm, a specific declaration that at the moment of His baptism, he was the Messiah, he began his reign, the Kingdom of God had arrived. This is particularly fitting, since the word *mashiach* means, "anointed one," and at that moment, Jesus was anointed with the Holy Spirit.

---

[28] If you've worked the math and come to 26 AD, you've forgotten that there was no year zero.

[29] Tishri was the seventh month of the Jewish religious calendar and the first month of the civil calendar.

[30] Many Futurists date the announcement of "Messiah the prince" at Jesus' triumphal procession into Jerusalem, shortly before his death. It is true that Jesus was at that time hailed as "the son of David," but that is not necessarily messianic. God's announcement, however, at Jesus' baptism, is a public proclamation of messianic status, thus satisfying the prophecy.

[31] One ancient Greek manuscript of this passage and several church fathers cite Ps 2:7 outright with, "You are my son, today I have fathered you."

Simple exegesis must not be allowed to divert us from the richness of this event. The Jews believed that the prophetic voice had been removed from Israel shortly after the Babylonian exile. When the proper time for renewal of prophecy had come, it would be restored. Until that time, the Jews were limited in direct communication from God to the *bat kol* or "daughter voice." It was the occasional voice of God, likened to the cooing of a dove.[32] Thus, the appearance of the Holy Spirit in the form of a dove brought the picture to the Jews that Jesus was indeed the predicted Messiah. Jesus himself confirmed that this event fulfilled the sixty-nine weeks.

> And after John had been taken into custody, Jesus came into Galilee, preaching the gospel of God, and saying, "**The time is fulfilled**, and the kingdom of God is at hand; repent and believe in the gospel." (Mark 1:14–15; emphasis added)

The completion of the sixty-nine weeks may be noted in several other passages. Hebrews 1:3 literally says that "at the end of these days" God spoke to us in His Son. 1 Peter 1:20 literally states that Jesus appeared "at the end of the times." Hebrews 9:26 speaks of Jesus being "manifested" "at the consummation of the ages." Galatians 4:4 states that "God sent forth His Son" "when the fullness of time came." Each of these statements points to the appearance of Jesus for ministry at the proper time in fulfillment of prophecy.

Students of prophecy in that day knew it was time for the Messiah to appear. John 1:19–24 describes an inquiry from the priests to know if John the Baptist was the Messiah. John 4 tells of the encounter between Jesus and the woman at the well in Samaria. She specifically asks if he is the Messiah (4:25).

But the most interesting of these accounts is that of the magi, recorded in Matthew 2. These scholars were of uncertain geographic origin. They arrived in Jerusalem seeking the "king of the Jews" (Matt 2:2). There was no doubt in their minds that the star they had seen indicated his birth. The only biblical prophecy indi-

---

[32] Brad H. Young, *Jesus the Jewish Theologian*, (Peabody, MA: Hendrickson, 1995), 13–26.

cating the date at which the Messiah would appear is Daniel 9:25. But that told of his arrival as "Prince," not his birth. However, if they added other Old Testament prophecies, it was possible to derive that he would be a priest (1 Sam 2:35–36) and that his sign would be a star (Num 24:17). Since priests were usually anointed at age thirty (Num 4; 2 Chron 31:15–16; cf. Luke 3:23), the magi could then add 483 years to 457 BC, subtract 30 years, and arrive at the proper time to look for the stellar sign.

We have not yet discussed the Futurist calendar, but the story of the magi is impossible if the Futurist schema is correct. They take 444 BC (Neh 2) as the starting point, and sixty-nine weeks of "prophetic years" are added to get to the supposed date of the triumphal entry.[33] Unfortunately, this then prevents the magi from working backward to identify the date of Jesus' birth. Unless Daniel 9:27 describes the length of Jesus' ministry,[34] there would be no information to allow them to subtract his 3 1/2 year ministry before subtracting the thirty year age at baptism. Their certainty as to the meaning of the star would be impossible.

Let's restate this important but confusing point. Historicists say that at the end of the 69th week, 483 actual years after the decree, the Messiah was anointed as priest and king. In the middle of the 70th week, 3 1/2 years later, he was killed, as the prophecy specifies. Knowing from the Scriptures that priests were anointed to their office at the age of thirty, and understanding that the Messiah would have both a priestly and a kingly role, the Magi could know approximately when the Messiah should be born.

Futurists, on the other hand, say the anointing and the cutting off happened at approximately the same time, 3 1/2 years later than Historicists say the anointing happened. If the magi worked backward thirty years from that time, they would have arrived in Bethlehem three years late. What is more, it's unlikely that they

---

[33] There are minor differences proposed by different Futurist interpreters. Some end a precise time period at the triumphal entry. Others count to the cross. Since these are less than a week apart, we can treat them as identical for practical purposes.

[34] In the Futurist plan, Daniel 9:27 discusses the career of a future "Antichrist" and the length of the Great Tribulation. This means that it cannot discuss the length of Jesus' ministry, leaving no Old Testament prophecy indicating the length of Jesus' ministry.

would have figured out the arcane math used by Futurists in fig-
uring that there are 483 years between 444 BC and 31 AD.[35]

The testimony of Scripture is quite clear. "Until Messiah the
Prince" speaks of the manifestation (John 1:31) of Jesus at his
baptism. The announcement by God is the clear confirmation
Jesus then repeats by saying "the times are finished." His assertion of "the acceptable year of the Lord" (Luke 4:19; cf. Isa 61:2)
in the synagogue is the third time the announcement is made
publicly. The fact that the both common people and the literati
understand that the Messiah is due is confirmed by apostolic
writers who also make that same declaration in other writings.

Counterpoint: The Futurist Chronology

Futurists suggest that the Bible tells us to calculate the length
of prophecies in "prophetic years" (Anderson, 67–75). The first
evidence adduced is the span of 150 days from the start of the
flood until the ark rested on solid ground (Gen 7:11; 8:3–4). This
extended from the seventeenth day of the second month to the
seventeenth day of the seventh month, and is supposed to imply
that months were exactly thirty days long. Twelve such months
yields a 360-day year.

If months were actually thirty days long, then this span would
include 151 days, not 150, since Hebrews used inclusive counting.[36] Therefore at least one month was less than thirty days long.
If we propose that the months were based on observation of the
new moon, as in historic Judaism, it would be easy to have the
new moon of the seventh month obscured by the horrible
weather of the flood, delaying the start of the month by one day.
The geographic displacement of the ark during the flood could
also have the same effect, even if the moon was clearly visible.

---

[35] Isn't that 475 years, rather than 483? Yes. How do Futurists massage 475 to
make it 483? They multiply 360 days per prophetic year times 483 years, yielding
173,880 days, then divide that number by 365 days per year, yielding 475 actual years.
This actually takes them to 32AD, a year after the cross, not the proper date of 31AD.
So 475 equals 483. Go figure—literally. Is that what Gabriel meant Daniel to understand? We think not.

[36] This method counts both the first and last days of the period to arrive at the total.

This would agree with the Jewish calendar in the time of Christ, where alternate months were thirty and twenty-nine days long and the new month start could easily be delayed.[37] It is therefore improper to infer a 360-day year from this passage.

Hebrew Months

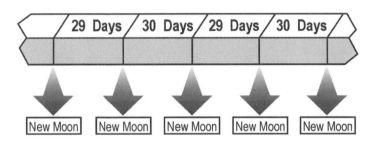

The second scriptural "proof" adduced by Anderson is the supposed time span of the desolation of Jerusalem. This is suggested to have lasted from the tenth day of the tenth month of the ninth year of Zedekiah (Ezek 24:1–2) to the twenty-fourth day of the ninth month of the second year of Darius (Haggai 2:10, 15–19). Anderson calculates this period as extending from 589 BC to 520 BC, including a span of 25,202 days, or two days longer than seventy times 360 days (70). There are three fundamental flaws with this bit of detective work.

First and foremost is the fact that Anderson has identified the wrong period. Zechariah 1:12–16 specifically identifies the end of the desolation as the completion of the rebuilding of the temple. Thus, the period of desolation extended from the destruction of the temple (2 Kgs 25:8–9) until the temple was fully rebuilt (Ezra

---

[37] Ibid, 102. "Treatise *Rosh Hashanah* of the *Mishna* deals with the mode in which, in the days of the "second temple," the feast of the new moon was regulated. The evidence of two competent witnesses was required by the Sanhedrim to the fact that they had *seen* the moon . . . ." Ibid, 99–100. "The new moon began at the *phasis* of the moon . . . and this happens, according to Newton, when the moon is eighteen hours old . . . But sometimes the *phasis* was delayed until the moon was 1d. 17h. old . . ." In other words, the observational new moon could also be delayed a day without weather obscuration.

6:15). This span was from the seventh day of the fifth month[38] of 586 BC to the third day of the twelfth month of 516 BC. This is the seventy years prophesied by Jeremiah (Jer 25:11).

Second, there is no evidence in any historical document or archeological find that any Hebrew was even aware that this interval constituted seventy years of 360 days. For that matter, there is no evidence that a year of 360 days was *ever* considered for *any purpose whatever* in the Jewish economy. Normal years were nominally 354 days long with twelve lunar months. Because the festivals had to be synchronized with the seasons, seven of nineteen years were leap years in which a thirteenth month was added. These years were a nominal 384 days long.[39] We must therefore declare Anderson's calculation to be anachronistic.

Hebrew Years

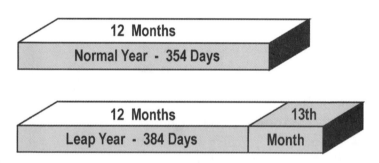

Even more devastating to this theory is that Anderson has his own dates wrong. The siege of Jerusalem began on January 15, 588 BC (189). Zerubbabel began the reconstruction of the temple in 536 BC. Rather than sixty-nine solar years, the span is only fifty-two. This leaves no Old Testament source for a 360-day

---

[38] Edwin R. Thiele, *The Mysterious Numbers of the Hebrew Kings* (Grand Rapids: Kregel, 1983), 190. This date is August 14, 586 BC.

[39] There was never a 360-day year in the Jewish economy. The actual length of any year could vary ±1 day from the nominal, depending on the specific lengths of the months due to the lunar cycle. The seven of nineteen frequency of leap years is based on the modern calculated calendar. Since the ancient calendar was observational, based on the time of the barley harvest, it is impossible to be completely specific. The calculated calendar did not come into use until centuries after Christ. However, even though the Jews didn't use a solar calendar, they knew what a solar year was—if not, they wouldn't have known when their lunar calendar needed an extra month. When dealing with a period of 483 years, the solar calendar would certainly have been assumed.

year. This is of great importance, since in Daniel 9:25 Gabriel tells Daniel he is to "know and discern" that from the issuing of the decree to the Messiah would be "seven weeks and sixty-two weeks." This 483-year period was to be understood long before any New Testament book was written. This cannot be over-emphasized. There is no biblical, historical, or archeological data to suggest that any Hebrew in that era could have understood the idea that God's intention was to define years as 360 days.[40] A year was a solar year, marked off in lunar months. No other definition was known to the Jews.

Having shown that "prophetic years" of 360 days are an un-scriptural concept, we will now assume for the sake of argument that they are true in order to examine another foundational diffi-culty of Futurism. The Futurist outline identifies the consent given to Nehemiah as the starting point of the sixty-nine weeks. Anderson calculates this as beginning on Nisan 1, 445 BC.[41] We must ask why Nisan 1 is chosen, since Neh 2:1 only identifies the date as "in the month Nisan." If it had been on the first of the month, that would have been easy to record. The language used implies that it was *not* the first of the month. Anderson "infers" that "Nehemiah also set out *early* in the first month." Such impre-cision of the record should disqualify it from use for precise cal-culations.

To this assumed starting point is then added sixty-nine years of 360 days to reach the triumphal entry.

The Julian date of that 10th Nisan was Sunday the 6th April, A.D. 32. What then was the length of the period intervening between the issu-ing of the decree to rebuild Jerusalem and the public advent of 'Mes-siah the Prince,' – between the 14th March, B.C. 445, and the 6th April, A. D. 32? THE INTERVAL CONTAINED EXACTLY AND TO THE VERY DAY 173,880 DAYS, OR SEVEN TIMES

---

[40] The calculation of 360 day years is based on Revelation 11:2–3, where 42 months are equal to 1,260 days. Simple arithmetic yields 360 day years. This is true in the context of the book of Revelation 11–13, but the Old Testament Jews would not have understood it in this way, so it would not have helped them determine the time of the Messiah's coming, since Revelation was written long after the cross.

[41] Anderson, 122–123. This date is off by a full year, but will serve for illustrative purposes. More modern interpreters correctly identify the consent as being issued in 444 BC. All Futurists accept the first of the month date for their calculations.

SIXTY-NINE PROPHETIC YEARS OF 360 DAYS, the first sixty-nine weeks of Gabriel's prophecy.[42]

Biblical Seventy Weeks

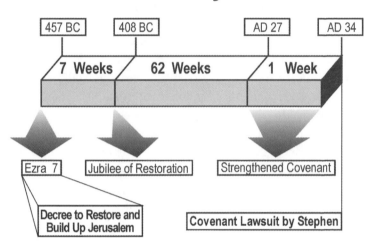

As already noted, the starting point is arbitrary rather than scriptural, and so the accuracy of the end point of the calculation is also suspect. But a second problem arises. Jesus' baptism was in the fall of 27 AD. His ministry was 3 1/2 years long, as identified by the sequence of festivals in the gospel of John. This places the cross in March or April of 31 AD.

A number of investigators have tried to use astronomical calculations to identify the year in which Passover fell on Friday. But since the pattern of leap years is unknown and the start of the month was dependent on observation of the new moon, it is impossible to determine from astronomical data just which day of the week Passover fell on in any year of that era. No helpful secular data exists, and so the only accurate source is the word of God. This forces us to reject Anderson's calculations as being a year too long. When modern calculations starting at 444 BC are done, they place the cross in 33 AD, two years too late. Therefore we must reject the Futurist approach to the seventy weeks on this ground as well.

---

[42] Ibid, 127–128; emphasis in the original.

"The Prince who is to come"

The key to understanding the seventieth week is found in this phrase. Because the people of this prince would destroy Jerusalem, Futurists identify Titus as the prince envisioned here. After all, he was the Roman general in charge of the army that destroyed Jerusalem in 70 AD. But this choice suffers by ignoring the immediate context.

The central thought in Daniel 9:25 is, "from the decree until Messiah the Prince comes will be sixty-nine weeks." That is, the prince who was to come (in sixty-nine weeks) would be the Messiah. This implies that the Jews would destroy Jerusalem, because it was the Prince's people who would do it. And this is exactly what Daniel admits in his prayer preceding the prophecy. The destruction of Jerusalem in 586 BC by Nebuchadnezzar is described there as a judgment by God against a rebellious people (9:11–12). Jeremiah refers to Nebuchadnezzar as God's servant in executing this judgment (Jer 27:6).

The responsibility of the Jews in Jerusalem cannot be denied. At the urging of the Zealots, they rebelled against their Roman overlords. Titus' army besieged the city, which fell into cannibalism when food supplies ran out. Eventually the Roman army was able to enter the city, but was under orders not to cause any harm to the temple. But Zealots inside the temple walls resisted, and eventually a torch was thrown in by a soldier. The resulting fire was so hot that the gold in the temple melted and ran out. Resistance to the last man led to total destruction of the city.

The Romans physically destroyed the city, but the Jews were responsible. In Hebrew thought, this was a judgment from God on a rebellious people. In fact, it was part of the covenant curses described in Deuteronomy 28. The Romans were the agents of God. Thus, the people of Jesus, the Jews, did destroy Jerusalem.[43]

By recognizing that the focus of the entire prophecy is on the Messiah and His people, we are now able to unravel the remaining threads. The first statement is that the Messiah would be "cut off." The Hebrew *karet* is a judicial term thought by many to

---

[43] It should be noted that "the people" refers to an ethnic identity, not a military one. The soldiers under Titus' command were not his people in this sense. That term would instead refer to Roman citizenry if it were applicable.

mean exclusion from the camp. This penalty for unconfessed sin on the Day of Atonement is parallel to the crucifixion, which occurred outside the city. The timing was certainly "after" the sixty-nine weeks, since Jesus' ministry was 3 1/2 years long.[44] This places it exactly in the middle of the seventieth week, as specified in 9:27.

Daniel 9:27 explains that the prince who is to come will "make a firm covenant with the many for a week." This translation misses the force of the Hebrew verb *higbir*. This word emphasizes the strengthening of an existing covenant. Since Jesus is the prince, the covenant he is strengthening is with the Jews as God's firstborn (cf. Exod 4:22).[45] His statement that his ministry was to the "lost sheep of the house of Israel" (Matt 15:24) points to the strengthened covenant. The covenant is explicitly noted in the last supper, where he states that the wine is "My blood of the covenant, which is poured out for many for forgiveness of sins" (Matt 26:28). The term "the many" is a technical description for Israel (Isa 53, esp. v. 11).

The prince who was to come would put an end to "sacrifice and grain offering." This speaks of an end to the sacrificial system instituted at Sinai. The first indication of this was the tearing of the veil of the temple by an angel at the moment Christ died. This signified to all that the glory of God was gone. The earthly temple was no longer important in the worship of God. All its services were now obsolete (cf. Heb 8:13). The entire sacrificial system had been replaced forever with Jesus' one sacrifice for all time (Heb 8–9).

All of the feasts and sacrifices typologically pointed forward to Christ (as a tutor teaches pupils—Gal 3:24). They all met their antitype in Christ. Christ's Melchizedek priesthood permanently replaced the Levitical priesthood. For Christ to become a priest required a change in the law that created the priesthood (Heb 7:12). The Levitical priesthood was hereditary, but the better priesthood of Christ (7:11) is based on the "power of an inde-

---

[44] "After" in this case implies a substantial interval between the event in view and the preceding event. In this sense, a five day span between the Triumphal Entry and the cross is not "after."

[45] This birthright blessing would be lost when the Jews failed to meet the conditions of their probation.

structible life" (7:16). And this priesthood is "forever" (7:17, 21, 24–25, 28). This permanent priesthood is the result of a permanent change in the law that prevents forever and renders utterly useless any reversion to a Levitical priesthood with its sacrifices.[46]

The Second Half of the Seventieth Week

Anderson states that, "History contains no record of events to satisfy the predicted course of the seventieth week" (76) If this is true, then the interpretation we have presented is incorrect. But Jesus so perfectly matches the details of Daniel 9:26–27 we have examined so far as to suggest that Anderson is wrong. But what can be found that can fill out the rest of the week? Scripture appears to be silent regarding this.

Jesus strengthened the covenant with the Jews as God's firstborn. Incarnate deity ministered predominantly with them and brought the prophetic ministry and the miraculous manifestations of God to them in an unequaled way. After the ascension of Jesus, the apostles continued this ministry. The first seven chapters of Acts detail the actions of the apostles in the Jewish community. But after Stephen was stoned (Acts 7:58–60) a great persecution of Christians in Judea began. All the believers except the apostles were scattered (8:1), and the gospel began to be actively spread outside Judea (8:4). In Peter's vision of the unclean animals (Acts 10), the Scriptures record the explicit divine approval of extending the ministry to the Gentiles. These events are consistent with the second half of the week, but so far lack any element allowing us to be certain that this is the intent of the prophecy.

The seventy weeks are defined as a period of covenant probation. God states that certain conditions must be met within that time. In accordance with His usual orderly way of dealing with mankind, at the end of the probation a covenant lawsuit was brought. These actions are well known to technical theologians, although the average reader will probably not be familiar with the

---

[46] This point will be discussed further when the Futurist idea of a "millennial temple" is explored.

term. Over thirty such lawsuits are recorded in Scripture, and they follow a standard form not unlike a modern court trial.[47] Since a covenant is a contract, covenant lawsuits are very similar to breach of contract actions. First, God identifies himself as present and as a maker of the contract. He then establishes the fact that he has carried out his obligations under the contract. He charges man with breach of the contract, and witnesses are called. A verdict is announced.[48] Stephen presents just such a lawsuit.

Prophets have three types of duties. The first is to bring instruction to the people from God (for-telling). The second is to tell the future as instructed by God (fore-telling). The last is to act as his prosecuting attorney in a covenant lawsuit (forth-telling). Stephen fulfilled this last role in 34 AD.[49]

Acts 6:8 identifies Stephen as "full of grace and power." Certain men opposed him and brought him before the Council on trumped-up charges. While false testimony was being presented, God made His presence known by causing Stephen's face to be "like the face of an angel." With the preamble complete, Stephen presents the historical prologue in Acts 7:2–50. The following indictment is particularly stinging.

"You men who are stiff-necked and uncircumcised in heart and ears are always resisting the Holy Spirit; you are doing just as your fathers did. Which one of the prophets did your fathers not persecute? And

---

[47] G. Ernest Wright, "The Lawsuit of God: A Form-Critical Study of Deuteronomy 32," in Bernhard W. Anderson, Walter Harrelson, eds., *Israel's Prophetic Heritage* (New York: Harper, 1962), 26–67.

[48] These steps are known formally as the preamble, historical prologue, indictments, witnesses, and verdict. The curses are the penalty for failure established in the original covenant. If the covenant is fulfilled, blessings are pronounced. In the case we are discussing, the covenant is the Sinaitic covenant, which is detailed at length in the book of Deuteronomy. The blessings are in 28:1–14 and the specific curses are found in 28:15–60. The best-known covenant lawsuit is probably that brought against David for his adultery with Bathsheba and murder of Uriah in 2 Samuel 12.

[49] The story of Stephen is dated to 34 AD as follows. Paul participated in the stoning of Stephen (Acts 8:1). He then met Christ on the Damascus road (Acts 9), after which he went to Arabia (Gal 1:17). "After three years" he returned to Jerusalem (1:18). Fourteen years later (2:1) he returned to Jerusalem, probably for the Jerusalem conference recorded in Acts 15. This conference is widely accepted as having happened in 49–50 AD. Using modern arithmetic, this would place Stephen's death in 32 AD, as DeMar does (Gary DeMar, *End Times Fiction* (Nashville: Thomas Nelson, 2001), 45.) But the Jews used inclusive counting, which, when applied to two succeeding intervals, reduces the total by two years. This places the death of Stephen in 34 AD.

they killed those who had previously announced the coming of the Righteous One, whose betrayers and murderers you have now become; you who received the law as ordained by angels, and yet did not keep it." (Acts 7:51–53)

We should notice specifically the charge of murder. The Council was the body which had sent Christ to the cross. They did it by breaking a number of rules of Jewish law. First, all capital trials had to be held in the daytime. They were sacred events, and must be done after the morning sacrifice so that the members could be ritually pure. Council members were bound to act as defense counsel, yet they sought testimony against him (Matt 26:59). It was the duty of the Council to acquit if any of a host of specific events took place. The perjured testimony (Mark 14:56–59) required acquittal. The high priest's intervention to change the legal theory of guilt (14:61) required acquittal.[50] Finally, the Council was not allowed to vote on a verdict until the next day. Yet they rendered an instant unanimous guilty verdict (14:63–64). Under Jewish law this was again a mandatory acquittal, since it smacked of mob action.

The Council members at Stephen's trial were nearly all the same people who had murdered Christ by shredding their own canon of laws. No witnesses were needed, since the Council members themselves knew of their own guilt. They began "gnashing their teeth" at Stephen (Acts 7:54). Then Stephen was granted a vision of the heavenly Court. He saw "the heavens opened up and the Son of Man standing at the right hand of God" (7:56). The Council members recognized this scene.

When a king heard a legal case, his regent, seated at his right hand, would stand to present the verdict. The scene Stephen presented was the judge of all mankind about to say "Guilty." This was more than the Council could stand, because they knew their guilt. They knew they had murdered the Son of God and would not allow that guilty verdict to be pronounced on them. So they rushed out and "shut up vision and prophet" (lit. trans.) by stoning Stephen to death. The seventy weeks were over. Probation for the Jewish nation had ended, and the birthright blessing was

---

[50] The high priest himself committed a capital offense by tearing his robe.

taken from them and "given to a nation producing the fruit of it" (Matt 21:43). Their "house was left to them desolate" (23:38).[51]

Biblical 70th Week

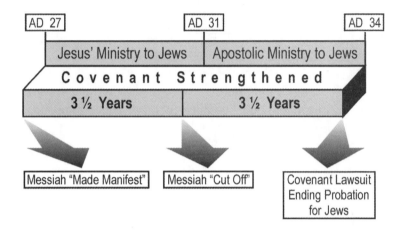

The fourth of the six elements in Daniel 9:24 has now been identified. The final two are "to bring in everlasting righteousness" and "to anoint the most holy." The first of these is familiar to all Christians. Jesus' death on the cross ended his perfect life, allowing righteousness for all of us. The second is a bit less obvious.

The Hebrew of "most holy" is *qodesh qodeshim*, "holy of holies." It is used over forty times in the Old Testament, and in every case it refers to a physical object. The only one of these objects ever anointed was the sanctuary, so this must refer to anointing a sanctuary or temple for worship. For this reason, Futurists suggest that it refers to the anointing of the third temple described by Ezekiel at the end of the Great Tribulation and beginning of the millennial kingdom on earth.[52] Unfortunately for them, Jesus' new ministry as our high priest in the heavenly sanctuary has *forever* ended the earthly ministry of priests. But this fact points us to the real sanctuary which was to be anointed.

---

[51] Wilson Paroschi, "The Prophetic Significance of Stephen," *JATS*, 9:1–2, 345–363, 1998.
[52] This will be discussed later.

The book of Hebrews describes in detail the ministry of Christ in the heavenly sanctuary. But just like in the earthly sanctuary, this ministry could not begin until the sanctuary was anointed for service. Then Jesus had to bring his sacrifice to apply in place of our own. Now that this is complete, we are able to come directly before the throne of grace through our mediator, Jesus Christ (Heb 4:16; 7:25). The seventy weeks are complete, exactly on time. But one part of the prophecy remains.

"On the wing of abominations"

The final segment of the prophecy has caused interpreters great difficulty. Because of the enigmatic nature of the statement, translators have rendered this in many different ways. The NASB is probably as good as any of them:

> . . . on the wing of abominations will come one who makes desolate.
> (Dan 9:27b)

The word for wing is *kanaph*. Its root meaning is "extremity," and it is used in a number of ways, including the common reference to a bird's wings. The Expositor's Bible Commentary notes of this passage that the expression "wing of abominations" must be familiar to Daniel and his readers. In other words, it is an idiomatic expression. The expression "on the wings of" occurs four other times in the Hebrew Bible, all in poetic passages. In 2 Samuel 22:11, Psalm 18:10, and Psalm 104:3, we find God traveling "on the wings of the wind." In Psalm 139:9 the psalmist considers traveling on "the wings of the dawn." In these verses, the expression suggests swiftness, immediacy, and inevitability. Thus, the phrase in Daniel means, simply, "the desolator will sweep in carried by the power of his abominations."

About AD 66, the Zealots and other groups of rebels fomented a revolt to throw off the Roman yoke. Although there were several leaders, such as Simon ben Giora, the most influential was John, son of Levi, of Gischala in Galilee. The revolt was in itself an abomination, but worse was to follow. The Zealots murdered over 12,000 priests. Later, as the revolt reached its peak in AD 70, over 8,000 were murdered in the Temple grounds and left unburied, a further abomination. The bloody rebels used the Temple itself as their final stronghold in Jerusalem. The end of the revolt was the complete destruction of Jerusalem at the hands of the Romans, with loss of a million Jewish lives. The desolation was complete.

> . . . even until a complete destruction, one that is decreed, is poured
> out on the one who makes desolate. (Dan 9:27c)

The " abomination" was the Jewish revolt and its aftermath. The one who made desolate was John, son of Levi, who stood *pars pro toto* as the corporate image of revolt against God. He, through his complicit countrymen, caused the desolation of Jerusalem. And complete destruction, just as decreed in Deuteronomy 28:15 and the verses following, was poured out on him and the Jews with him. The handful of survivors was dispersed, and Jerusalem became a Roman city, off limits to Jews.

The destruction of Jerusalem did not take place within the seventy weeks, nor should it have. The destruction was a covenant curse poured out on rebellious Jews. This curse could not be imposed until after the completion of the covenant lawsuit, which could not take place until the close of the seventy weeks. The delay in the execution of the judgment is similar to the modern gap between the pronouncement of a capital verdict—a death sentence—in court and the time when the condemned felon dies.

Summary

The seventy weeks were cut off from the 2,300 days of Daniel 8:14 as a probationary final phase of God's covenant relationship with the Jewish people as his firstborn. The six items listed in 9:24 are not blessings to be received at the end of the Great Tribulation, but probationary conditions of God's covenant with the Hebrews. The Jews were to bring themselves fully into compliance with God's laws. This period began in the Jubilee year of 457 BC, when the decree to restore and build up Jerusalem went out to Palestine from Artaxerxes. It was 483 solar years later that Jesus was baptized in the Jordan and the arrival of the Messiah was announced for all to hear, first by God the Father at Jesus' baptism, then by Jesus in the synagogue. The people knew it was time for the Messiah, and the scriptures repeatedly confirm this knowledge. After the sixty-nine weeks, in the middle of the seventieth week, Jesus was cut off by crucifixion. This brought in everlasting righteousness. Jesus then anointed the most holy sanctuary in heaven at his ascension.

The remaining 3 1/2 years passed with the active ministry of the apostles to the Jews. When the seventy weeks expired without the required repentance, Stephen prosecuted the covenant lawsuit. The Council responded by shutting up vision and prophet when they stoned him. The birthright blessing of kingdom power was removed from the Jewish people and given solely to the body of believers, whether they be Jewish or Christian. The covenant curses defined in Deuteronomy 28:15 and the verses following were then inevitable, and they fell in 70 AD, the direct result of the actions of the Zealots and other rebels, led by John. He is the desolator, standing *pars pro toto* for the entire rebellious people. Destruction also came exactly as prophesied. It also came *after* the end of the probation, exactly as required by God's orderly covenant lawsuit procedure.

Biblical Seventy Weeks

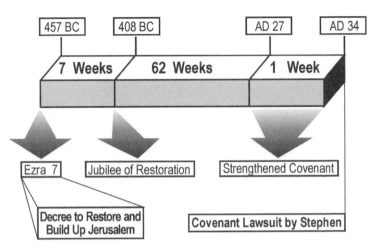

Finally, the Bible knows of no such concept as a 360-day prophetic year meant to be mathematically configured into a 365 day actual year. Such calculations of the supposed exact day of Christ's triumphal entry are mere sleight of hand. Nor does it know of a seven-year "Great Tribulation." Yes, there will be great tribulation, as predicted, but it will not involve a rapture of the church, an Antichrist persona, or a mass conversion of Jews. These topics await us in future chapters.

CHAPTER FOUR:

TRIBULATION . . .

Plainly, if the church were to go through the Tribulation, she would not survive it. (LaHaye, 62)

Severe troubles will come upon the earth. Many, including our Savior, describe this.

"Therefore when you see the abomination of desolation which was spoken of through Daniel the prophet, standing in the holy place (let the reader understand), then let those who are in Judea flee to the mountains; let him who is on the housetop not go down to get the things out that are in his house; and let him who is in the field not turn back to get his cloak. But woe to those who are with child and to those who nurse babes in those days! But pray that your flight may not be in the winter, or on a Sabbath; for then **there will be a great tribulation, such as has not occurred since the beginning of the world until now, nor ever shall. And unless those days had been cut short, no life would have been saved**; but for the sake of the elect those days shall be cut short." (Matt 24:15-22; emphasis added)

Jesus draws our focus to the fact that a time of nearly unimaginable trouble is coming. Futurists identify this period as a time of wrath poured out by God.[1] They suggest that God will remove the saints from the earth prior to the commencement of this judgment in order to protect them. Pentecost comments:

Since the church is the body, of which Christ is the Head (Eph. 1:22; 5:23; Col. 1:18), the bride, of which he is the Bridegroom (1

---

[1] Jeremiah 30:7 describes it as "the time of Jacob's trouble." Deuteronomy 32:25 calls it the "day of their calamity." Isaiah 61:2 identifies it as "the day of vengeance of our God."

Cor. 11:2; Eph, 5:23) . . . there exists between the believer and the Lord a union and a unity. The believer is no longer separated from Him, but brought into the closest oneness with Him. If the church is in the seventieth week, she is subjected to the wrath, judgment, and indignation which characterizes the period, and because of her oneness with Christ, He, likewise, would be subjected to that same visitation. This is impossible according to 1 John 4:17, for He can not be brought into judgment again . . .

Again, Revelation 13:7 makes it clear that all who are in the seventieth week are brought into subjection to the Beast and through him to Satan, who gives the Beast his power. If the church were in this period she would be subjected to Satan, and Christ would either lose His place as Head, or He, Himself, because of his union with the Church, would be likewise subjected to Satan's authority. Such a thing is unthinkable. Thus it is concluded that the nature of the church and the completeness of her salvation prevent her from being in the seventieth week. . . .

. . . the church is a mystery . . . This whole mystery program was not revealed until after the rejection of Christ by Israel. . . . It must logically follow that this mystery program must itself be brought to a conclusion before God can resume His dealing with the nation Israel, as he has shown previously He will do. The mystery program, which was so distinct in its inception, will certainly be separate in its conclusion. This program must be concluded before God resumes and culminates His program for Israel. This mystery concept of the church makes a pretribulation rapture a necessity. (Pentecost, 200-201)

"Rapture" is not a term found in Scripture. It is drawn from Latin translations of the New Testament, where it is used to describe the time when the saints are "snatched up" from the earth to be with Christ. It is functionally equivalent to translation, as happened to Enoch and Elijah. As a concept, it also includes the resurrection of the righteous dead Paul describes in 1 Corinthians 15:50-52. LaHaye calls the rapture the "blessed hope" (Titus 2:13) of the Christian. This it truly is, for at that time we will be removed from this sinful world to a place where sin will no longer have dominion. Before we can discuss the timing and nature of the rapture, we must first consider events preceding it.

Historical Tribulation

Throughout recorded history, Satan has worked to kill off the faithful whenever and wherever possible. Cain's jealousy led him to kill Abel. Elijah ran from Jezebel for fear of his life. Daniel's three friends were thrown into the furnace when they would not worship the image. Antiochus IV Epiphanes pronounced a death sentence on anyone who observed the Jewish ordinances. By the time of Christ, persecution was an established historic fact of life. In the Sermon on the Mount, Jesus said that his followers would be persecuted (Matt 5:11). The disciples were told that they would be imprisoned and killed (Luke 21:12, 16). Paul echoes this warning.

> And after they had preached the gospel to that city and had made many disciples, they returned to Lystra and to Iconium and to Antioch, strengthening the souls of the disciples, encouraging them to continue in the faith, and saying, "Through many tribulations we must enter the kingdom of God." (Acts 14:21-22)

The history of persecution of Christians is well known. Tradition tells us every apostle was sentenced to death, with only John surviving. Christians were executed in large numbers in the most barbaric fashions. And yet through the deaths of millions the faith was preserved. Today the memory of this horrific persecution has faded in the western world.[2] But Jesus said that the persecution of the last days would be worse than ever before.[3]

The Nature of Tribulation

The time of trouble spoken of by Christ has a number of features. There will be false messiahs and false prophets (Matt 24: 24) working lying wonders (2 Thes 2:9). Such a time would seem

---

[2] Persecution is a present-day fact of life for Christians who live in the less developed parts of the world. Voice of the Martyrs magazine repeatedly asserts that over 100,000 are killed annually for their faith in Jesus.

[3] Bear in mind, however, that this sort of language is a characteristic form of Jewish expression common in Old Testament prophecies—referring to events that happened before Christ's time. Also, hyperbole (deliberate exaggeration) is typical of Jesus' teaching. Thus, we needn't necessarily seek out the worst catastrophes anywhere, then say, "Much worse than that." The tribulation will be terrible—some places worse than others, no doubt—but God's remnant people will remain faithful and will survive.

to be here now, with such persons as Sun Myung Moon, Maharishi Mahesh Yogi, James Jones, David Koresh, and others leading messianic movements. Various televangelists claim to perform healings and other miracles, then request generous "love offerings." When we find either the evangelist or his works to be phony, his "miracles" are shown to be lying wonders such as predicted by Paul.

The persecution of Christians will increase—in some places more than others—such that the evils of history will be eclipsed by greater satanic campaigns. The apparent protection of laws will become a mirage with no substance. Jesus' prediction to the disciples on the Mount of Olives will directly affect the members of the church, in order to "refine, purge, and make them pure until the end time" (Dan 11:35).

Pre-trib Futurists[4] will object strongly at this point, insisting that the church will have been raptured away before this time of trouble begins. Yet Jesus' remarks were addressed to the disciples, who became the very foundation of the church (Eph 2:20). And LaHaye himself notes that second and third century Christians thought themselves to be in the great tribulation (LaHaye, 198). We ought to take our Lord's comments as authoritative and accept that our own lives may be threatened in the near future because of our faith. No statement within the Olivet discourse (or any other eschatological oracle, for that matter) distinguishes between ethnic Jews and the church with regard to passing through the tribulation. Only faith or lack thereof is in view with regard to redemption.

The first segment of tribulation is one where mankind becomes more and more evil under the influence of Satan. Eventually every person on planet Earth will have chosen sides (Rev 13:8). In an attempt to gain complete control over mankind, Satan's surrogate will impose a death decree on all who will not worship him (13:15). At this point, all who will choose for God have done so, and the mark of the beast and the seal of God will

---

[4] This is one of the occasional places where it becomes necessary to discuss the separate camps of Futurism. The shortened "pre-trib," "mid-trib," and "post-trib" forms will be used as appropriate in place of the longer expressions describing the time each group believes the church will be raptured in relation to the non-existent seven year tribulation period.

be applied. Probation will close,[5] and a new era will begin. The plainest description of this sequence is found in the seals, trumpets, and bowl plagues of Revelation. We must examine these prophetic series in some detail because Futurists use them to map out a detailed chronology of their hypothetical seven-year "Great Tribulation."

One Futurist scholar has written, "A cursory examination of the book of Revelation will indicate that all seven trumpets are contained in the seventh seal, and the seven bowls are contained within the seventh trumpet."[6] But such a cursory examination will not allow us to properly comprehend these prophetic sequences. To properly understand them we must begin at the opening of the scene in Revelation 4. Because our concern is primarily with chronology, some details of these prophecies will not be explored.

The Heavenly Throne Room

After these things I looked, and behold, a door *standing* open in heaven, and the first voice which I had heard, like *the sound* of a trumpet speaking with me, said, "Come up here, and I will show you what must take place after these things (Rev 4:1).

Futurists generally see John in this passage as a symbol of the church being raptured, so that all that follows is subsequent to that event. That is, the church is in heaven, with ethnic Jews and wicked Gentiles left behind on earth.

John is shown a room in heaven with a central throne. The occupant of this throne (4:3) is God, described in terms drawn

---

[5] Rarely does one encounter the term "probation" to describe man's status on earth, but it is in fact appropriate. Probation means a "proving" or "testing." Released prisoners often go through a period of "probation" so they can prove they've changed their ways. Likewise, everyone alive is on "probation," with angels of God as our probation officers, guiding us through our consciences and reporting to the judge whether we are reformed (converted) or not. Each person has the opportunity to choose salvation, but most will not. When God determines that the proper time has come, there will no longer be an opportunity to be converted. Probation for mankind will have closed. At that time, every person who is righteous will "still be righteous," and whoever is filthy will "still be filthy" (Rev 22:11).

[6] Marvin Rosenthal, *The Pre-Wrath Rapture of the Church* (Nashville: Thomas Nelson, 1990), 132.

from Ezekiel (1:26; 24:10; 28:13). Around this throne are twenty-four more, occupied by "elders" (4:4). The elders are dressed in white, the color of robes given to victorious saints (3:5), and are wearing *stephanoi*, the crown given to victors (2:10). These features identify them as being from the earth. Their number seems likely to refer to the twenty-four divisions of the Levitical priesthood (1 Chr 24:1-5), since there is no other group of twenty-four in Scripture—if only to remind us of the nature of their work. Their acts of worship (Rev 4:10-11; 5:14; 7:11; 19:4) and presentation of incense (5:8) again suggest that they are performing priestly functions.[7] Pentecost notes that, "Since, according to Revelation 5:8, these twenty-four are associated in a priestly act, which is never said of angels, they must be believer-priests associated with the Great High Priest."[8]

The promise of the eternal priesthood has been given to both Jews and the church (1:6; 5:10; cf. Exod 19:6), implying that there is no difference between Israel and the church. Further, in an event where only the church is alleged to be in heaven, it is incongruous to have the defining features of the scene drawn not from the church era but from the Hebrew sanctuary. We can only conclude that, as was found in chapter two, the church is the Israel of God (Gal 6:16).

Filling out the sanctuary scene is a sea of glass before the throne of God (Rev 4:6; cf. 1 Kgs 7:23). This reference to the laver in Solomon's temple (1 Kgs 7:23-26) identifies this as the courtyard. Four living creatures surround the throne (Rev 4:6-8), exactly as in Ezekiel's vision of the glory of God (Ezek 1ff). This setting, where all the priestly courses are present and the slain lamb is in the courtyard (5:6), identify this as a Passover scene. Even John would have seen nothing to allow him to separate the church from Israel in a time when the church would supposedly be raptured away from the Jews.

---

[7] In the Old Testament another important function of priests is judging, not only in law cases, but among the clean and the unclean, the repentant and the unrepentant.

[8] Pentecost, 209. Of course, Pentecost is partially wrong about this—an angel performs priestly duties in the heavenly sanctuary in 8:3-5, and in 15:5-8 seven angels and one of the living creatures are involved with priestly ministry—but he is probably right in seeing the twenty-four elders as having a priestly function of a sort.

Revelation 5 presents a paean of praise to Christ. He is identified as the "Lion from the tribe of Judah," and the "Root of David" (5:5). The next verses present Christ as a sacrificial lamb. Such a conflation of messianic titles occurs nowhere else in Scripture other than Isaiah 9:6. Jesus is "worthy to take the book [from God's right hand (5:1)], and to break its seals" (5:9) because of his status as paschal sacrifice. Again the Hebrew sanctuary permeates the scene, denying a separation between Israel and the church.

LaHaye argues that these passages, so steeped in Hebraism, indicate that the church is not present. In fact, he goes so far as to say "the church is not mentioned in Revelation 4:6-18:1" (LaHaye, 212). To this we must respond that this Jewish Temple-like scene, occurring when the church is supposedly absent from the earth, is in exactly the location where LaHaye thinks the church has been taken!

The next step will be for the Lamb to open the seals. But before we proceed with the opening of the scroll, let us note the nature of the event laid before us. A scroll sealed with seven seals was the form of a last will and testament in the Roman Empire at the time Revelation was written. We know that Jesus, the Lamb of God, is to receive his kingdom as an inheritance (Exod 15:16-17; Deut 9:26; Dan 7:14). Thus, the process of opening of the seven seals will reveal Jesus' kingdom. And because this kingdom is made up of saints, the seals which must be opened to bring them to view will naturally be related to the drama of redemption.

Seven Seals

The seals describe the contour of redemptive history from First to the Second Advent. Immediately Futurists will object. For the sake of completeness, let us briefly consider their position.

In the Futurist schema, the seventieth week of Daniel 9 begins with the rapture of the church and the rise of the Antichrist.[9] This person will unify the world and make a peace treaty with the Jews, allowing the restoration of sacrifices in a rebuilt temple in

---

[9] This is where the pre-trib Futurists place the rapture of the saints.

Jerusalem. After 3 1/2 years he will break the treaty, desecrate the temple, and begin a terrible oppression of believers and Jews.[10] The seven years will end with the "Glorious Appearing," when Jesus returns to set up his millennial kingdom of peace on earth.

Futurist 70th Week

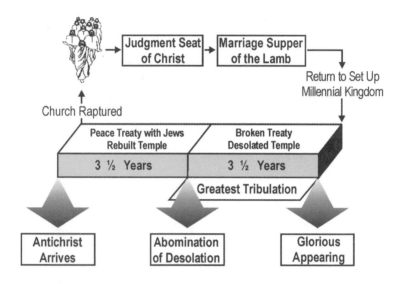

The first problem with this view is that Paul says, "The mystery of lawlessness (antichrist) is already at work" (2 Thes 1:7). Thus, antichrist is both a past and present-day satanic force and office. It is not a single person in the future. The second problem is that Futurists identify "the one who makes desolate" in Daniel 9:27 as the "Antichrist." We have already shown that the desolator was John, son of Levi, leader of the Jewish rebels in 66-70 AD. Finally, the covenant in Daniel 9:26 was "strengthened," not made new. Therefore Scripture mentions *no* new peace treaty for this fictional character to create with anyone. And of course, the seventieth week, in which all this supposedly will take place, ended in 34 AD. No basis exists for the Futurist framework.

Returning to Revelation, we have already seen how the introductory temple scene portrays the Passover service at the Tem-

---

[10] This is where the mid-trib Futurists place the rapture of the saints.

ple. As the narrative moves into Revelation 5, the entire Levite corps of twenty-four priestly elders is still present. This was required at Passover, Pentecost, and the Feast of Booths. Here (Rev 5:6), at the same time that we see the sacrifice of Passover, a specific reference is made to the Spirit of God being sent into the world. From Acts 2 we know this occurred at Pentecost. Thus, God has included the Mosaic festival of Pentecost in the tapestry of the vision. But even more important for our perspective, this includes an apostolic church constituent. The "Jewish" and "Christian" elements are completely melded.

The four horsemen come forth from heaven. A brief look at them shows a complex of war, plague, famine, and death. These are the four standard judgments sent against rebellious Israel in the past (cf. Lev 26:23-26; Deut 32:23-25, 42, etc). Compare the horsemen with God's promise to his unfaithful "sons and daughters" (Deut 32:19) in the "Song of Moses":

> I will heap misfortunes on them;
> I will use **my arrows** on them.
> *They will be* wasted by **famine**, and consumed by **plague**.
> And bitter **destruction**;
> And the teeth of **beasts** I will send upon them,
> With the venom of crawling things of the dust.
> Outside the **sword** will bereave,
> And inside terror— (Deut 32:23-25; emphasis added)

John writes, regarding the four horsemen, "Authority was given to them over a fourth of the earth, to kill with **sword** and with **famine** and with **pestilence [plague]** and by the **wild beasts** of the earth" (Rev 6:8; emphasis added). The four horsemen are "God's arrows" (Deut 32:23, 42), serving as preliminary judgments intended to bring apostate Israel to repentance.

These are not literal horsemen. If they were, we would see riders physically passing through the earth carrying out the acts described. But since such literalism[11] is not representative of

---

[11] Literalism refers to the rigid requirement that any scriptural statement must be taken in a physically literal sense. LaHaye proposes a "golden rule of interpretation" [Tim LaHaye, *Revelation Unveiled*, (Grand Rapids: Zondervan, 1999), 17]: "When the plain sense of Scripture makes common sense, seek no other sense; therefore take every word at its primary, ordinary, usual, literal meaning unless the facts of the immediate

God's actions or intentions, we should recognize that the horsemen are symbolic representatives of God's preliminary judgments. The details of their descriptions are intended to depict
aspects of redemptive history. When the second, third, and
fourth horsemen are sent out, they join others already in the
earth. Thus, the four horsemen are contemporaneous (Zech 1:7-
11; 6:1-8).[12]

The first rider is on a white horse. Futurists identify him as
the "Antichrist." But white is the color of righteousness, never
used in Scripture to describe anything of satanic origin. In particular, lying and deceit would disqualify the "Antichrist" from
being this rider. The first horseman is given a *stephanos*, the victor's crown (Rev 6:2), such as the twenty-four elders wear in 4:4,
the woman wears in 12:1 and Jesus wears in 14:14. Satan and his
followers are never described in Scripture as victors, and are certainly never given any insignia of victory. Such a conquering person of righteous character strongly suggests that Christ is in view,
at least typologically. The structure of the book of Revelation
confirms this view. The first horseman appears again in 19:11-16,
where he is explicitly named "the Word of God."[13] Both ride
white horses. Both come to conquer. And both are announced by
identical introductions: "And behold a white horse, and he who
sat upon it . . ."[14] This strongly implies that the horseman on the
white horse in the seals is also Christ. The first horseman carries a
bow, a fit implement with which to send "God's arrows" into the
world, while the latter has a sharp sword coming from his mouth
to "strike down the nations." (In Deut 32:42, God says, "'I will
make My arrows drunk with blood, and My sword will devour

---

text, studied in the light of the related passages and axiomatic and fundamental truths,
clearly indicate otherwise." While this seems reasonable on its face, this effectively denies the figurative use of language which permeates Hebrew writing and is an integral
part of apocalyptic prophecy. By interpreting in this way, Futurists frequently mis-apply
the hermeneutic they espouse.

[12] The fact that they are continuing concurrently may be seen from current events,
where death at the World Trade Center, famine in the Sudan, and plague in the AIDS
epidemic have brought many to Christ. War is represented by the aphorism, "there are
no atheists in foxholes." Thus, all four horsemen are currently active.

[13] This is the same name given to Jesus in John 1:1, 14.

[14] The Greek is *kai ho kathémenos ep auton* in both texts.

flesh, with the blood of the slain and the captives, from the long-haired leaders of the enemy.'") The span of the seals is defined by the fifth seal (6:9-11), where the blood of the saints murdered for their faith cries out "How long" from beneath the altar.[15] Such martyrs have been a feature of history since Cain killed Abel (Matt 23:35) shortly after the fall. These saints are given white robes—symbolizing the surety of their righteousness—and told to wait "a little while longer" (Rev 6:11). An alternate reading of the Greek of this passage states that the martyrs are to wait "until those who were yet to be killed have been made perfect."[16] This points to future martyrs who must be sealed before the Lord can proceed to avenge them (cf. Eph 4:30). This "little while" suggests that the sealing must be complete before the sixth seal follows with its cosmic signs of impending final judgment on the wicked (Rev 6:12-17).[17] The sixth seal contains the same signs Jesus declared would immediately precede his return (Matt 24:29-31). Thus, the span of the seals is at least from the ministry of Christ to the end of the age, and a strong case can be made that the first five seals have been a repetitive feature of virtually all of mankind's history.

At this point Futurists argue that the saints in the fifth seal are limited to those converted and martyred during the seven-year Great Tribulation. But this complaint is without substance. As we have repeatedly noted, there will be a great tribulation, but there will be no *seven-year* "Great Tribulation."[18] Since the seventi-

---

[15] The text actually says "the souls." They are located where the blood of sacrifices was poured out, not in the Israelite sanctuary, but at the base of the altar of burnt offering in the courtyard of the sanctuary, from whence it seeped "under the altar" and formed a symbolic foundation of atonement. Since life "is in the blood" (Lev 17:11), and Genesis records Abel's "blood crying out from the ground" (Gen 4:10), the imagery is truly that of the sacrificial altar, where the shed blood of martyrs cries out. The "blood of the slain and the captives" in Deut 32:42 that leads God to slay the enemy leaders calls to mind the fifth seal.

[16] Erwin Gane, *The Holy Spirit and the Latter Rain* (Harrisburg, PA: American Cassette Ministries, 1998), EG-4.

[17] A cosmic sign may be defined as a real-time celestial event observable in much or all of the earth which indicates the imminent return of Christ to execute judgment on the wicked. It may result in substantial damage and death among the lost, although the saints will not be harmed.

[18] Some Futurists finely subdivide the supposed seven year period into smaller periods where the "great tribulation" is a segment of the seven years. We will not involve

eth week of Daniel ended in AD 34, we have no way of knowing how long this time of trouble will be, but it may last only a few months. Futurists also argue that these saints must be on earth, and are thus the "left behind" wicked who have converted and are therefore supposed to be different from the church. But this scene is in the throne room of God in heaven. The altar is seen there, in the presence of God.[19] No distinction is made as to whether these souls are Jew or Gentile. The only scriptural basis for identifying the souls is what the text itself declares. The martyrs are persons killed "because of the word of God and because of the testimony which they had maintained" (Rev 6:9). Since the word of God and its testimony extends from Eden to the second coming, people of all ethnic origins and times are necessarily included.[20]

The image of the first horse seems most reasonably to represent the victorious gospel preached by the faithful church, the Israel of God. This is the cause of Christ, who is represented as seated on the horse. He goes forth as the victor over sin, making his conquest of the world through the Holy Spirit and the faithful witness of believers. The next horse presents the absence of the true gospel and the consequent dissensions and strife.[21] Such conflicts have led to the loss of millions of lives, sacrificed at the altar of false orthodoxy. The third horse, black rather than white, represents a famine of the spirit, the opposite of the conquest of the gospel. The oil and wine symbolize the care with which God watches over His people. While the love of most men has grown cold (Matt 24:12), those who still have faith will never be sepa-

---

ourselves in such discussions, since they all rely on the same mistaken idea of a seven-year "tribulation" period based on Daniels seventieth week.

[19] This scene is symbolic, assuring God's people that the faithful who have died are not forgotten. God's vengeance on the wicked is *in response* to these cries for justice and vindication. Note that if this scene is literal, then the fate of the souls of the millions of martyrs, until Christ's return, is to be cooped up under an altar, as if in a dungeon, bleating for help. This is hardly a picture of souls enjoying heavenly bliss.

20 Another possibility, though less likely, is that "word of God" should be seen, as in 19:13, as referring to Jesus. In that case the "souls" under the altar would be martyrs since the time of Christ, whether Jewish believers or Gentile.

[21] The story of Cain and Abel, which defined the beginning of the fifth seal, may also be seen in the second. There Cain tried to substitute his own false worship for God's true worship. This led to strife in the family and the death of Abel—a reflection of the fourth seal.

rated from their lifeline to Christ. Finally, death rides a pale horse. This represents the cumulative force of evil, permitted to kill a fourth of all mankind.[22]

Excursus on Futurist Interpretation

LaHaye and Jenkins updated LaHaye's technical work in 1999. Their discussion of the first seal states:

"The first seal introduces the initial member of the famous 'four horsemen of the Apocalypse.' The rider is said to have a bow but no arrows, indicating that although he is militarily strong, in the beginning he does his conquering by diplomacy. Since he wears a crown, we know that he is successful in his efforts. And who is the rider on this white horse? There can be no doubt that it is the Antichrist, who through deceit and clever maneuvering will bring a false peace to the world. But that peace will not last"[23]

Up to this point I have been considerate of Futurist methods of interpretation. In this passage I have quoted LaHaye and Jenkins' *entire discussion of the first seal.* To say that this interpretation is shallow would be to understate the obvious. But this discussion is more complete even than that in Pentecost's extended technical work (Pentecost, 360), of which Walvoord states, "This work merits classification as a standard and comprehensive text in biblical eschatology…"[24] The first thing that we should note is that there is not a single Old Testament scriptural reference used in either comment on the first seal.[25] This violates a key principle of

---

[22] Much more could be said about the seals, but that would distract us from the chronological focus of our discussion. While we complain about the brevity of the LaHaye and Jenkins commentary on the first horse, please note that unlike them, we are not writing a detailed commentary, but a response to their work. Further, it is notable that while in the imagery of the horsemen may be seen shadows of the history of the church; they are not primarily intended to present chronological information. That they evoke such images at all is a testimony to the infinite genius that inspired the apocalypse.

[23] Timothy LaHaye, Jerry Jenkins, *Are We Living in the End Times?* (Wheaton, IL: Tyndale, 1999), 179.

[24] Pentecost, cover comment by John F. Walvoord.

[25] LaHaye's updated commentary on the book of Revelation, *Revelation*, 142-144, devotes over two pages to the identity of the first horseman, since he is the "key to understanding the three that follow him." Unfortunately, LaHaye does not use a single Bible text to assist him in this work, either.

context. Every scripture is to be understood by comparison with other scripture.

> But know this first of all, that no prophecy of Scripture is a matter of one's own interpretation, for no prophecy was ever made by an act of human will, but men moved by the Holy Spirit spoke from God. (2 Peter 1:20-21)

Here Peter points out, as Paul does in 2 Timothy 3:16, that God has inspired all biblical prophecies through the Holy Spirit. Thus, Scripture speaks with one voice. As Jamieson, Fausset, and Brown comment, "No Scripture is an isolated composition of the individual man, but part of an organic whole, to be solved by comparison with the rest of the Spirit-inspired Word."[26] In order to understand John's apocalypse, it is absolutely necessary to consider the rest of Scripture. In particular, since Revelation drips with Hebraisms, one must consider the Old Testament sources from which John has drawn his imagery. And in this, these Futurists have utterly failed. They treat the New Testament as a "church" testament unrelated to the "Jewish" Old Testament. In this they deny the apostles' own method of using the Old Testament to prove every point of doctrine.

LaHaye and Jenkins say, "The rider is said to have a bow but no arrows . . ." Their statement is demonstrably false. All that John records in Revelation 6:2 is that the rider has a bow. Had LaHaye and Jenkins bothered to check the Old Testament, they would have discovered at least forty texts where the archer's bow is used *without* any mention of the arrow. Only sixteen Old Testament texts mention both bow and arrows. The image of the first horseman is drawn from Isaiah 41:2. No mention of arrows is present, yet the bow is a powerful weapon in God's hands.

> "Who has aroused one from the east
> Whom He calls in righteousness to His feet?
> He delivers up nations before him,
> And subdues kings.
> He makes them like dust with his sword,
> As the wind-driven chaff with his bow." (Isa 41:2)

---

[26] Jamieson, Fausset, and Brown Commentary, Electronic Database (BibleSoft, 1997)

Lest the reader think I am picking on a single lapse by Futurist writers, Pentecost devotes a total of only five pages to the seals, trumpets, and bowl plagues without a single supporting Scripture reference from the Old Testament. LaHaye and Jenkins do a far better job, spending forty-two pages, with three Old Testament references. Unfortunately, not one text is used to help explain the prophecy. The "interpretation" is composed entirely of geo-political speculation. When context is utterly ignored as these Futurists have done, their "interpretation" should be expected to coincide with God's intention only by chance. And this in a book that begins with five chapters explicitly devoted to "Context"! Such a work does not contain the elements required for it to be considered "interpretation." It should therefore not be taken seriously.

The Church in Great Tribulation

While there is little religious persecution in the United States today, elsewhere many thousands every year die for their faith, whether in Sudan, Indonesia, Mexico, China, or one of many other countries. This indicates that the work of the pale horse in particular is as yet unfinished.[27] His power over all people will increase as we approach the end of the age. The troubles of the saints will grow, and many will die (Rev 2:10, 13; 6:11). Jesus said that if this evil of man against man were not terminated, no one would be left alive (Matt 24:22). Only God's grace will terminate this stage of trouble before the saints are all killed. (This will be discussed in more depth in the trumpets and bowl plagues.)

A great faith will be required to persevere through these troubles. And in this lies the greatest danger presented by the Futurist schema. Prophecy has been given so we will have faith when it is fulfilled (John 13:19; 14:29). Thus, past fulfillments stand as a firm foundation on which we can rest our faith in the future guarantees. But if those future promises are misunderstood, their apparent failure will seem to be a failure of God to

---

[27] "Pale," by the way, does not mean "white." The Greek word translated "pale" is *chloros*, a sickly yellowish-green the color of Clorox liquid chlorine bleach.

keep His word. Christians who believe in a pre-trib rapture will be severely shocked when they personally face terrible tribulation. Did God lie? On what will Futurists rely at that time? They would be better off to have never studied prophecy (cf. Eccl 4:3; 6:5)!

Christians who properly understand that there will be terrible troubles ahead will not be disappointed the way the pre-trib believer will be. They will face a crisis when threatened with death. But if their eyes are firmly fixed on the Savior, knowing their oppressors can "kill the body, but after that have no more that they can do" (Luke 12:4), they will be able to stand firm (Acts 14:22; 1 Thes 3:3; 1 Pet 4:13). In support of our belief that the Futurist scenario may lead believers to despair if it does not come true, we present LaHaye's own comments:

> Hope in this biblical context signifies confident expectation that Christ is coming. Of that there is no doubt because it is based on the certain Word of God that 'abides forever,' 'will never pass away,' and is 'settled in heaven.' . . . If Christ does not rapture His church before the Tribulation begins, much of the hope is destroyed, and thus it becomes a 'blasted hope.' (Rapture, 69)

> Paul's 'blessed hope' is the Rapture, for it is unique to the church. No one else will take part in it... The Glorious Appearing, on the other hand, is not for the Christian, but for the remnant at the end of the Tribulation. It will primarily affect the Jews and those who have been good to them, who somehow survive the Tribulation. His appearing literally turns the world into the kingdom of Christ. (Rapture, 68-69)

Saints throughout history have faced death without flinching. Thousands willingly went to the lions in the Roman games rather than renounce Christ. Reformers allowed themselves to be burned at the stake, singing as they died, rather than abandon the gospel. Many Christians in the Third World live in mortal danger today. It is only a wealthy Laodicean Christianity that considers tribulation to be capable of destroying hope. Those who have laid up their treasure in heaven (Matt 6:19-21) will not be unwilling to give up this temporary existence. When they open their eyes, it will be to the voice of the archangel (1 Thes 4:16). As they listened to the call of God in this life, they will rejoice at the call of God in the next.

The Fifth and Sixth Seals

The cry of the martyrs for vengeance in the fifth seal (Rev 6:10) reveals the thematic organization of the seals. The horsemen present God's call to repentance. Then the martyrs cry, "We repented and were killed for your name! How long will it be before you avenge our deaths?" God begins his answer with, "I must wait until all who will have come to me" (6:11). Then the sixth seal continues the answer with, "When that is done I will come in judgment to begin to avenge you."[28] Thus, the underlying theme of the seals is the covenant of salvation. God is not willing that one should be lost (2 Pet 3:9), and pledges to all lost sinners that if they will only come to him, he will save them (John 3:16; 1 John 1:9). In the messages to the seven churches (Rev 2-3), God lays out his covenant. In each message he offers salvation for all who will overcome with his help. For all who reject the offer, covenant curses will fall.

The final signs in the sixth seal are essentially the same as those described by Christ in Matthew 24. Since Jesus said that he was returning right after them, the cosmic signs[29] in the sun, moon, and stars mark his imminent return. Most commentators suggest that these signs identify the Day of the Lord, when Jesus comes in final judgment against the wicked (Beale, 396, 398). But details within the sixth seal suggest that the majority of analysts have erred in degree on this point. First, the cosmic signs are not the signs which accompany destruction in the seventh trumpet and bowl judgment. Those signs are thunder, lightning, and sounds (Rev 11:19; 16:18, 21).

Second, God's wrath "has come" (6:17),[30] but the wicked have not yet been destroyed. Put simply, the wicked are experi-

---

[28] G. K. Beale, *The Book of Revelation* (Grand Rapids: Eerdmans, 1999), 395. All three quotations here are paraphrased.

[29] These signs are also described in a number of Old Testament prophetic passages, where they are generally not literal but symbolic harbingers of disaster, idiomatic expressions. At Christ's return, however, they may well be literal. The predicted actions of the wicked in response to them (Rev 6:15-17) suggest they will be literal then.

[30] The Greek of this is in the aorist tense, indicating the fact that God's wrath has already arrived.

encing the wrath of God, but are still alive. There is only one period where this happens—the first six bowl plagues (16:1). This is the time when God's angels pour out covenant curses on the wicked prior to their complete destruction at Jesus' second coming. Therefore, the sixth seal covers the time of the first six bowl plagues and presents the beginning of the Day of the Lord.

Finally, although the sixth seal contains an earthquake (6:14), it is different from the earthquake in the seventh bowl judgment (16:18, 20). The earthquake in the sixth seal speaks of every mountain and island being moved. The earthquake in the seventh bowl judgment doesn't just move the islands and mountains. It causes them to vanish. This is a much stronger earthquake than in the sixth seal.

The sixth seal earthquake is drawn from Zechariah 14:4-7ff. There we see the Lord's feet on the Mount of Olives which splits in two, forming a valley to the east. This prepares the escape route of the saints. The "kings from the east" (Isa 41:2; Rev 16:12) use this route to rescue the saints (Dan 12:1).[31] This may also be seen as an echo of Paul's description of the second coming in 1 Thessalonians 4:13-17.

When the wicked see the cosmic signs, they recognize that the great day of God's vengeance has arrived (Rev 6:16-17). As God's wrath pours over them they try to hide, and they ask the crucial question, "Who will be able to stand?"[32] Just as the harbingers of final judgment in the sixth seal answer the cry of the saints in 6:10, the scenes recorded in 7:1-8:5 answer the query of the wicked.

In 7:1 John sees a new vision of four angels holding back the four winds of the earth.[33] They will be held back until all the saints on earth are sealed. The timing of this event is of crucial importance. In literary sequence it appears to occur *after* the sixth seal. But Jesus cannot pour out the covenant curses of the bowl plagues until after all of his saints have been sealed. This suggests that the seals are presented primarily in thematic rather than

---

[31] LaRondelle, 386-388. The "Kings from the East" describes Jesus and the hosts of heaven. See chapter six for discussion on this point.

[32] This cry is a quotation from Joel 2:11.

[33] The new vision is signaled by the formulaic phrase, "After this I saw."

chronological sequence. The content of the fifth seal suggested that the sealing was on-going then, and would be completed before the sixth seal. Later, as we explore the trumpets, it will become clear that this scene is in fact between the fifth and sixth seals.

A great many scholars acknowledge that Revelation is *not* a sequential prophecy, as asserted by LaHaye (*Rapture*, 212). It has numerous recapitulations, which is to say, it covers the same time period several times, each time seeing it from a different perspective with a different emphasis. Even the Futurist Walvoord writes, ". . . it pleased God to reveal various aspects of future events in other than their chronological order" (*Revelation*, 243). In doing so, the book follows the typical pattern of Hebrew apocalypses.

After the command to the four angels, John "hears" the number of the saints that are to be sealed. The number is 144,000, 12,000 from each of twelve tribes of Israel. This immediately suggests to the Futurists that these are not from the church, but are Jews. Several facts prevent this conclusion.

The most obvious problem is the way in which the scene is presented. John "hears" the number and description, then turns and sees "a great multitude, which no one could count, from every nation and all tribes and peoples and tongues" (7:9).[34] That this presentation is intended to represent a single group may be inferred from the presentation of Jesus in 5:5-7 and the New Jerusalem in 21:9ff. In the first scene, John is told that the Lion of Judah is worthy to open the *biblion*, but instead sees a sacrificial lamb receive the scroll. In the latter he is told that he will be shown the bride of the Lamb, but is instead shown a city. This form of being told one thing but seeing something apparently

---

[34] The idea of uncountable numbers is frequent in the Old Testament, but is never literal. The number "no man can count" is an idiom meaning "a great many." However, given that John *hears* the number 144,000 and is familiar with that, the actuality of what he *sees*, an uncountable "great multitude," should be understood to be much greater than 144,000, and 144,000 should be seen as a symbolic number. The number twelve symbolizes completeness, so twelve times twelve, 144, symbolizes even more perfect completeness, and that is multiplied by a thousand, yielding 144,000, suggesting that a large and utterly perfect number (in God's eyes) will be saved. Everyone willing will be saved, and God will make no mistakes.

different is the same mode of presentation utilized in the sealing scene.

The great multitude is in heaven, where the church is supposed to be in the Futurist schema. Since these two representations present the same group in different places, it is impossible for the description to be physically literal. The number must be symbolic. The true number sealed is far larger than 144,000 and is drawn from people of every description.

Next, the exact equality of 12,000 from each tribe is highly improbable in any real sense. But as a symbolic number, it is made up of multiples of twelve and ten to represent the complete number of those saved (Walvoord, *Revelation*, 28). Third, the tribes listed do not match any list of the twelve tribes anywhere else in Scripture. This again implies a symbolic meaning for the names of the tribes, rather than a literal accounting. At least one possible accounting of the symbolism has been suggested.

Name:	Meaning:
Judah	"Praise" (Israelites enter God's spiritual Jerusalem through gates called "Praise." See Isa 60:18.)
Reuben	"A Son" "Firstborn" (Gen 49:3; John 1:12; Rom 8:14-17, etc.)
Gad	"A Company" (Rev 7:9; 19:1, 6, etc.) – of sons, redeemed
Asher	"Happy" (John 13:17, etc.) – after
Naphthali	"Wrestling" (Gen 32:24-30, etc.) – in prayer
Manasseh	"Forgetting" (Phil 3:13; Isa 65:17) – self and the past
Simeon	"Hearing" (1 Sam 3:10: "Speak, for thy servant heareth.") – God's Word
Levi	"Joined" (John 15:1-7; Acts 2:47) – to God
Issachar	"Servants" (Rom 6:16-22, etc.)
Zebulun	"Dwelling" (Ps 91:1; Isa 33:14, etc.) – with
Joseph	"Added" (2 Pet 1:2; 5-11, etc.) – joys and special blessings

Name:	Meaning:
Benjamin	"Son of the right hand" (not "son of sorrow") "In thy presence is fullness of joy; at Thy right hand there are pleasures for evermore." (Ps 16:11; Eph 2:6)[35]

This list of tribes evokes a number of characteristics of saints. The Israel of God *praises* Him continually. They are adopted as *sons* to make a *company*. They are *happy* after their salvation. They *wrestle* in prayer until the second coming. They *forget* themselves and their past in the service of God, which they perform by *hearing* His voice. They are *joined* as *servants*, *added* to God as *sons*, seated *at his right hand*.

The scene greeting John when he turns is very comforting. First, the number of saints is immense, and they are from every conceivable heritage. This is without doubt a view of the church in heaven. But even more comforting are the details. This view calls to mind the Feast of Booths (Tabernacles).

This Feast was a joyous memorial. It commemorated the protection of God for the Israelites in the wilderness (Lev 23:42) and was a feast of thanksgiving for the harvest (Deut 16:13-15). It was celebrated with the waving of the *lulav* (Lev 23:40), made of branches such as palms (Rev 7:9). The people lived in booths—temporary shelters of saplings and branches—like the shelter the Lord spread over them (7:15) at the time of the exodus from bondage in Egypt. These booths protected them from the harsh desert sun (7:16).[36] The saints follow the Lamb (7:17) to springs of water (cf. Isa 12:3; Exod 17:6). This "following" recalls the leading of the Lord in the wilderness by the pillar of fire at night and the pillar of smoke in the day (Exod 13:21-22).

This distinctly Jewish event is in heaven, where LaHaye insists the church will have been taken at the time this scene represents. Once again we find that the Futurist schema stands in direct opposition to the pattern of Scripture. The Bible presents the

---

[35] Modified slightly from Desmond Ford, *Crisis!* vol. 2 (Newcastle, CA: Desmond Ford Pub, 1982), 391.

[36] The shade of the booth (*sakkath*, from the same root as *sukkot*, the word for booth or tabernacle) was a tremendous protection from the summer sun. As a result, "shade" became a symbol of divine protection, and is seen in a number of passages. Ps 17:8; 27:5; 31:20; 36:37; 57:1; 63:7; 91:1; Isa 4:6; Amos 9:11; Hos 14:7, etc.

outline of end times in totally Jewish form. The spring festivals were the pattern of Jesus' first advent, and the fall festivals are the pattern for His second. There is no provision in this pattern for separating Jews and the church. All saints of all ages are treated as a single people of God.

The Seventh Seal

When the seventh seal is broken in Revelation 8:1, there is a period of silence in heaven for about half an hour.[37] As in every interpretive element before, "the key to the significance of the 'silence' must lie in the connotation that it has in the OT and in Jewish writings . . ." (Beale, 445). And the significance is great indeed.

Our view has returned to the throne room of God. This is the heavenly tabernacle, and the events there echo the earthly counterparts that are a type and shadow of the true tabernacle in heaven (Heb 8:1-2).[38] In the daily services of the temple, instrumental music and singing were constantly present.[39] But when it came time for the priest to come before the Lord with the offering of incense, everyone became silent. This was a time of expectation of the "unfolding of God's judgments."

The daily events of the temple foreshadowed the final events of the annual Day of Judgment, the Day of Atonement. The half hour duration of the silence in 8:1 points to the time of the High Priest's ministry in the presence of God. As in the daily service, the High Priest offered incense. But during the Atonement ceremony, he added two hands full of incense to the censer, rather than the customary half mina (Lev 16:12-13). This created a bil-

---

[37] John F. Walvoord writes, in *The Revelation of Jesus Christ*, 151, "Though thirty minutes is not ordinarily considered a long time, when it is a time of absolute silence portending such ominous developments ahead it is an indication that something tremendous is about to take place. It may be compared to the silence before the foreman of a jury reports a verdict; for a moment there is perfect silence and everyone awaits that which will follow."

[38] The actual echo is in the earthly services which are the shadows, but since we have concrete knowledge of them, the heavenly is represented using symbols drawn from the earthly.

[39] Alfred Edersheim, *The Temple: Its Ministry and Services* (Peabody, MA: Hendrickson, 1995), 50-54. Jamieson, Fausset, and Brown on Revelation 8:1.

lowing cloud of fragrant smoke so that the High Priest was screened from the glory of God over the mercy seat (16:2), allowing him to survive in God's presence. He would then be able to carry out the other tasks of the Atonement ritual. At the same time, everyone else had to leave the tabernacle precincts (16:17). The entire populace waited silently outside the tabernacle to hear the bells on his robe tinkle, signaling that he had finished his task (Exod 28:35).[40]

Habakkuk 2:20 and Zechariah 2:13 present God in his temple, preparing to execute judgment. The inhabitants of the earth are to stand silently in awe before him to hear the verdict.[41] And this is exactly the scene on the Day of Atonement. The camp waited silently in anticipation of judgment in favor of God's people (cf. Dan 7:22), which would be signaled by the tinkling of the bells on the High Priest's robe as he left the Holy of Holies (Mishna Tractate *Yoma*, 53b). Confirmation was complete when they heard him pronounce the full name of Yahweh after leaving the presence of God.[42] This also completes the answer to the question in Revelation 6:17. Those who are able to stand are those who have answered the call to repentance. They have washed their robes in the blood of the lamb (Rev 7:14), and have been sealed as God's property. The verdict on the Day of Atonement is "not guilty," and they have been given clean robes (7:9; cf. Zech 3:4).

The book of Hebrews points out that the ultimate Day of Atonement is coming.

> Let us hold fast the confession of our hope without wavering, for He who promised is faithful; and let us consider how to stimulate one another to love and good deeds, not forsaking our own assembling

---

[40] Edersheim, 231. M. L. Andreasen, *The Sanctuary Service* (Hagerstown, MD: Review & Herald, 1947), 181. Douglas Ezell, *Revelations on Revelation—New Sounds from Old Symbols* (1977), 48-49. The New English Translation renders this passage "And the robe is to be on Aaron as he ministers, and his sound will be heard when he enters the Holy Place before the Lord and when he leaves, so that he does not die."

[41] Other Old Testament texts that present this same idea are Isaiah 41:1 and Psalm 76:6-9.

[42] Ibid, 66a. Although direct references to the silence of the camp are scanty, the ability to hear the bells and the spoken name of Yahweh require it.

together, as is the habit of some, but encouraging one another; and all the more, as you see the day drawing near. (Heb 10:23-25)

"The day" in this passage would have reminded Hebrew readers of the Day of Atonement, which in Jewish thought and writing is simply referred to as "The Day,"[43] although in the Old Testament prophecies "the day" is shorthand for the "Day of the Lord," usually meaning the time when God returns to rescue his people and punish those who have enslaved or hurt them.[44]

For if we go on sinning willfully after receiving the knowledge of the truth, there no longer remains a sacrifice for sins, but **a certain terrifying expectation of judgment**, and the fury of a fire which will consume the adversaries. Anyone who has set aside the Law of Moses dies without mercy on the testimony of two or three witnesses. **How much severer punishment do you think he will deserve who has trampled under foot the Son of God**, and has regarded as unclean the blood of the covenant by which he was sanctified, and has insulted the Spirit of grace? For we know Him who said, **"Vengeance is Mine, I will repay."** And again, "The Lord will judge His people." **It is a terrifying thing to fall into the hands of the living God.** (Heb 10:26-31, emphasis added)[45]

The "Day of the Lord" and the "Day of Atonement" are closely related. The "Day of the Lord" points to the punishment of those who have refused to confess and the sending of the scapegoat into the wilderness, nearly the last part of the day's ac-

---

[43] This identification is so ingrained that the Mishna tractate on the Day of Atonement is simply titled "Yoma," or "The Day," rather than being given the full title "Yom Kippur." The Mishna is a compilation from about 200AD of the oral Torah. This in turn was a collection of the rabbinical traditions amplifying the written instructions of God in the first five books of the Bible, the Torah.

[44] It's possible that in some cases "the day of the Lord" is speaking not of the end times, but of various Old Testament times when God executed judgment on the enemies of his people. However, it always seems to refer to an overwhelming physical event that is really God's execution of judgment, even when God uses some king and his army to do the work for him. As will become apparent later in the book, the Day of Atonement and the Day of the Lord will occur at the same time, even though the language of the Old Testament may seem to treat them separately. Even in Old Testament times the Hebrews understood the Day of Atonement to be the Day of Judgment, which is generally synonymous with the Day of the Lord.

[45] The inseparability of the Old and New Testaments is made particularly clear by this passage, since in it Paul makes his case by quoting Isaiah 26:11 and Deuteronomy 32:35-36 while also making direct reference to Deuteronomy 17:2-6 and 19:15.

tivities. On the other hand the Day of Atonement points to God covering over the sins of his people. Paul exhorted the believers to encourage each other in faith in anticipation of the Day, since judgment would accompany its arrival, just as it did in Levitical times. At the same time it will be a woeful time for the wicked, since their rejection of the atonement will result in the arrival of the Day of the Lord to punish their evil.

Revelation 8:3-5 concludes the Day of Atonement description in the seventh seal. First, an angel is given a large amount of incense in a censer to offer with the prayers of the saints on the golden altar of incense. The smoke went up "before God" (8:4). This parallels the offering of large amounts of incense on Yom Kippur (Lev 16:13). It also recalls the prayer of the martyrs in Revelation 6:10,[46] tying this action to a theme already noted in the seals. When the Atonement is over, the incense burns out, and only coals are left in the bottom of the censer. To these the angel adds fire from the altar. With the judgment in favor of the saints complete, the fire is cast to earth in final judgment on the wicked (8:5).

The vision of Ezekiel confirms this view. One year before the destruction of Solomon's temple in Jerusalem, as the glory of God was preparing to depart from the temple, a man clothed in linen was told to take coals from the fire beneath the wheels of the cherubim and spread them over Jerusalem (Ezek 10:2). The clothing of this person is the linen of the High Priest's white robe on the Day of Atonement. This suggests that this person is the High Priest, which we recognize to be an office of Christ (Heb 7:26). The action is judgmental in character, another task of Christ, since the Father "has given all Judgment to the son" (John 5:22). Thus, the coals represent judicial action by God. This scene, drawn from Ezekiel 10:2, presents the wrath of God poured out to destroy the wicked after they have rejected the atonement.

The fire thrown to earth is a form of "hail" (Ps 18:12-13; 105:32; Isa 30:30). It also evokes the image of the fire and brimstone that destroyed Sodom and Gomorrah (Gen 19:24-25). Hail

---

[46] The text says "the prayers of all the saints," so this is not limited to the prayer of the martyrs in 6:10.

is an agent used by God to destroy the wicked (Exod 9:19; Isa 28:2). This indicates that the seventh seal includes the conclusion of the Day of the Lord in which nothing wicked will survive (Isa 13:6, 9; Ezek 30; Joel 2:11; Obad 15-16; Zeph 1:14-15). Once the atonement was completed in the earthly sanctuary, another annual cycle began. But at the close of probation, the final atonement will be completed in the heavenly sanctuary. No new prayers for forgiveness may then be made. Everyone who is righteous will be righteous still, and everyone who is wicked will be wicked still (Rev 22:11).

Parallels with the Trumpets and Bowl Judgments

The sixth seal contains cosmic signs in the heavens where the saints have their hopes fixed. And in this they follow the pattern of the first theme of the seals—salvation. But this set of signs does not recur in the trumpets or bowl judgments. Instead, there is a different set of signs. The seventh seal (Rev 8:5) includes four—thunder, sounds, lightning, and an earthquake. This exact set is also found in the seventh trumpet (11:19) and the seventh bowl plague (16:18). The occurrence of the identical signs in all three sequences gives us a solid chronological peg. The seventh seal, trumpet, and bowl all describe the same event, and therefore are parallel, not sequential. As we will later discover, all of them also include the Day of Atonement.

There is only one Day of Atonement in heaven, not three. There is only one second coming and Day of the Lord, not three. Therefore, rather than describing a sequence of twenty-one sequential events, as the Futurist "Great Tribulation" scenario proposes, the seals, trumpets, and bowl judgments are partially concurrent sets of seven items. As we study the trumpets and bowl judgments, a grand design will become clear. The seals primarily point to the reproof, repenting, refining, and salvation of the saints. The trumpets primarily point to the rejection of salvation by the wicked, and the bowl judgments are the covenant curses that result from the rejection our Lord. In the end, all three series conclude at the same moment: the revealing of Jesus Christ in power and glory (Matt 24:30; Mark 13:26; Luke 21:27).

Seven Seals

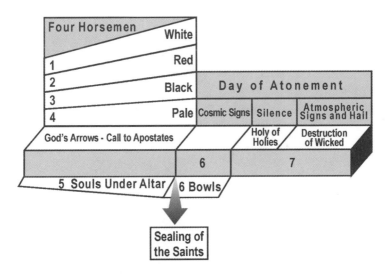

Four Horsemen
White
1   Red
2   Black   Day of Atonement
3
4   Pale   Cosmic Signs   Silence   Atmospheric Signs and Hail

God's Arrows - Call to Apostates   Holy of Holies   Destruction of Wicked

6   7

5 Souls Under Altar   6 Bowls

Sealing of the Saints

CHAPTER FIVE:

... GREAT TRIBULATION ...

"Woe, woe, woe, to those who dwell on the earth, because of the remaining blasts of the trumpet of the three
angels who are about to sound!" (Rev 8:13)

The seven trumpets are introduced in the middle of the seventh seal (Rev 8:2). Then the narrative returns to the final elements of the Day of Atonement in the seventh seal. But the next
three verses do not stand as only a part of the seals. They also
look forward to the trumpets. The offering of incense was a part
of the process of forgiveness offered to sinful mankind. But the
wicked will ultimately refuse the offer and reject God. When the
atonement is complete, the wicked will have placed themselves
directly in the path of the wrath of God. With the incense gone,
only coals are left, and they become a hail of fire and brimstone
to destroy the wicked. In this short space the end of the seventh
seal has presented a brief sketch of the theme of the trumpets.
This passage is thus a "duo-directional"[1] link that ties the seals
and trumpets together.

---

[1] The primary work on this is in Jon Paulien's "Looking Both Ways: A Study of
the Duodirectionality of the Structural Seals in the Apocalypse," a paper presented to
the Hebrews, General and Pastoral Epistles, Apocalypse Section of the Society of Biblical Literature Annual Meeting, Chicago, Nov. 19–22, 1988, though many other scholars, such as Beale, agree with Paulien, whether or not they use this term. According to
the principle of duodirectionality, this passage serves as both the conclusion of one
section (the seals) and the beginning of the next section (the trumpets). This occurs a
number of times in Revelation.

The Nature of the Trumpets

"The object of [blowing trumpets] is expressly stated to have been 'for a memorial' (Num 10:1–10), that they might 'be remembered before Jehovah,' . . . [and] was a public acknowledgment of Jehovah as King" (Edersheim, 231). When the trumpets are blown at the Feast of Trumpets, ". . . the Rabbis hold that the blowing of the trumpets is intended . . . as a call to repentance – as it were, a blast to wake men from their sleep of sin" (Maimonides, *Moreh Nev.* iii. 43, in Edersheim, 236–237). The Jewish people of Christ's day understood that Yom Teruah (the Feast of Trumpets; lit. "the day of blowing"), which fell ten days before the Day of Atonement, was the beginning of the heavenly trial. The books would be opened, and every person's destiny would be decided.

An additional element is present here. Just as there was a holy sabbatical cycle of days (Gen 2:2–3; Exod 20:8–11) and years (Lev 25:2–17), Yom Teruah demarcated the holy sabbatical cycle of months. On the first day of the first six months the shofar was blown. This began in the month of Nisan, which began the spring festivals that were fulfilled in the First Advent of Christ. On Yom Teruah the silver trumpet was blown throughout the day. This heralded the beginning of the judgment. This sequence of trumpets spanning the gap between the spring and fall festivals links them together. The fall festivals will be fulfilled in the Second Advent of Christ. And just as the seven monthly trumpets announced the annual judgment, the seven apocalyptic trumpets proclaim the great eschatological judgment and span the time from the First to the Second Advents.

The Purpose of the Trumpets

The trumpets present a series of calamities. There is hail and fire (8:7; cf. Exod 9:23), water turned to blood (8:8; cf. Exod 7:19–21), bitter water (8:11; cf. Exod 7:21), darkness (8:12; cf. Exod 10:21–22), locusts (9:3; cf. Exod 10:12–15), and death of a third of mankind (9:15; cf. Exod 12:29). Just as the seals represented God's arrows, used to bring apostate Israel back to God, the trumpets re-present the plagues of God against Egypt, where His people were held captive. These plagues served two purposes. First, God said, "I will lay My hand on Egypt, and bring out My hosts, My people the sons of Israel, from the land of Egypt by great judgments" (Exod 7:4). In a similar way, God's people in the end time will be brought out of spiritual Egypt (Rev 11:8) by great judgments. Thus it is legitimate to identify the trumpets as judgments against the wicked. Second, the plagues were intended to show that Yahweh was the one true God (Exod 7:5).

The Keys to the Chronology of the Trumpets

The Day of Atonement and the signs of the Day of the Lord provide us with keys to unlock the sequence of the trumpets relative to the seals (and later the bowl judgments). This is true because the heavenly Day of Atonement only happens once, and the Day of the Lord also happens only once.[2] If we can identify when these events take place in each sequence, then we have identified matching points in their chronologies.

There are at least ten Old Testament "Day of the Lord" passages that describe cosmic and atmospheric signs.[3] The signs listed in individual passages vary. For example, Amos 5:18–20 only describes darkness, while Joel 3:15 tells of celestial darkness, thunder, and an earthquake. And this variability is also seen in Revelation. The sixth seal includes celestial darkness and a great earthquake. The seventh seal, trumpet, and bowl judgment all include lightning, thunder, sounds, and an earthquake. Since all of these signs are Day of the Lord signs, we should have no difficulty agreeing that all of them describe the Day of the Lord.[4] And

---

[2] Printers preparing for color printing use what are known as "color separations" in cyan, magenta, and yellow. If these are properly "registered," matched up exactly, the result will look like a color photo. If they are not, the separate color separations will be seen and the picture will look blurry. On each color separation there are "registration marks," usually little targets or crosses. When these are matched up exactly on the printed page, the result looks like a photo. Similarly, the atmospheric signs of the seventh seal, trumpet, and bowl judgment serve as "registration marks." When the same "one time only" signs are found elsewhere in the Bible and matched up, the chronology becomes clear. If this is ignored, the chronology will be wrong.

[3] Isa 13:9–12; 24:17–23; Ezek 32:3–9; Joel 2:1–11, 31; 3:15; Amos 5:18–20; Zeph 1:14–18; Zech 14:6–7.

[4] The signs listed in the Day of the Lord texts have little other use in scripture. While thunder appears in a number of other places, it almost always refers to the voice

since the Day of the Lord is a singular event in earth's history, it is not difficult to identify all of these signs as describing God's definitive final action against the wicked. But this does not imply that the sixth seal, which contains only the cosmic signs, is the time of the destruction of the wicked. As we discussed in the previous chapter, the cosmic signs are only seen in the sixth seal. While they are happening, the wicked are still alive, but aware of the Day of the Lord. This implies that the concluding action on the Day of the Lord, the destruction of the wicked, is still future.

The seventh trumpet opens with a paean of praise (Rev 11:15–18). God's ultimate reign has begun, and the time has come to judge the dead (11:18). This is then broken down into two actions—rewarding the saints and destroying the wicked. And in parallel fashion these two actions are presented.

First, the temple of God is opened, revealing the "ark of His covenant" (11:19). This is the view greeting the High Priest on the Day of Atonement as he enters the Holy of Holies. In the normal course of events, he was the only person who would ever see the ark, and then only on the Day of Atonement (Lev 16:1–6; 23:26–28). As discussed in chapter four, this is the process by which the saints are finally cleansed and prepared to receive their reward.

Next come the atmospheric signs of the Day of the Lord— lightning, thunder, sounds, and an earthquake. These are followed by hail, which destroys God's enemies. Once again the two aspects of the final judgment are presented. The Day of Atonement language is progressive, moving from outside the tabernacle in the seventh seal to inside in the seventh trumpet, while the Day of the Lord language is identical in both. There can be no mistaking the fact that these two symbolic series conclude at exactly the same moment. This is the strongest possible evidence that the two series are parallel and denies the Futurist assertion that Revelation is a sequential prophecy. The seals and trumpets cover the same general span of time, but with differing purposes.

---

of God. Earthquakes are even more exclusive, and hail, while not appearing in the Day of the Lord texts, has a nearly exclusive scriptural use as a weapon of God against the wicked.

Our next chronological key is found in the fifth trumpet. There (9:4), the agents of judgment are told they will not be allowed to harm anyone who has the seal of God. Prior to the completion of the sealing, the saints will also be exposed to the trumpet judgments. They are still at risk at the time of the fifth seal,[5] and the cosmic signs of the sixth seal point to the Day of the Lord. Therefore God's people must be sealed before the sixth seal, and the fifth and sixth trumpets must be after the fifth seal. It seems clear, thus, that the sealing of the saints is completed between the fifth and sixth seals and before the fifth and sixth trumpets. The question remaining is just when the trumpets begin. As always, Scripture will be allowed to interpret itself. We will look to the Old Testament for keys that unlock for us the meaning of the trumpets.

The Time Span and Detailed Character of the Trumpets

A detailed interpretation of each of the trumpets is beyond the scope of this book. The emphases of the seals and trumpets are different, since the seals recall "God's arrows" that called apostates to repentance, while the trumpets recall the plagues against the wicked people of Egypt. Thus, the most important difference between them appears to be the target population. This ought to be a sufficient discussion for a book focusing on chronology, but because Futurists are so accustomed to "thorough" presentations of the particulars of the symbols, it is necessary for us to go beyond a simple outline to their sources. In order to do so we must first consider the literary nature of the book of Revelation.

Virtually all expositors recognize that the book of Revelation is an apocalypse.[6] The primary purpose of this type of writing is to give assurance to the faithful in the midst of persecution, not

---

[5] In Rev 6:11 the martyrs under the altar are told they must stay there until more of their "fellow servants" and "brothers" are slain as they have been, so clearly martyrdom continues at least until the end of the fifth seal period.

[6] A number of apocalypses exist in Scripture. The most important are Daniel and Revelation, but the books of Isaiah, Joel, Ezekiel, Zephaniah, and Zechariah contain apocalyptic elements. Further, Revelation 1:1 calls the book an "*apokalupsis*," using the Greek word from which the term "apocalypse" is derived.

to serve as a demonstration of God's prophetic prowess (Walvoord, *Revelation*, 14). In order to reinforce the message of redemption contained within an apocalypse, the revelation is repeated from different perspectives. In the case of Daniel, the grand prophetic outline in Nebuchadnezzar's dream (Dan 2) is amplified in the vision of the four beasts (Dan 7), the ram and the goat (Dan 8), the seventy weeks (Dan 9), and the kings of the North and South (Dan 11–12). In a similar way, the book of Revelation uses repetition to amplify various aspects of what is to come, different views of God's protection and judgment.

Many expositors consider the messages to the churches to contain a general outline of the course of church history since the apostolic era (Walvoord, *Revelation*, 52). This is then revisited from different perspectives in the seals and trumpets. Additional expansions are found in the measuring of the temple (Rev 11), and so on. Because of this repetition and recapitulation, it is improper to deal with the apocalypse as if it were a linear prophecy.

In common with other apocalypses, the book of Revelation is written primarily in symbolic language.[7] Some have suggested that this use of symbols was to avoid offending the civil authorities who were causing trouble for the saints. These writers propose that if the language had been more direct, it would have been regarded as seditious. Certainly even Jesus used symbolic language in his parables so that those who had open minds would understand, but others would be baffled (Mark 4:11–12).

It might be tempting to suggest that the choice to use symbols was the author's. This would then place upon John the responsibility of choosing the specific symbol for each situation and lessen the divine import that biblical language carries. But all Scripture is inspired by God (2 Tim 3:16). While this does not mean that God dictated every word, God did ultimately direct John to record (or not to record) specific scenes (Rev 1:11; 10:4). While John chose the words describing the scenes, the symbols he recorded were present in the vision and not his literary inven-

---

[7] Ibid, 25. In Rev 1:1 John writes that Jesus Christ "signified" what he revealed, which means he used "signs" or "symbols" (the root word in Greek is the same word from which we get the word "Semiotics," the study of signs, especially linguistic signs, which always serve as "symbols" of the things or ideas they represent).

tion. Put differently, John saw angels with trumpets. When the angels blew the trumpets, various things happened. John wrote down the contents of each scene in his own way, but did not concoct the scenes.[8]

Since God presented the scenes to John, we may legitimately expect that the substance of those scenes was put there to be meaningful to God's people. Therefore, the images used must be either unambiguous present-day (to John) material or recapitulations of older scriptural material. As we examine the specifics of the trumpets, it will become clear that God presents new scenes to John with old symbols. In doing so, he brings to view a large amount of prophetic imagery from the OT. This allows God to speak volumes in a short space.

To illustrate this concept, let us consider a modern colloquial expression: "to hit a home run." If taken literally, this describes a baseball game in which the batter succeeds in striking the pitch so as to cause the ball to leave the field of play in fair territory. The batter and any runners on base score. However, the literal physical events that make up the image do not apply in many cases where the expression is used.

A businessman may lead his company into a highly successful business venture, such as happened when Sony first marketed the Walkman portable tape player. A politician may make a speech that appears to propel his party into a markedly superior popular position relative to its opposition. In both cases the act may be spoken of as "hitting a home run." But in neither case is the sport of baseball in view. Rather, in each case the metaphor speaks of dramatic success in the face of opposition or competition. An image from one universe is imported into another in order to convey a larger meaning than simple language limited to the specific area might provide.

The first trumpet (Rev 8:7) tells of hail mixed with fire that burns up a third of the trees and grass. This is a mixed metaphor, to say the least. Since hail is ice, it does not mix with fire. Next, it burns up "all the green grass." But in the fifth trumpet (9:4), the

---

[8] Ibid, 11. The Greek grammar of the book of Revelation has been frequently criticized. If God were to have dictated the book on a word-by-word basis, we would expect to see formally perfect grammar and syntax.

plague of locusts is told that it cannot "hurt the grass of the earth." Thus, the first trumpet plague must not literally destroy every blade of grass. This implies that the language used is in fact symbolic, as stated by Walvoord (*Revelation*, 12–13). Having identified the character of the image, we must investigate its origin in order to understand the intent of the first trumpet.

"'[H]ail' was an essential part of God's holy wars against His enemies (Job 38:22, 23): against Egypt (Exod. 9:18, 22–26), against the Amorites (Josh. 10:11), against David's enemies (Ps. 18:12–14), against an apostate, rebellious Israel (Isa. 28:2, 17) and Judah (Ezek. 13:11, 13)."[9] In eschatological oracles, hail is one of God's weapons against the wicked (Job 38:22–23; Isa 28:2, 17; 32:19). But even in the Old Testament, the metaphorical nature of "hail" can clearly be seen. Isaiah 32:1–2 describes rulers as shelters from the storm, which includes hail (v. 19). David describes his deliverance from Saul (Ps 18) in such hyperbolic language that it clearly cannot be literal. Certainly David did not see smoke rising from God's nostrils (v. 8), and "hailstones and coals of fire" were not literally the means by which he escaped. But such hyperbole presents the picture of an angry God whose acts of retribution against the wicked cannot be escaped.

The imagery of the first trumpet includes fire with the hail, leading us to further sources. The most obvious is the fire and brimstone that destroyed Sodom and Gomorrah (Gen 19:24). Their destruction was so complete that no one who stayed in either city survived, and archeologists have not been successful in identifying their ruins.

The first trumpet results in a third of the earth and a third of the trees being burned up, as well as complete destruction of all the grass. This imagery is not mathematically rigorous. The idea that *exactly* one third of specific groups would be destroyed is drawn from Ezekiel 5. There, Ezekiel is told that thirds of Judah would suffer specific fates (Ezek 5:12). Yet the exactness of the image was not matched by history. The terms were fulfilled in approximate proportion, in keeping with the prevailing Hebrew imprecision in mathematics. Similarly, we must not ascribe to

---

[9] Hans K. LaRondelle, *How to Understand the End-Time Prophecies of the Bible*, (Sarasota, FL: First Impressions, 1997), 169.

Revelation absolute exactness in such numbers (Walvoord, *Revelation*, 28). The intent in their use is to state that a large portion suffered the same fate.

The specific imagery of trees in the first trumpet comes directly from the plague of hail in Egypt, where "every tree" was shattered (Ex 9:25). But since it is clear that the intent in Revelation is symbolic, we must look further. We find tree imagery in 2 Chr 25:17–20, where a thistle tries to marry its son to the daughter of a cedar of Lebanon, but is instead trampled by a wild beast. Ezekiel wrote four oracles in which trees feature significantly. In the parable of the great cedar (Ezek 17:1–24), the tree is the house of Judah, and other trees are other kingdoms. In the oracle against the forest of Teman (20:45–48), the forest is the people of the evil kingdom. The trees in the oracle against the wicked in the land of Israel (21:1–32) are the people. Assyria is referred to as a "cedar in Lebanon" (31:3). Other prophets use similar symbolic language. In Daniel 4, king Nebuchadnezzar is symbolized by a tree in his dream. Judah is "God's fig tree" (Joel 1:7). Olive trees are the "anointed ones standing by the Lord" (Zech 4:14). And who can forget the olive tree representing true Israel in Romans 11 (cf. Hosea 14:6)?

We may now reasonably expect "trees" to represent nations, people, or leaders of people. Grass would appear to be likely to represent the "little people" or the population of an affected area. Certainly a visual people such as the Hebrews would seem likely to use such a description, and indeed, this is what we find. But the image is not just "grass," but "burned grass." This image is seen a number of times in the Old Testament, each time referring to evildoers. The inhabitants of Assyria will become as scorched grass (2 Kgs 19:26; Isa 37:25). Evildoers will wither like grass on the rooftops (Ps 37:2; 129:6). The wicked will become like grass burned by fire (Isa 5:24; 15:6). But the most direct source of this image is Isaiah 40:6–8, which is also quoted by Peter (1 Pet 1:24) and James (James 1:10–11).

A voice says, "Call out." Then he answered, "What shall I call out?"
All flesh is grass, and all its loveliness is like the flower of the field.
The grass withers, the flower fades, when the breath of the LORD

blows upon it; surely the people are grass. The grass withers, the flower fades, but the word of our God stands forever. (Isa 40:6–8)

This passage is an oracle of comfort for God's people. In keeping with all of the other Old Testament sources using this image, Isaiah presents the vivid picture of God's retribution on the peoples who have oppressed them. Finally, in Hebrew thought, the land[10] was their home, in keeping with the promise to Abraham (Gen 12:7). And this brings us full circle. We are ready to "hit a home run" in understanding the first trumpet.

The people of God in the days of John had been students of Scripture (Acts 17:11). Inspired students of Scripture had preached to them. This preparation, using imagery from the Old Testament, was far deeper than this brief examination of symbols. We may explore the origins of the symbols, but they "heard and understood" (Rev 1:3, lit.). When the first trumpet was read, the original churches would have immediately called to mind the plague of hail in Egypt, the fire and brimstone at Sodom and Gomorrah, the imagery of leaders as trees and wicked people as grass. The addition of blood into the mixture would have indicated the carnage that would accompany the plague. Then they would have called to mind Deuteronomy 29:19–28. This covenant curse on the unrepentant in Israel calls out that God will "smoke" (lit.) with fire and brimstone like Sodom and Gomorrah. The people would be "uprooted from their land" and "cast into another land." The hearers of the first trumpet would most likely understand it as an oracle against apostate Israel, and would identify its fulfillment in the destruction of Jerusalem and the dispersion of the few survivors to far portions of the Roman Empire (Matt 23:38).[11]

---

[10] "Land" is a literal translation of the Greek *ge*.

[11] The alert reader will recognize that the destruction of Jerusalem was in AD 70, and the commonly accepted date for the book of Revelation is about AD 94. This would place the first trumpet in the past, even though the vision is apparently future. This difficulty is resolved when we note that the child of chapter 12 is generally identified as either Christ or the church. Either identification is also past when compared to the date of the writing of the book. A second option is that the earlier proposed date of Revelation (ca. 65AD) is correct, and that this oracle is in the immediate future. This interpretation of the first trumpet could suggest the plausibility of that thesis.

It would be possible to spend similarly large amounts of space on the other trumpets, but this would divert us from our chronological task. By identifying the first trumpet with the destruction of Jerusalem, in fulfillment of covenant curses, we have determined the length of the series. It extends from AD 70 to the heavenly atonement, from the First Advent to the Second. The only remaining details of chronological importance are the sealing of the saints and the close of probation for sinners. But since we have given such a large amount of space to the details of the first trumpet, it would seem inappropriate to casually dismiss the second, third, and fourth. Therefore we will very briefly mention a few high points.

The second trumpet has "something like a mountain" thrown into the sea (Rev 8:8). In Scripture, mountains refer to kingdoms. In particular, this image is drawn from Jeremiah 51:24–32, where God declares that He is against the "destroying mountain" (v. 25) that "destroys the whole earth." This oracle against "Babylon" is adapted by John to apply to the more modern Babylon, which Peter identifies as Rome (1 Peter 5:13). The second trumpet therefore points to the destruction of the Roman Empire in the fourth and fifth centuries.

The third trumpet (Rev 8:10–11) depicts the fall of a star named Wormwood. Wormwood is the name given to idolatry in Deuteronomy 29:17–18 and Jeremiah 9:13–15. Idolatry poisons the waters of life, leading to death. This trumpet may reasonably be taken to depict judgment on those who follow the lead of Papal Rome in its apostasy.[12]

The fourth trumpet (Rev 8:12) portrays the darkness of a third of all celestial bodies. In particular, stars are a symbol of the "lights" of the church, as drawn from Daniel 12:3 and Revelation 1:16, 20 and 12:1. Darkness symbolizes blindness or ignorance. While this expression permeates Paul's epistles, it is drawn from several Old Testament sources. The key is Micah 3:6–7 (see also Isa 8:20, 22; 42:7; Ps 107:10–11).

---

[12] Ibid, 69. The issue of apostasy in the Roman Catholic Church is large, and is beyond the scope of this book. But many respected scholars identify this church as the home of idolatry in the worship of Mary, prayers to saints, and so on. Readers who wish a careful discussion of the issue may wish to obtain *The Roman Catholic Controversy*, and *Mary: Another Redeemer?*, both by James R. White (Minneapolis: Bethany House).

> Therefore it will be night for you—without vision,
> And darkness for you—without divination.
> The sun will go down on the prophets,
> And the day will become dark over them.
> The seers will be ashamed
> And the diviners will be embarrassed.
> Indeed, they will all cover their mouths
> Because there is no answer from God.

This imagery suggests that the darkness is spiritual ignorance and blindness. In particular it describes the failure of vision of false prophets ("diviners") on whom the apostate secular world depends. This calamity (Isa 45:7) is an apt description of our modern condition. Rationalism—the religion of science—is the rule of the day. Evolutionary theory has replaced the biblical creation account as an explanation for the origin of life. God has been declared dead, or at least irrelevant.[13] The result of this darkness will be the death of many.

Woes

The fifth trumpet begins the "woes" (Rev 8:13). These three woe trumpets are more severe than the first four. And special restrictions which give us chronological clues are present in them. First, no sealed saint may be affected by them (9:4), and no one may be killed (9:4–6), although the torment is severe enough to cause men to wish for death. The time is limited to "five months" (9:10). Whether this time is literally five months, or representative of some other period, we may rest assured that it is defined and limited by God.

Because no sealed saint may be harmed, the fifth trumpet cannot sound until the sealing of the saints is complete (the fifth seal). This places the fifth and sixth trumpets after the fifth seal and before the seventh seal, since the seventh trumpet contains the same Day of the Lord events as the seventh seal.

---

[13] Stephen Jay Gould, *Rocks of Ages: Science and Religion in the Fullness of Life* (New York: Ballantine, 1999).

The sixth trumpet becomes more severe in that men are killed (9:18). But even after the difficulties it creates for mankind, the wicked still will not repent (9:20–21). And this shows us the purpose of these two trumpets. God knows who is willing to be saved. But he is not willing to foreclose any possibility for repentance. The wicked will have failed to respond to God's goodness. Therefore he will allow Satan[14] to work nearly unfettered[15] so that all will see the utter depravity of sin. Now they will refuse to reject Satan's wickedness. Even with the demonstration of the effects of evil in the fifth and sixth trumpet, no one will accept this final opportunity to repent.[16]

The Close of Probation

God is not willing that any person should be lost (2 Pet 3:9). Throughout the trumpets he has been issuing a call to come to him for salvation. This call has gone out in parallel to the appeals in the seals to those who have known the truth but have left it. Eventually the time will come when all will have made an irrevocable decision for or against him. At that point the saints will be sealed, but God will continue in a further demonstration of his willingness to reach out. That plea will fail, and the door of opportunity will close. Probation for mankind will end. The seventh trumpet announces this fact.

> And the angel whom I saw standing on the sea and on the land lifted up his right hand to heaven, and swore by Him who lives forever and ever, who created heaven and the things in it, and the earth and the things in it, and the sea and the things in it, that there shall be delay no longer, but in the days of the voice of the seventh angel, when he

---

[14] Satan may be identified as the instigator of the woes, since he is the enlightened being who fell to earth (Rev 8:10; cf. Luke 10:18). He is then identified in 9:1 as the one to whom the key to the bottomless pit is given. Thus he has power over the demonic horde that comes out like smoke.

[15] The command in the sixth trumpet (Rev 9:13–14) comes from the golden altar of sacrifice, indicating that God remains in ultimate control, even during this time of unimaginable trouble.

[16] The discussion of the contents of the fifth and sixth trumpet has been severely truncated for two reasons. First the imagery of these trumpets is very complex, and would require an extended discussion adding nothing to our chronological pursuit. Second, they are future, and fail in their mission of repentance. Since our mission is to try to help Christians who might otherwise fall away because of tribulation prior to these events, a detailed discussion of them will add nothing to this task.

is about to sound, then the mystery of God is finished, as He preached to His servants the prophets. (Rev 10:5–7)

This trumpet contains both the Day of Atonement (12:19) and the atmospheric signs. The angel in 10:5–7 points out that that moment will indicate the conclusion of the "mystery of God." Paul repeatedly identifies the term "mystery of God" as the gospel message.[17] Thus, the gospel call to repentance will end at the time of the seventh trumpet. Just as the seals describe the salvation of the saints, the trumpets describe the call to the lost, ending in their final judgment. And just as the signs in the seals were sited where the saints would look, the signs in the trumpets are located where the wicked will look. They will have signs in the earth: lightning, thunder, sounds, and earthquakes.

God is sovereign over all regardless, but wishes all created beings to willingly follow in his way. Why hasn't he brought an end to sin before this? If we can fairly use Job 1 and 2 to suggest an answer, it is because of Satan's accusations, which essentially add up to a charge of injustice. God is proving the righteousness of his government by allowing sin to run its destructive course. The security of every moral being in the universe is at risk. God must be found blameless, ultimately. Everyone must accept and confess that God's judgment against sin and his rescue of those willing to come home with him are right, appropriate, and loving (Isa 45:23–24; cf. Rom 14:11; Rom 3:4; cf. Ps 51:4).

Love can render this universe eternally secure only if it becomes grounded on unquestionable trust. An attitude of trust and loyalty cannot be demanded, it must be freely given. It is only when we have had occasion to see the integrity, fairness, and trustworthiness of a person that we develop an attitude of trust toward such a person. A vital function of the pre- and post-Advent judgments is to provide an opportunity to the moral beings of the universe to deepen their trust

---

[17] Rom 11:25; 16:25; 1 Cor 2:7; 15:51; Eph 1:9; 3:3–4, 9; 5:32; 6:19; Col 1:26–27; 2:2; 4:3; 1 Tim 3:9, 16. Futurists repeatedly refer to the church as a mystery which was not foreseen in the Old Testament. This position can only be maintained if the New Testament is treated as if it did not exist when interpreting the Old Testament. If Scripture is allowed to interpret Scripture, then Paul's identification of the gospel as "the mystery" is unavoidable.

in God by verifying, validating, and vindicating the justice of His judgments.[18]

The seventh trumpet is also the third "woe trumpet" (Rev 8:13; 9:12). The hail which falls on the wicked is God's weapon to destroy them. Whether, as suggested by the seventh bowl judgment, he uses literal hail or whether this is a figurative description of the end is unimportant. All the wicked will be destroyed at the second coming.

Once the mystery of God is finished, there will be no going back. The gospel door will close, and probation for mankind will end. No wicked person will have another opportunity to repent and be saved. His destiny in the lake of fire will have been sealed. And truly this will be the greatest woe of all.

Seven Trumpets

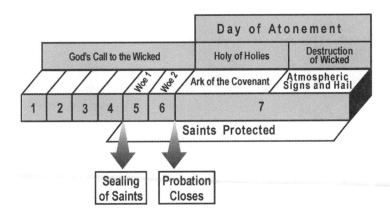

[18] Samuele Bacchiocchi, "The Typology and Theology of the Pre-Advent Judgment," *EndTime Issues* 74 (September 6, 2001).

CHAPTER SIX:

... AND WRATH

The term "wrath of the Lamb" (Rev 6:16–17) is not recognized as capable of being directed only at the wicked if
the church is still on earth. (LaHaye, *Rapture*, 108)

The Time of Jacob's Trouble

Jeremiah describes the last part of the tribulation in the passage which gives it its name.

Now these are the words which the LORD spoke concerning Israel
and concerning Judah,
"For thus says the LORD,
'I have heard a sound of terror,
Of dread, and there is no peace.
Ask now, and see,
If a male can give birth.
Why do I see every man
With his hands on his loins, as a woman in childbirth?
And why have all faces turned pale?
Alas! for that day is great,
There is none like it;
And it is the time of Jacob's distress,
But he will be saved from it. (Jer 30:4–7; emphasis added)

In figurative language God here declares that while there will
be great distress in the world, by His power He will break the
hold of sin on His people. Deliverance from the difficulties at
this stage is guaranteed. It will be "the time of Jacob's distress,"
implying a great worry and fear on the part of true Israel, but "he

will be saved from it."[1] It is important to notice that at this time, the final days before Christ's return; true Israel will not suffer injury.

> Behold, the tempest of the LORD!
> Wrath has gone forth,
> A sweeping tempest;
> **It will burst on the head of the wicked.** (Jer 30:23; emphasis added)

The target of God's wrath will be the wicked. The saints will be saved because God has good aim. He achieves His goals without any concern for failure, since God cannot fail. Similarly, most of the plagues of Egypt fell only on the Egyptians, leaving the Israelites unscathed, even though they were in the land when the plagues fell. Unlike the Futurist worry, the church has nothing to fear from this time of trouble. Daniel points this out.

> "Now at that time Michael, the great prince who stands *guard* over the sons of your people, will arise. And there will be a time of distress such as never occurred since there was a nation until that time; and at that time your people, everyone who is found written in the book, will be rescued." (Dan 12:1)[2]

The prince who stands for the people is their advocate in court. He always "stands" for them. But in this scene he is pictured as rising from a seated position to become the judge standing to present the verdict. And this judge declares two verdicts. The first verdict imposes a time of trouble worse than ever in history. This is the last part of the time of trouble pictured in Matthew 24. The language is nearly identical, so there can be no doubt. The Hebrew *tsarah* (distress, adversity) suggests the actions of an adversary to the wicked who causes this adversity, evoking the picture of God pouring out bowls of wrath on them (Rev 16:1).

---

[1] Once again we see Jacob used *pars pro toto*, one part standing for all, as Jacob was of course many centuries dead when Jeremiah was alive.

[2] The word "guard" is italicized, indicating that it is not present in the original Hebrew text. "Stands" indicates that "the great prince" is the *representative* and *advocate* and *champion* of his people against the "accuser." "Stands guard" is not really what is meant.

The second verdict declares that all the saints—all those who are truly God's people—will be rescued from the trouble poured out on the wicked. The verb translated "rescued" here, *malat* (to be delivered, to give birth) suggests slipperiness, raising the possibility that the saints might indeed slip away before the trouble begins. But this is not consistent with God's pattern throughout history. Noah was not removed from the earth during the flood. He had to go through it, but was protected in the ark. When Daniel's three friends were faced with the death sentence (Dan 3), God did not prevent them from being thrown into the furnace. Instead, He rescued them out of the furnace. When Daniel refused to pray to Darius (Dan 6), God did not keep him from entering the lions' den, but he protected him in it. Paul and Silas were not kept from being sent to jail, but were rescued from inside it (Acts 16). This pattern of action by God strongly suggests that the proper way to understand *malat* is that the saints will be rescued from within the tribulation.

"Kept out of the hour"

Revelation 3:10 states that God will keep the saints of Philadelphia "out of" the hour of adversity that is to test the entire world.[3] LaHaye identifies this as one of four texts guaranteeing that all the saints in the church will be removed from the earth during the tribulation. We are not destined for wrath (1 Thes 5:10). We will be "saved" (Rom 5:9) or "delivered" from the wrath (1 Thes 5:9). While the certainty of our protection is very clear from these passages, the mechanism is not so clear. LaHaye suggests that the only way to protect the church is to remove it from the earth during Daniel's seventieth week (LaHaye and Jenkins, 62).

---

[3] We are translating the preposition *ek* as "out of" in keeping with LaHaye's line of argument.

Futurist 70th Week

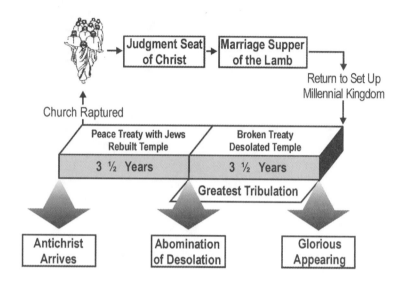

To support the idea that the saints will not be on the earth during the tribulation, LaHaye presents an entire chapter dedicated to the meaning of the little Greek word *ek* ("out of").

> "While it may be proposed that the Lord can keep His own *from trial* simply by keeping them *safely through* it, it does not seem to us that this can be stated with equal force in regard to the hour of temptation that the whole world will experience. The *hour* itself must be lived through by all who are in the world contemporaneous with it, when the only way that one can be *kept* from that *hour* is to be taken *out* of the world when it strikes."[4]

We must reject this assertion because the phrase "keep out of the hour" does not mean "prevent from being present" at that time. *Tereo* (to keep) means to protect and preserve. Thus, it is legitimate to translate the passage to say that God will "protect the saints during the tribulation and deliver them safe at the end of it." There is no need for them to be absent during the tribula-

---

[4] "The Preposition *Ek* Means *Out Of*," *Our Hope Magazine*, October 1949: 86–88; in LaHaye, *Rapture*, 217–219.

tion. This becomes clearer when we consider the very first paragraph of LaHaye's discussion.

> "The word rendered 'from' is from the Greek preposition *ek*. It has various connotations that denote *exit out of* or *separation from* something with which there has been connection; from a place, from the midst of a group, from a condition or state, etc."

The root meaning described here speaks of removal from a state "with which there has been a connection." That is, in order for the saints to be "kept *out of* the hour," they must have a connection with the hour. The saints must be present during the tribulation, or they will have no connection with it. Rather than revealing their removal from the earth prior to the tribulation, this passage describes their presence. Walvoord confirms this understanding of *ek* by stating that Jesus' resurrection was "*out of* the mass of men who died."[5]

This usage of *ek* is discussed by Pfandl.[6]

> ". . . the preposition *ek* has the basic meaning of 'out of,' 'from' referring to coming out of something or from somewhere. Another Greek preposition [*apo*] expresses the idea of separation, 'away from.'
>
> "In His high-priestly prayer Jesus says: 'I do not pray that You should take them out [*ek*] of the world, but that You should keep [*téreó*] them from [*ek*] the evil one' (John 17:15, NKJV). To 'keep from the evil one' does not mean that Satan could not tempt the disciples, but Jesus is asking the Father to keep the disciples safe in the temptation, to watch over them, and to prevent Satan from overcoming them.
>
> "Similarly, in 2 Peter 2:9 the apostle writes: 'the Lord knows how to deliver the godly out of [*ek*] temptations [*peirasmos*]' (NKJV). The apostle here is not saying that God's people will be kept away from [*apo*] temptations, but that He will deliver them out of [*ek*] the midst of them. In the same way the apostle John in Revelation 3:10 is not saying that the believers will be kept away from [*apo*] the hour of trial ... but that they will be kept safe during that time.

LaHaye is not wrong in applying Revelation 3:10 to the modern church.[7] But one other part of the text draws our attention.

---

[5] John F. Walvoord, *The Revelation of Jesus Christ*, (Chicago: Moody, 1966), 38.

[6] Gerhard Pfandl, "The Rapture: Why it Cannot Occur Before the Second Coming," *Ministry*, 74/9 (September 2001): 5–7.

The word translated "testing," "trial" (NIV), or "temptation" (KJV) is *peirasmos*. It has the root meaning of "putting to the test." In the message to Philadelphia *peirasmos* refers to the process of proving the status of the wicked to be correctly identified. It does not mean testing the saints to prove their righteousness. As such, the testing is not even related to the saints. It only applies to the wicked.[8]

The Pattern and the Prophecy

The alert reader will have noted that we have observed the pattern of the fall festivals of Israel in John's apocalypse. Futurists insist that this cannot be the case, since in their view Israel and the church have to be completely separated. They believe that the "seven annual feasts predicted the redemption of Israel as a nation and did not in any way contemplate the church."[9] This premise must be compared to the testimony of Scripture.

The spring festival types were all fulfilled in the life of Christ and in the apostolic church. Jesus became our Passover (1 Cor 5:7). He was the First Fruits (1 Cor 15:20). The spring festival of harvest, Pentecost, met its true antitype on the Day of Pentecost when the Holy Spirit was poured out in power and over three thousand souls were harvested (Acts 2). These events were specifically identified by inspired writers who linked the church with them. The continuity of Israel from the Old Testament into the New Testament is specifically demonstrated by this linkage. Further, since the spring festivals all met their antitypical fulfillment in the gospel era, the pattern of the festivals should require that the fall festivals also be fulfilled within the gospel era and not in a revived old covenant Jewish era.

---

[7] "He who has an ear, let him hear what the Spirit says to the churches" (Rev 2:7, 11, 17, 29; 3:6, 13, 22) indicates that the audience who is to respond to the message is not limited to churches themselves, but includes anyone willing to hear and respond.

[8] The phrase "entire world" could be taken as including the saints, which would contradict what we have said. But many Old Testament passages use similar language to refer only to the wicked, so we can discount this potential difficulty. Revelation 3:10 literally says "those who dwell on the earth," not "the entire world," and in Revelation this refers specifically to the wicked and excludes the righteous (see Rev 17:2).

[9] Terry C. Hulbert, *The Eschatological Significance of Israel's Annual Feasts*, Doctoral Dissertation, Dallas Theological Seminary (Dallas: 1965), 293.

Paul described the Levitical law as a "tutor" (Gal 3:4) leading us to Christ. Its tabernacle services and festivals pointed forward to the Messiah. Each time a sin offering was brought, innocent blood was shed (Heb 9:22), pointing to the eventual death of the Messiah (Isa 53:5–8). Similarly, every other aspect of the tabernacle also pointed in some way to the Messiah.

Just as the furnishings and observances of the tabernacle were types[10] of Christ, so the festivals pointed forward to Him. The spring festivals were typologically fulfilled in Christ's first advent. The monthly trumpets linking the spring and fall festivals are the end-times alarm that links the First and Second Advents. The fall festivals provide the blueprint for the events we are studying in the book of Revelation. Trumpets announce the coming judgment, and then the Day of Atonement brings in the final judgment. When the atonement is complete, all that remains is to execute the verdict. The saints will be forever clean, and are the completion of the harvest of which Christ was the first fruits. The wicked have sealed their own fate and will suffer the death penalty their sin requires. Satan, as the scapegoat, will bear his sins "to a place not inhabited" (Lev 16:22 KJV), and Jesus will "tabernacle" with the saints forever.

Bowls Full of Wrath

The bowl plagues (often called the seven last plagues) begin with another throne room scene. This time, the imagery evokes the exodus of Israel from Egypt. First there is a "sea of glass mixed with fire" (Rev 15:2). This is a "Red Sea." The saints are standing on it, just as the children of Israel walked on dry land across the Red Sea to escape from Pharaoh. Next, the victorious saints sing the song of Moses and the Lamb (15:3–4; cf. Exod

---

[10] A "type" is an acted-out prophecy. It does not have to be recognized as such initially, but it becomes identified as a type when an inspired author employs it as one. Such an author may specifically use the *tupos* (type) terminology or may simply construct an argument or narrative in such a way as to identify the type/antitype correspondence. The identification of a typological relationship does not have to be fully explicit, but may instead be implied. Further, typology is characterized by progression from lesser to greater, so that the antitype is always larger and more important than the type.

15:1–18), recalling the deliverance of true Israel from Egypt.[11] And in exactly the same manner, God has delivered the saints from "Egypt" (Rev 11:8) by "great judgments" (Exod 7:4).

Seven angels dressed in priestly garments come out of the temple (15:5–6). They are given the bowls which had been full of incense in 5:8. The normal purpose of these utensils was to pour out libations to God (Exod 25:29). But now they are to be used to pour out the wrath of God (Rev 15:7), an event anticipated many times in the Old Testament. "The seven (bowls of wrath) are not a vindictive outburst of an offended God, but are the well-ordered demonstration of the final covenant curses."[12] Sevenfold punishment is declared for disobedience in Leviticus 26, and seven specific punishments are found in 26:18–34. They serve for all time to expose the hearts and the works of man in their attitude toward Christ.

The close of probation—the end of the period when repentance is possible and salvation available—is now expressed graphically.

> After these things I looked, and the temple of the tabernacle of testimony in heaven was opened, and the seven angels who had the seven plagues came out of the temple, clothed in linen, clean and bright, and girded around their breasts with golden girdles. And one of the four living creatures gave to the seven angels seven golden bowls full of the wrath of God, who lives forever and ever. And the temple was filled with smoke from the glory of God and from His power; and no one was able to enter the temple until the seven plagues of the seven angels were finished. (Rev 15:5–8)

This picture is drawn from Old Testament images. In the revolt of Korah, Dathan, and Abiram (Num 16:5, 19ff.) the Lord issued judgment from the door of the tabernacle. It was filled with smoke and the glory of the Lord, preventing entry. The Day of Atonement—the annual Day of Judgment—reflects this in the time when only the high priest was able to be in the temple (Lev 16:17). The time for repentance and individual sacrifice for sin

---

[11] Notice Revelation 11:8, where Egypt is one of the mystical names given to Babylon. Pharaoh is a shadow of antichrist, and the death of the Egyptian army in the Red Sea is a shadow of the death of the wicked at the second coming.

[12] LaRondelle, 382.

had ended. Up till then, anyone was able to bring a sin offering to the tabernacle. Their sins were forgiven and transferred to the tabernacle in anticipation of the cleansing of the sanctuary on the Day of Atonement. But once the Atonement ceremony began, this daily process ended.

In the same way we make our daily supplication for forgiveness (Heb 4:16). We each come before the judgment seat of God, begging for Christ to cover our unworthiness with his righteous blood. When the angels with the bowls full of wrath leave the tabernacle, this will no longer be possible. But daily forgiveness will not be needed, since we will have been sealed and will have the full measure of grace manifested in us to keep us from further sin. The wicked will have demonstrated their unchangeable unwillingness to repent, so from this point forward, all access to the temple will be terminated. Probation will close. This moment is seen symbolically as the cloud of smoke preventing entry.

The imagery is also drawn from Ezekiel 10, where as the glory of the Lord was preparing to leave the temple, the cloud of His glory filled the temple (10:4). This double application of the imagery will shortly become very real as the Lord leaves His heavenly tabernacle at the end of the bowl plagues. With the Day of Atonement in heaven ended, He will come to earth to reap the harvest of the saints (Rev 14:6). At the end of that harvest, the wicked will be reaped (14:19–20). This will be discussed in more depth in chapter seven.

The bowls present a series of covenant curses which will pour out "the wine of the wrath of God, which is poured out without mixture into the cup of his indignation" (Rev 14:10 KJV). No grace will remain for the wicked. God's wrath will clearly be the *greatest* tribulation.

Futurists of all stripes will protest that the saints have definitely been removed from the earth, so they will not be affected by these incredible punishments. After all, the church is not destined for wrath (1 Thes 5:9), and this will be a time of great wrath. To this we must suggest that the Futurists have again neglected to consider God's power. Just as He was able to cause the seven last plagues of Egypt to fall only on the Egyptians, God will place a division between the saints and the wicked to protect the saints (Exod 8:23). His wrath is not against his own people, but against those who persecute them, the wicked, but if the righteous were not present on earth to be persecuted, the reason for his wrath against the wicked would be less clearly seen.

Further, in Ezekiel 9 God presents the picture of surgical execution of judgment. First, a man in priestly linen (9:2, 4) places a mark on the forehead of all who "groan over the abominations." Then a cadre of executioners is sent to kill everyone who does not have the mark (9:5). Righteous people are untouched. We have already seen that the saints are protected during fifth and sixth trumpets because they have the seal of God. That this is again the nature of the bowl plagues is confirmed in Psalm 91.

> A thousand may fall at your side,
> And ten thousand at your right hand;
> But it shall not approach you.
> **You will only look on with your eyes,**
> **And see the recompense of the wicked.**
> For you have made the LORD, my refuge,
> Even the Most High, your dwelling place.
> **No evil will befall you,**
> **Nor will any plague come near your tent.**
> For He will give His angels charge concerning you,
> To guard you in all your ways. (Ps 91:7–11; emphasis added)

Verse 8 specifically identifies this scene as the time of the wrath of God by pointing out that all of the troubles constitute the "recompense of the wicked." This reward is made up of the curses pronounced in Scripture for failure to keep the covenant. Clearly, the saints will be within the carnage, since there will be many who fall at their left and right hands. But they will not be harmed, since they have placed their faith in God. He will send angels to guard the saints and prevent them from being harmed in any way. They will not even be able to injure a toe (91:12). This is in full agreement with the promise of rescue in Daniel 12:1.[13] A paraplegic in a wheelchair has nothing to fear from the wrath of God, as long as his eyes are fixed on the Savior.

---

[13] The same promise is also found in Jer 30:7; Joel 3:16; Obad 17; Zech 12:4–9; and Rom 11:26.

Contrast this with Tim LaHaye's statement quoted at the beginning of this chapter (and chapter 4). He feels that the church would be destroyed if it went through the tribulation. Such a thought implies that God has poor aim when he targets his judgments at the wicked. God has promised to take care of his saints when the troubles come. Finite man must not attempt to limit infinite God.

God's promises have profound implications for the interpretation of Revelation 13. There we see a death sentence decreed against those who have the seal of God. Pentecost states that this implies that the saints are subject to the antichrist power. But Scripture does not say that the death decree will be carried out. In other places we find that the woes will "kill" (9:15) and that saints were "beheaded" (20:4). The absence of this kind of language suggests that the death decree will not be enforced. This would be perfectly consistent with the protection during tribulation that Scripture repeatedly promises.

The Timing of the Bowl Judgments

The first six bowl judgments cause great calamities to fall on the wicked, yet many remain alive. This allows them to cry out to the rocks, "Fall on us and hide us from the presence of Him who sits on the throne, and from the wrath of the Lamb; for the great day of their wrath has come; and who is able to stand?" (6:16–17). They know that their time is up, and there is no escape. They would rather die in a natural calamity than to suffer the wrath of God. These covenant curses fall as soon as the opportunity to comply with the covenant ends. As probation closes, the heavenly Day of Atonement begins, and the bowls begin to be poured out. As we found in chapter four, this coincides with the sixth seal.

The bowl judgments are parallel to the trumpets in an important way. The target of each bowl judgment is exactly the same as its sequential counterpart in the trumpets. This recapitulates the fact that the trumpets and bowl judgments both act on those who refuse God's offer of salvation. At the same time, there is an important difference. While the first six trumpets all recall plagues of Egypt, only the first five bowls echo them. The sixth and seventh bowls are oracles against Babylon. While this is a change of language, it is not a change of focus. Revelation 11:18 speaks of "the great city which is mystically called Sodom and Egypt, where also their Lord was crucified." The reference to the crucifixion identifies this as Jerusalem, but the allusion is not literal. "The great city" is an exclusive reference in Revelation to Babylon (16:19; 17:18; 18:10, 16, 18, 19, 21). And Babylon is not used in the apocalypse to refer to the physical city, but to false religion. When this is combined with the names "Sodom," "Egypt," and Jerusalem of the time of Christ (Acts 9:1; 22:3–4) it becomes a general reference which draws together a number of major oppressors of the Israel of God.

"It is Done."

The seventh bowl judgment describes the Day of Atonement with the statement "It is done" spoken from the throne with a loud voice (16:17). This can only be the voice of God, declaring that the mystery is finished (10:7). The saints have all received the atonement and will be clean forever (cf. Lev 23:30). No reason will remain to delay the final destruction of the wicked and the rapture of the saints. With the atonement finished, there will be great signs announcing the appearance and presence of the holy God, King of the universe (16:18; cf. 8:5 and 11:19). Again, because the focus of the bowl judgments is on the curses on the wicked, it includes the Day of the Lord signs in the earth. Walvoord comments:

> "'It is done!' In the Greek, the statement is one word, *gegonen*, in the perfect tense, indicating action accomplished. It is the final act of God preceding the second coming of Christ…
> "Chronologically the next event is that prophesied in 19:11 where Christ Himself descends from heaven to take over His kingdom . . .
> ". . . the unmistakable impression of the Scriptures is that the whole world is being brought to the bar of justice before Christ as King of kings and Lord of lords." (*Revelation*, 240–242)

Seven Bowls

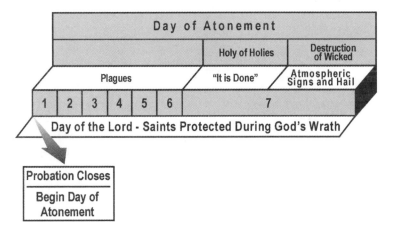

It is valuable for us to consider in detail just what will happen. The earthly sanctuary was an acted-out prophecy of Christ's atonement for us. And just as every part of the tabernacle pointed toward Christ's atoning sacrifice, every part also pointed toward the process of cleansing the heavenly sanctuary. This is necessary for two reasons. First, every sin ever committed defiles the heavenly sanctuary and calls forth further evidence of God's mercy and long-suffering. Second, the sanctuary stands as a demonstration of God's grace and justice to "the rulers and the authorities in heavenly places" (Eph 3:10; 1 Cor 4:9). God's "administration of the mystery" of the gospel (Eph 3:9) is at issue, and God himself is on trial (Rom 3:4).

The high priestly ministry on the Day of Atonement was designed to "cover over"[14] all the confessed sins of the people. There was an elaborate sequence of sacrifices and presentation of blood. The sacrifice of the bull (Lev 16:6, 11–14) atoned for the high priest and his family. This rendered him fit for the service to come. Then the two goats were presented and lots cast for them (16:7–10). The goat "for the Lord" was sacrificed, and atonement was made for the people. The final atonement was that for the

---

[14] "Cover over" is a literal translation of *kippur*, the Hebrew word for "atonement."

"altar before the Lord" (16:18–19).[15] At this point, atonement was "done." As Moses recorded, "atonement shall be made for you to cleanse you; you shall be clean from all your sins before the LORD" (16:30).

Paul recorded for us the fact that it was essential for the same action to occur in heaven.[16] "Therefore it was necessary for the copies of the things in the heavens to be cleansed with these, but the heavenly things themselves with better sacrifices than these" (Heb 9:23). The cleansing required in heaven comes from the same defilement as on earth. And only blood can atone for that defilement. Fortunately God has provided the better sacrifice in Jesus.

The Sixth Bowl

Having identified the nature and timing of the bowl judgments, we have no chronological need to look at the details of the first six bowls. But the sixth bowl has a specific application to other parts of our prophetic journey, so we will devote a bit of attention to it.

The sixth bowl judgment is poured out on the Euphrates to dry it up and prepare the way for the kings from the east. LaHaye comments:

> "The literal rendering of the expression is 'the kings from the sunrising,' a reference to the kings from the Oriental nations of the world. Since it refers to them en masse, it indicates that they do not amalgamate or lose their identity (for they are 'kings'), but instead form a massive Oriental confederacy. This confederacy may be preparing to oppose Antichrist, whose capital lies in Babylon, but because of the lying tongues of the demons we are about to study, they will be brought across the Euphrates River on the side of Antichrist in opposition to Christ." (LaHaye, *Revelation*, 255–256)

This is LaHaye's entire substantive discussion of the identity of "the kings from the east." And like his prior efforts at exegesis,

---

[15] This was the golden altar of incense.
[16] I am assuming that Paul wrote Hebrews. This is a subject of some scholarly controversy, but that will not be addressed here.

since it completely ignores the other parts of scripture which might help in understanding, it should be disregarded.

The Euphrates was the river of Babylon. It ran through the city, inside the walls. This was thought to be a completely insurmountable problem for any army that might besiege the city, since the city's water supply was inexhaustible. There was enough land in the city to grow food, so it could withstand any length of siege. But God told Isaiah that Cyrus would have the "two-leaved gates"—the river gates of Babylon—opened before him (Isa 45:1 KJV) so that he could conquer the city. In this way Cyrus— God's anointed—would free the Jews from their captivity (45:4).

Cyrus achieved his victory over Babylon by the stratagem of diverting the Euphrates from its banks. No water flowed through the city, and his army was able enter by walking under the walls on the river bed. Because this was done on a great feast day, wine "loosened the loins" of Belshazzar and his army (Dan 5:1–4), and the army of Persia conquered the city virtually without resistance. Since Persia was east of Babylon, Cyrus and his allied kings were "kings from the east." They "dried up the Euphrates" in order to rescue the Israel of God from oppression. And thus the type is established. But a full understanding requires a further exploration of the terms.

We have already seen how the river Euphrates fed the Babylonians who literally held the Jews captive. In the same way, "Euphrates" is used in the sixth trumpet as the source of life for spiritual Babylon. The satanic angels who command the immense demonic horde are resident in the Euphrates until released to work their evil (Rev 9:14–16). So when the "Euphrates" is dried up (Hos 13:14–15), every source of satanic power evaporates.[17] This "clears the decks" for the final rescue of the saints.

While Cyrus is a type of Christ, the typological identification does not stand alone. Malachi 4:1–3 describes the Day of the Lord. Verse 2 specifically identifies the savior on that day as the "sun of righteousness." This sun will "rise with healing in its wings." Since the sun rises in the east, this is the place where Jesus will be seen on the Day of the Lord. 2 Peter 1:19 describes

---

[17] Revelation 17:16 describes this same event as "eating the flesh of the harlot," which is another name for Babylon.

Jesus as the "Day Star" that will "rise in our hearts."[18] Since the Day Star also rises in the east, this again points us to Christ as the king who will arrive from the east. And Isaiah describes God as a deliverer from the east (Isa 41:2). But we must note that this is the *cosmic east*, not the *geographic east*. An interpretation such as LaHaye's is geocentric and ignores the war between Christ and Satan while focusing on politics. If we recognize that the nature of war in the apocalypse is primarily spiritual, with only incidental reference to physical battle, then we will have no problem accepting the scene as it is intended to be seen.

Christ is God's anointed, the antitype of Cyrus, God's "anointed," his "shepherd" (Isa 44:28–45:1) who delivers Israel. He and his angels are the kings from the east coming to rescue the saints. This was prophesied by Zechariah.

> Then the LORD will go forth and fight against those nations, as when He fights on a day of battle. And in that day His feet will stand on the Mount of Olives, which is in front of Jerusalem on the east; and the Mount of Olives will be split in its middle from east to west by a very large valley, so that half of the mountain will move toward the north and the other half toward the south. And you will flee by the valley of My mountains, for the valley of the mountains will reach to Azel; yes, you will flee just as you fled before the earthquake in the days of Uzziah king of Judah. Then the LORD, my God, will come, and all the holy ones with Him! (Zech 14:3–5)

On the Day of the Lord, as Christ comes to destroy the wicked, the Mount of Olives is portrayed as splitting in two, creating a valley to the east. This becomes the route by which the saints escape and through which the hosts of heaven come. From the east comes rescue, not invasion!

---

[18] The New English Translation notes, "The reference to *the morning star* constitutes a double entendre. First, the term was normally used to refer to Venus. But the author of course has a metaphorical meaning in mind, as is obvious from the place where the morning star is to rise— "in your hearts." Most commentators see an allusion to Num 24:17 ("a star shall rise out of Jacob") in Peter's words. Early Christian exegesis saw in that passage a prophecy about Christ's coming. Hence, in this verse Peter tells his audience to heed the OT scriptures which predict the return of Christ, then alludes to one of the passages that does this very thing, all the while running the theme of light on a parallel track."

The Seventh Bowl

When the seventh bowl is poured out, God speaks those fateful words, "It is done" (Rev 16:17). The heavenly atonement is complete and the saints are clean. Jesus may now remove his priestly garments and don the crown of the conquering king (19:12). While signs of God's wrath fill the earth (16:18), God rains the hail of destruction on the wicked (16:21), turning them from living men into a feast for the birds (18:17–18). God's people will witness the carnage (Ps 91:8), then be lifted up to join their Lord in the air (1 Thes 4:16–17).

Summary of the Seals, Trumpets and Bowls

The seals portray God's appeal to mankind to come to him for salvation. The trumpets signify to the wicked the approach of final judgment and condemnation. And the bowls are the wrath of God, covenant curses poured out on unrepentant mankind. All three series end with the Day of Atonement and the Day of the Lord.

The seals present the close of probation as the beginning of the Day of the Lord, which coincides with the beginning of the Day of Atonement. When the atonement ceremony proceeds into the Holy of Holies—the seventh seal—the camp becomes silent (Rev 8:1). This part of the Day is presented again in the seventh trumpet when tabernacle is opened and the Ark of the Covenant is seen by the High Priest (11:19). It is also seen in the seventh bowl when God pronounces the atonement complete (16:17). With the atonement complete, the saints are forever clean, and the punishment of the wicked can be completed.

The atonement is the final judgment.[19] On that Day everyone who comes pleading before the throne of grace (Heb 4:16) will be declared clean. "Whoever does not believe stands condemned already" (John 3:18 NIV). As Daniel states, this is judgment "in favor of the saints" (Dan 7:22). This judgment is the ultimate

---

[19] It is beyond the scope of this discussion to explore the fact that all judgment issues from the sanctuary. For an Old Testament example, the reader should study the revolt of Korah, Dathan, and Abiram recorded in Numbers 16. The New Testament prototype is the Great White Throne Judgment in Revelation 20.

good news of the gospel (Rev 14:6–7). It is to be more desired than fine gold (Ps 19:9–10).

The saints will all have "come before the judgment seat of Christ" (2 Cor 5:10) to be rewarded for their faithfulness, while the wicked will be "cut off from the camp" (Lev 23:29). As a result of these judgments, the heavenly jury will be able to sing,

> "Hallelujah! Salvation and glory and power belong to our God; because His judgments are true and righteous; for He has judged the great harlot who was corrupting the earth with her immorality, and He has avenged the blood of His bond-servants on her" (Rev 19:1–2).

The book of Revelation contains a tremendous amount of material we have not begun to discuss. Even the seals, trumpets, and bowls are far larger topics than these chapters can adequately cover. But Scripture provides enough keys to unlock their chronological outline in a relatively short space. Despite LaHaye's claims, Revelation is *not* a sequential prophecy. It is full of flashbacks and recapitulations, with many interludes that give additional perspectives on one issue or another. When the landmarks within each sequence are matched with the others, the mosaic can be seen.

The key to understanding that the seals, trumpets, and bowl plagues are not consecutive but recapitulative is seeing that the seventh seal, trumpet, and bowl describe the same event, always including an allusion to the Day of Atonement, the same atmospheric and global phenomena alluding to the Day of the Lord, and some sort of hail falling to the earth. If the same phenomena occur three times, consecutively, then we seem to have allusions to three Days of Atonement, rather than the one Day of Atonement we should expect in light of the yearly sanctuary calendar.

Grand Design of Seals, Trumpets, and Bowls

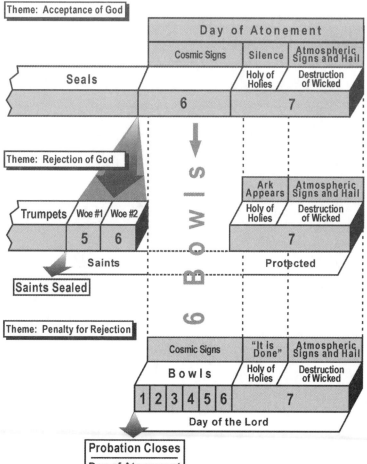

The following table helps clarify this. Look up the texts and see for yourself.

7ᵗʰ Seal: 8:1–5	7ᵗʰ Trumpet: 11:19	7ᵗʰ Bowl: 16:17–21
Day of Atonement Language: Silence in Heaven, Large amount of Incense	*Day of Atonement Language:* Ark Seen in Temple	*Day of Atonement Language:* Voice from Throne, "It is done"
Day of the Lord Language: Thunder Lightning Sounds Earthquake Fire hurled to earth (coals from altar—fire & brimstone; cf. "hail and fire" in 8:7)	*Day of the Lord Language:* Thunder Lightning Sounds Earthquake Great hailstones	*Day of the Lord Language:* Thunder Lightning Sounds Earthquake Huge hailstones

The prophecy of Daniel 9 is a bit more difficult, primarily because of translation issues. But again, Scripture contains within it sufficient data to allow us to be confident of the conclusion that it has been fulfilled. With these chronologies established, certain conclusions fall into place.

The premise that there will be a *seven-year* tribulation is based on the incorrect idea that the seventieth week of Daniel 9 is yet in the future. Since that week ended in 34 AD, every interpretive element based on a proposed fulfillment in the future is incorrect. There will be no *seven-year* "Great Tribulation." But there will be horrendous troubles. "The true Christian is called upon to swim upstream against powerful currents and treacherous riptides until his Lord returns. That's not the exception, that's the rule."[20] We do not know how long this tribulation will last, except that the time will be shortened for the sake of the saints.

Certainly many saints will die (and have died) during the time of the first five seals and the first four trumpets. But once the final sealing has been done, no saint will ever suffer injury again.

---

[20] Marvin Rosenthal, "Love Not the World," *Zion's Fire* 12:3 (July-August, 2001): 3–5.

Because the saints will be safe throughout the remainder of the great tribulation, there will be no need to remove them from the earth. In fact, in the early stages God will be allowing the drama of sin to play itself out as live testimony to the heavenly jury. The death decree of Revelation 13 will be a final act of ultimate hatred directed at true Israel. A host of witnesses will have all doubt as to the wickedness of unbelief removed when everyone makes an irrevocable decision to stand for or against God. The actions of the lost will show without any doubt the nature of their choice. Once this becomes clear, God can then show the justice which is due. In his mercy, he will not prolong the agony.

The Futurist construct has Jesus returning to rapture the saints before the *seven-year* "Great Tribulation." They then go before the judgment seat of God, attend the marriage supper of the Lamb, and return at the Glorious Appearing to assist in the establishment of the millennial kingdom of peace on earth. While the church is absent from the earth, God will supposedly complete His plan for the Jews and any unconverted Gentiles during the *seven-year* "Great Tribulation."

> Pretribulation rapturism rests essentially on one major premise – the literal method of interpretation of the Scriptures. As a necessary adjunct to this, the pretribulationist believes in a dispensational interpretation of the Word of God. The church and Israel are two distinct groups with whom God has a divine plan. The church is a mystery, unrevealed in the Old Testament. This present mystery age intervenes within the program of God for Israel because of Israel's rejection of the Messiah at His first advent. This mystery program must be completed before God can resume His program with Israel and bring it to completion. These considerations all arise from the literal method of interpretation. (Pentecost, 193)

As we noted in the first chapter, the historical-grammatical method of interpretation—which Futurists espouse but do not apply—is truly the only proper way to understand Scripture. End-times prophecies are built primarily out of symbolic figures, which are understood by exploring those figures in the rest of Scripture. Instead of allowing all of scripture to bear on any question of interpretation Futurists reject literal meaning in favor of literalism. This literalistic method loses the true meanings of prophecies in artificial tunnel vision that separates the Old and New Testaments into an "Israel Bible" and a "Church Bible." Words are thus denied the application to which the author put them. For example, because the word "church" is "missing" from Revelation 4:6–18:1, LaHaye insists, "the church is not there!" (LaHaye, *Rapture*, 53–54, 212). This ignores the fact that the word "saints," which is, according to the New Testament, synonymous with the church, appears nine times in that space.

When the historical-grammatical method is applied to the definition of Israel, it properly leads to the conclusion that the root meaning of Israel is now, as it always has been, the body of believers. The original congregation in the wilderness was the church. It was defined in exactly the same way as the church is today. Therefore, we must reject Pentecost's assertion that there are two separate redemptive programs for the Jews and the Gentiles. In fact, as we discovered in chapter three, the birthright blessings God conveyed on ethnic Israel were revoked permanently in 34 AD, when Stephen brought God's covenant lawsuit against them. True Israel was never affected, but the mission the Hebrews were supposed to carry out was removed from the unfaithful. Faithful believers, regardless of ethnicity, are the recipients of both the birthright blessings conveyed through the power of the Spirit and the duty to spread the gospel. Since the church has been in existence for the entire span of redemptive history,[21] the claim that it constitutes an unrevealed mystery which must be concluded prior to the onset of tribulation is unfounded. We must therefore explicitly deny this Futurist claim. Finally, since the seventy weeks of Daniel 9 were completed in 34 AD, the chronological rationale for a rapture of the church prior to a *seven-year* "Great Tribulation" is incorrect.

Three key points bear repetition. First, since the seventy-week time period has long since expired, it cannot describe events in the future. Second, desolation (Dan 9:27) was a punishment meted out on ethnic Jews as a result of breaking the covenant, not devastating troubles that will affect all peoples. Its key charac-

---

[21] We have not discussed the idea that the church existed in the times prior to Abraham. But the same redemptive plan can easily be seen in those years, so it is no stretch to extend the term all the way back to creation.

ter was the lack of ability to worship God in the Temple. Third, the desolator was a rebellious Jew, not a future Antichrist character. The events proposed by Futurists are based on an incorrect understanding of the prophecy, and thus are incorrect themselves.

The book of Revelation fills out the final pieces of the story of redemption. There will truly be great difficulties in the last days of earth's history. Many saints will die in persecutions. But eventually every living human will have taken a stand either for or against God. At that time, God will place His protective hand on the true Israel of God from every nation, while still keeping the doorway to salvation open for the wicked. But they will refuse to repent, and probation will then be closed forever as the heavenly atonement begins. Only then will God's wrath be poured out on the wicked.

The pattern of these events has been foreshadowed again and again in the history of the Hebrew people. God provided a repetitive object lesson for them and for us in the sanctuary. And just as every part of the tabernacle and its services pointed to Christ, every part and service also pointed forward to Christ's actions in end times. Type will meet its antitype in the last days. The shadowy Day of Atonement on earth will reverberate through heaven in vivid reality. Probation will close and the final sacrifice for sin on the cross will have its final application to our sins.

At this point, the only parts of the Day of Atonement not yet discussed are the exit of the high priest from the Tabernacle and the banishment of the scapegoat to the wilderness. These events will take us into the next chapter.

CHAPTER SEVEN:

LIKE A THIEF IN THE NIGHT

> I see no contradiction in viewing the Second Coming as
> a single event in two phases. (LaHaye, *Rapture*, 38)

In the Futurist model the church is raptured out of the world before the seventieth week of Daniel 9 and its associated *seven-year* "Great Tribulation" begin. At the end of the week, the church then returns to the earth in the "Glorious Appearing" with Christ to set up the millennial kingdom of peace. They join with the Jews and "tribulation saints" in this era of peace. As we have repeatedly noted, since the seventieth week ended in 34 AD, the foundation for this idea is incorrect. But once again, completeness requires us to consider the specifics of this outline.

Imminence

Tim LaHaye devotes the very first chapter of his technical work to the idea that there will be absolutely no warning that the rapture is near (*Rapture*, 19–27). Then the second half of the book is largely devoted to debunking those who support mid-trib, pre-wrath, and post-trib positions (*Rapture*, 101–216). His major argument is that these positions "destroy imminency." He credits the expectant hope of true Christianity to the idea that Christ will take the church out of the world utterly without warning.

> Historically, belief in the any-moment-coming of Christ has three vital effects on Christians and their churches.
> 1. It produces holy living in an unholy society like ours. John said, 'He that has this hope in Him [the return of Christ] purifies himself, just as He is pure' (1 John 3:3).

2. It produces an evangelistic church of soul-winning Christians, for when we believe that Christ could appear at any moment, we seek to share Him with our friends lest they be left behind at His coming . . .
3. Belief in the imminent return of Christ impels Christians and churches to develop a worldwide missionary vision . . . (*Rapture*, 23)

This assertion may be answered at two levels. First, any Christian knows that he may die at any moment, due to events beyond his control. The recent destruction of the World Trade Center in New York drives this home with awful authority. Thus, if the Christian is not ready at this very moment, his eternal destiny may be at risk. Such a moment-to-moment walk with God is clearly important. And of course, Jesus gave the gospel commission to the apostles in Matthew 28:19–20. But these arguments still admit LaHaye's thesis. So we must consider the inspired testimony regarding the coming of our Lord.

The key passage adduced by Futurists is Christ's own statement from the Olivet Discourse.

> "But be sure of this, that if the head of the house had known at what time of the night the thief was coming, he would have been on the alert and would not have allowed his house to be broken into. For this reason you be ready too; for the Son of Man is coming at an hour when you do not think *He will*." (Matt 24:43–44)

Taken in isolation, this statement sounds like it is impossible to know the season of Jesus' return. After all, only two verses later Jesus says that only the Father knows the day or hour. But such a conclusion completely misses the point of Jesus' discussion and ignores the fact that even in this passage Jesus implies that the alert saint will *not* be surprised by the second coming.

In Matthew 24:14 we learn that the gospel will be preached in the entire world. Verses 15–26 tell of false teachers, messiahs, and a great tribulation. Verse 29 tells of cosmic signs that will follow the tribulation, which verses 30–31 say will be promptly followed by the coming of Jesus to gather the elect. This certainly lays out a program of events for the saints to see. While it doesn't tell the exact moment, it definitely gives "signs of the times" allowing the saints to know Jesus' return is near.

In the next paragraph, Jesus makes exactly that point. By telling the parable of the fig tree (vs. 32–33), he emphasizes that the signs he has just discussed will tell that, "He is near, *right* at the door" (v. 33). Jesus recognizes that His audience is somewhat dense, so He reinforces His point again.

> "For the coming of the Son of Man will be just like the days of Noah. For as in those days which were before the flood they were eating and drinking, they were marrying and giving in marriage, until the day that Noah entered the ark, and they did not understand until the flood came and took them all away; so shall the coming of the Son of Man be." (Matt 24:37–39)

First Jesus says the time of the end will be like the days of Noah. Then He tells how the people of Noah's day kept about their routine daily lives, completely oblivious to their impending doom. They died because they had no clue about the consequences of their spiritual stupor. We know that this was not due to a lack of preaching by Noah, but was a result of their own blindness. Then Jesus reiterates that the time of His return will be like those days. The saints will be like Noah and will be aware of the signs. The wicked won't care and will be taken completely by surprise, just as if robbed by the thief in the night.

Jesus is not content to stop with this illustration. In v. 43 he again points out that an alert head of the house would not have allowed himself to be robbed. Jesus then tells the parable of the faithful servant (vs. 45–51). Again the issue is watchfulness (v. 50). Proceeding to the parable of the ten virgins (Matt 25:1–13), he again points out that we should "be on the alert" (v. 13).

In the Olivet Discourse alone (Matt 25–26), Jesus points out at least six times that the saints should be watchful. They will not know the exact moment, but they will be aware of its nearness, because they will see the signs of the times. The wicked, on the other hand, will be taken completely by surprise. Paul parallels Jesus' illustrations when he writes to the church in Thessalonica.

> Now as to the times and the epochs, brethren, you have no need of anything to be written to you. For you yourselves know full well that the day of the Lord will come just like a thief in the night. While they are saying, "Peace and safety!" then destruction will come upon them

suddenly like birth pangs upon a woman with child; and they shall not escape. But you, brethren, are not in darkness, that the day should overtake you like a thief. (1 Thes 5:1–4)

The saints will not need to know the specific moment of Jesus' return, because they will be living in the light. Whenever Christ returns, they will still be His people. That day will *not* overtake the saints like a thief because they will have seen and identified the signs of the times. But the wicked will be carrying on their daily activities, as oblivious as the wicked people in Noah's day.

Remember therefore what you have received and heard; and keep *it*, and repent. If therefore you will not wake up, I will come like a thief, and you will not know at what hour I will come upon you. (Rev 3:3)

("Behold, I am coming like a thief. Blessed is the one who stays awake and keeps his garments, lest he walk about naked and men see his shame.") (Rev 16:15)

The return of Christ will be sudden, but it will not be without warning. The concern expressed by LaHaye for the doctrine of imminence is misplaced. Christ's return will surprise only the wicked. They will be jolted from complacency, but too late to do anything about it. The saints will not know the exact moment, but because they will have been aware of prophetic signposts, they will know his coming is soon.

Secret? Sudden?

Futurists consistently interpret Scripture as telling of the removal of the church from the earth in order for God to complete his program for the Jewish people. But since "Israel" has always identified the body of believers, this artificial separation is incorrect, and thus all doctrine based on it is necessarily incorrect. But once again, completeness leads us to consider the Futurist blueprint.

The Blessed Hope is definitely a reference to the Rapture of the church . . .

The Glorious Appearing is quite a different matter. It heralds that special day when Christ will return to this earth in triumph to be acknowledged by all men as KING OF KINGS and LORD OF LORDS. The Glorious Appearing is the literal, physical stage of His Second Coming, the coming of the church to the earth. The Rapture is His return for the church . . .

Our "gathering together to Him" cannot mean the Glorious Appearing, since that is when all living creatures are congregated for the judgment of the nations and the establishment of Christ's kingdom. The "gathering together to Him" refers to the Rapture . . . (LaHaye, *Rapture*, 78–79)

The elements LaHaye points out are two: the Rapture, where the church is removed from the earth, and the Glorious Appearing at the end of the "Great Tribulation," where Jesus returns from heaven with the church. These are referred to as the "two phases" of Jesus' second coming. In the pre-trib scenario, they are separated by seven years, and in the mid-trib by three and a half years. Such a curious interpretation should immediately raise our eyebrows, for even LaHaye admits that, "no one passage of Scripture teaches the two aspects of His Second Coming separated by the Tribulation" (*Rapture*, 75).

LaHaye cites three main passages of Scripture: John 14:1–2, 1 Thessalonians 4:13–18, and 1 Corinthians 15:51–58. These directly speak of the hope of resurrection and transformation to immortality. To these he adds Titus 2:13 as presenting both descriptions, supposedly as separate phases.

For the grace of God has appeared, bringing salvation to all men, instructing us to deny ungodliness and worldly desires and to live sensibly, righteously and godly in the present age, looking for the *blessed hope* and the *appearing of the glory* of our great God and Savior, Christ Jesus; who gave Himself for us, that He might redeem us from every lawless deed and purify for Himself a people for His own possession, zealous for good deeds. (Titus 2:11–14; emphasis after LaHaye)

This text points out that our hope "in the present age" is "the blessed hope and the appearing of the glory." The parallel structure suggests that the blessed hope of the Christian *is* the glorious appearing of the Savior. A similar parallel structure also appears in what at first glance appear to be two separate purposes: to "redeem us" and to "purify a people." But since redemption and purification "from every lawless deed" are intertwined and inseparable aspects of a single process of salvation, both terms indicate a single purpose.

The "blessed hope and the appearing of the glory" leads to the final redemption of God's people. Because redemption will be completed by the removal of the saints from this sinful planet, this is the "blessed hope" as expressed here by Paul and asserted by LaHaye. But this passage indicates that the redemption of the saints is also the purpose of the "glorious appearing!" In the Futurist scenario, the timing of the "glorious appearing" seven years after the redemption prevents the "glorious appearing" from serving the purpose of redeeming the saints. Since Paul clearly indicates that redemption is the objective of the "glorious appearing," the Futurist scenario must be incorrect.[1]

LaHaye also appeals to 2 Thessalonians 2:1–12 (*Rapture*, 79).

> Now we request you, brethren, with regard to the coming of our Lord Jesus Christ, and our gathering together to Him, that you may not be quickly shaken from your composure or be disturbed either by a spirit or a message or a letter as if from us, to the effect that the day of the Lord has come.

Paul here expresses a concern that the church in Thessalonica not be misled by any message that the Day of the Lord had already come. This is a single event which he describes here as "the coming of our Lord Jesus Christ and our gathering together to him." LaHaye correctly identifies the parallel description as the removal of the church from the earth.[2] But because LaHaye erro-

---

[1] Perhaps the best book on the meaning of "the blessed hope" is *The Blessed Hope: A Biblical Study of the Second Advent and the Rapture* (Grand Rapids: Eerdmans, 1956), by one of the greatest Evangelical scholars of Revelation, George Eldon Ladd of Fuller Theological Seminary. Ladd accepted the Futurist rapture scenario for many years until he bothered to actually study the verses used to support it, upon which he concluded that the idea has no biblical support at all. While this is a scholarly study, it is brief and still in print, and students of Revelation owe it to themselves to read it.

[2] We must be careful here not to take LaHaye's correct identification too far. In the Futurist schema, the church only refers to the New Testament church, and excludes the Old Testament saints. As we found in chapter 2, that assumption rests on an incorrect foundation and is therefore itself incorrect. The church removed from the earth is in fact all saints from all ages.

neously uses this text to support two separate phases of the second coming, let us paraphrase Paul's inspired statement.

"Brothers! With regard to the coming of Jesus and our rapture, don't be shaken up by any message that the Day of the Lord has come. It's not true."

Paul is talking about only *one* event: the Day of the Lord. Both the rapture and the second coming are part of it. The second issue to be addressed is the manner in which the church will be raptured.

Through the years some have tried to discredit the pre-Tribulation rapture theory by calling it the *secret rapture*. Of course, nowhere in Scripture is the term *secret* applied to this event. However, anyone who does not participate in the Rapture will not actually see it, for it will occur in the 'twinkling of an eye.' The word *twinkling* has been defined as 'a gleam in your eye,' which is faster than the eye can see. The occurrence would much better be labeled the *sudden rapture* . . .

I expect the Rapture to be electrifyingly sudden but not secret, for when Christ calls His living saints to be with Him, millions of people will suddenly vanish from the earth. An unsaved person who happens to be in the company of a believer will know immediately that his friend has vanished. There will certainly be worldwide recognition of the fact, for if over two hundred million people suddenly depart this earth, leaving their earthly belongings behind, pandemonium and confusion will certainly reign for a time. (*Rapture*, 39–40).

We must ask just what the difference is between LaHaye's "sudden" rapture and the "secret" rapture that has been taught by Futurists for almost two centuries. In fact, there is no difference whatever. LaHaye has simply chosen to soften the language so as to divert criticism away from it. The elements are the same. In it none but the saints are aware of the presence of Jesus, to whose presence they are instantly removed. The wicked merely become immediately aware of the fact that the righteous have been whisked away somewhere (see LaHaye's novels for the spellbinding results of this sudden disappearance).

The Biblical Doctrine of the Second Coming

The Bible does not leave us in doubt as to the nature of the second coming. Its truth is presented in John 14:1–3, where Jesus tells the disciples that He will return for them so they can be with Him "in [His] Father's house." Other passages expand this to include all believers. The first substantial details are given in the Olivet Discourse.

"But immediately after the tribulation of those days THE SUN WILL BE DARKENED, AND THE MOON WILL NOT GIVE ITS LIGHT, AND THE STARS WILL FALL FROM THE SKY, and the powers of the heavens will be shaken, and then the sign of the Son of Man will appear in the sky, and then all the tribes of the earth will mourn, and they will see the SON OF MAN COMING ON THE CLOUDS OF THE SKY WITH POWER AND GREAT GLORY. And He will send forth His angels with A GREAT TRUMPET and THEY WILL GATHER TOGETHER His elect from the four winds, from one end of the sky to the other." (Matt 24:29–31)

In this short statement Jesus laid out the essential sequence of events the saints should expect. The tribulation would come first. This is the great time of trouble that He said would be cut short (24:22) to prevent the death of all the saints. As we noted in the last chapter, the "saints" includes *both* the Old Testament saints and the church era saints. Scripture makes no separation between them at any time. Next we note several quotations from Old Testament prophecies, indicated in the NASB by small caps.

The first such quotation describes the cataclysmic signs discussed in chapter four. The NASB margin indicates nine separate Old Testament locations where these signs are mentioned.[3] In some of these verses they clearly refer to the Day of the Lord, and in others they may well refer to judgments fulfilled long ago. In those passages these signs actually became idiomatic metaphorical language pointing to catastrophic battle and destruction. This suggests a difficulty in knowing whether Jesus means them literally or symbolically. Since the same cosmic signs in the sixth seal (Rev 6:12–17) are accompanied by a great earthquake where "every mountain and island were moved out of their places" (Rev 6:14), however, we would propose that when this language refers

---

[3] Isa 13:10; 24:23; Ezek 32:7; Joel 2:10, 31; 3:15ff; Amos 5:20; 8:9; Zeph 1:15.

to the Day of the Lord, it should be taken as referring to actual events, even though it is possible that the language may exaggerate to some extent, as the Old Testament prophetic language does so often.

Next "the sign of the Son of Man will appear in the sky." It should be noted that this does not say there will be a sign that the Son of Man is coming. Rather, it says that the Son of Man *is* the sign. Futurists place this at the end of the fictional *seven-year* "Great Tribulation." This means that this would be Jesus' *third* coming. After all, they believe the church was raptured out earlier in the "first phase of the second coming." But to allow such an interpretation is to violate every rule of language *and* even the Futurists' own rules of interpretation.

First, in John 14:1–3, Jesus says he will come again to receive the saints. He does not say it will occur in two phases. In fact, there is not a single passage of Scripture that envisions two phases. Every prophecy of hope is of a single event. A two-phase coming is not discussed in 1 Corinthians 15, 1 Thessalonians 4, or any other passage on this topic. The message is always "I am coming back for you." Futurists impose the idea of a two phase coming on Scripture because their artificial separation of Jews and the church requires it.

When Futurists discuss Daniel 9, they are quite happy to count an exact number of days to the triumphal entry. Then they declare that the cross, which came only five days later, nicely fulfills the requirement of being "after" the sixty-nine weeks (Dan 9:26).[4] And indeed, Daniel does specifically note that these are two separate events. But when it comes to the second coming, they are equally happy to declare that two events *seven years apart* are the *same event* (LaHaye, *Rapture*, 38). A consistent application of the literal reading of Scripture, so vigorously espoused by Futurists, *must* stand in contradiction to this form of interpretation. But because consistency would require abandonment of their theory, this interpretation is forced into the Scripture. And in doing so, they commit a cardinal error. It is called

---

[4] In actual fact, as discussed in chapter 3, the cross came 3 1/2 years after the end of the sixty-nine weeks. This error is not corrected in the text so as to emphasize the character of another error.

eisegesis (forcing a meaning *in*), and it is properly condemned in every textbook on principles of biblical interpretation.

The proper process of scriptural interpretation is called *exegesis*. This is the process by which the interpreter examines Scripture to bring its meaning *out*. There are rules of interpretation, called hermeneutics, which govern the process. Futurists have made errors along the way by misunderstanding Daniel 9 and the seals, trumpets, and bowl plagues of Revelation. We can excuse such errors for now, since they can be made from a lack of information. So far we have supplied information to rectify those mistakes. But at this point, applying standard rules promoted even by Futurists, we have found that the second coming is a single event at a single point in time. Futurists could have found this just as easily as we have, since the statements of Scripture are very clear. Had they allowed the plain meaning of Scripture to guide them, the second coming scriptures would have shown them the error of their prior conclusions. But personal commitment to an erroneous conclusion has prevented this self-correcting mechanism from working.

Futurists have correctly identified that the second coming texts are associated with two kinds of events. First, the saints are gathered to the Lord. Second, the wicked suffer in the "Day of the Lord." But it is not necessary to arbitrarily require these to be at separate times. Scripture tells us that if we understand the pattern of the tabernacle service, we can properly understand the second coming.

> When I pondered to understand this [the apparent prosperity of the wicked],
> It was troublesome in my sight
> Until I came into the sanctuary of God;
> Then I perceived their end. (Ps 73:16–17; parenthesis added)

The Day of Atonement in Heaven

The seals, trumpets, and bowl plagues all end with a view of the Holy of Holies ministry of the High Priest on the Day of Atonement. The seals show the beginning, as the heavenly host waits silently for the High Priest to perform his ministry (Rev 8:5;

cf. Exod 28:31–35). The trumpets reveal the Ark in the Holy of Holies as the High Priest enters to perform the atonement (Rev 11:19; Exod 26:31–34; Lev 16:1, 12–13). Then the voice of God from the throne declares that the atonement is finished as the High Priest applies the last blood to the altar of incense (Rev 16:18; Exod 25:21–22; Lev 16:19–20, 30).

Two groups of people are in view in this process. The first is made up of all who apply for atonement, regardless of ethnicity. In Old Testament times Gentiles who believed became natives by belief (Exod 12:48). As long as they humbled their souls in contrition and confession of sin, they were regarded as "sons of Israel" (Lev 16:16, 21). If anyone refused to humble himself, he was cut off from the sons of Israel (Lev 23:29). Since the earthly sanctuary was a shadow of the heavenly (Heb 8:5), the same process must be in view in both places. As long as we confess our sins, our High Priest, Jesus, will atone for them (1 John 1:9), for as our sacrifice he has already paid the price. We can apply for forgiveness as often as needed (Heb 4:15–16).

The atoning ministry of the High Priest began at the end of the confession of the people. Probation for that year had closed. Confession and sin offerings on earth resumed that very night. But Jesus will have made a permanent end of sin (Dan 9:24) once the atonement in heaven is complete. God's people will be in every way clean (Lev 16:30), and probation will have closed forever. So those who will not accept the cleansing blood of Christ will be forever lost. In the language of Scripture, they will be "cut off from the camp" (Lev 23:29). The mystery of God (Rev 10:7) will be completed.

God cannot leave His people among wickedness at this time. Nor can he leave wickedness to continue in the universe. There must be a complete resolution of the accusations brought by Satan against God. Since God's people are forever clean, it is time for them to be brought home.

And I looked, and behold, a white cloud, and sitting on the cloud was one like a son of man, having a golden crown on His head, and a sharp sickle in His hand. And another angel came out of the temple, crying out with a loud voice to Him who sat on the cloud, "Put in your sickle and reap, because the hour to reap has come, because the harvest of the earth is ripe." And He who sat on the cloud swung His sickle over the earth; and the earth was reaped. (Rev 14:14–16)

John saw the gathering of the saints as a "reaping." This image is used in Isaiah 24:13 and in Hosea 2:9 and 6:11 to tell of the harvest of the saints. Jesus uses this specific image to speak of his return.

And He was saying, "The kingdom of God is like a man who casts seed upon the soil; and goes to bed at night and gets up by day, and the seed sprouts up and grows—how, he himself does not know. The soil produces crops by itself; first the blade, then the head, then the mature grain in the head. But when the crop permits, he immediately puts in the sickle, because the harvest has come." (Mark 4:26–29)[5]

The harvest of saints will leave one other crop to be reaped.

And He answered and said, "The one who sows the good seed is the Son of Man, and the field is the world; and *as for* the good seed, these are the sons of the kingdom; and the tares are the sons of the evil *one*; and the enemy who sowed them is the devil, and the harvest is the end of the age; and the reapers are angels. (Matt 13:37–39)

And another angel came out of the temple which is in heaven, and he also had a sharp sickle. And another angel, the one who has power over fire, came out from the altar; and he called with a loud voice to him who had the sharp sickle, saying, "Put in your sharp sickle, and gather *the clusters from* the vine of the earth, because her grapes are ripe." And the angel swung his sickle to the earth, and gathered the clusters from the vine of the earth, and threw them into the great wine press of the wrath of God. And the wine press was trodden outside the city, and blood came out from the wine press, up to the horses' bridles, for a distance of two hundred miles. (Rev 14:17–20)

In the Day of the Lord, after the saints have been rescued, the final measure of God's wrath is poured out on the wicked. In imagery drawn from Joel 3:13, John described the death of the wicked. Their blood is described as filling the entire area of the sacred district outlined in Ezekiel 45:1.[6] The picture of slaughter

---

[5] See also Matt 9:37–38; 13:30; Luke 10:2.

[6] That the volume of blood is not literal can be determined by calculating the volume of space in the prophecy. It is more than twice the total blood volume of all the people who ever lived on the earth.

presented here is indeed overwhelming. No wicked person will survive.

The Glorious Appearing

As the time for Jesus to return approaches, the saints will be aware of its nearness, while the wicked will be blindly going about the business of the day. A great earthquake and incredible celestial events will take the wicked by surprise, leading to a call of distress.

And the kings of the earth and the great men and the commanders and the rich and the strong and every slave and free man, hid themselves in the caves and among the rocks of the mountains; and they said to the mountains and to the rocks, "Fall on us and hide us from the presence of Him who sits on the throne, and from the wrath of the Lamb; for the great day of their wrath has come; and who is able to stand?" (Rev 6:15–17)

The wicked will have simply kept on "eating and drinking . . . and marrying and giving in marriage" (Matt 24:38). When all creation is shaken, they will finally wake up, not to repentance, but to panic. The bowls of wrath being poured out on them cause them to curse God, while the saints "lift up [their] heads, because [their] redemption is drawing near" (Luke 21:28). Both of these developments will happen at once. And this is exactly what Jesus says next.

In a statement parallel to the description of the sixth seal, Jesus declares that, "all of the tribes of the earth will mourn" (Matt 24:30). Who can blame them? They willingly made the worst decision possible by refusing Jesus' free gift of salvation, and now they are facing this fact in the starkest possible way. At this very moment Jesus will send his angels to gather the elect "from the four winds" (24:31). It cannot be overemphasized that Jesus placed both of these events at the same moment. And it should be contrasted with the description given by LaHaye and Jenkins.

"Local television stations from around the world reported bizarre occurrences, especially in time zones where the event had happened during the day or early evening. CNN showed via satellite the video of a groom disappearing while slipping the ring onto his bride's finger. A funeral home in Australia reported that nearly every mourner disappeared from one memorial service, including the corpse, while at another service at the same time, only a few disappeared and the corpse remained. Morgues also reported corpse disappearances. At a burial, three of six pallbearers stumbled and dropped a casket when the other three disappeared. When they picked up the casket, it too was empty."[7]

LaHaye and Jenkins describe a vanishing which leaves the remainder of the population puzzled, but otherwise unaffected. Could anything be further from the description given by Christ and the prophets? It certainly does not square with the next part of Jesus' discussion on the Mount of Olives.

"For the coming of the Son of Man will be just like the days of Noah. For as in those days which were before the flood they were eating and drinking, they were marrying and giving in marriage, until the day that Noah entered the ark, and they did not understand until the flood came and took them all away; so shall the coming of the Son of Man be." (Matt 24:37–39)

Jesus makes the story plainer and plainer. In a short passage book-ended with "My coming will be just like the days of Noah," He adds the final detail. The wicked people simply kept on with their lives, oblivious to Noah's message. In the same way, the wicked in the end time will ignore calls for repentance. When the Son of Man appears in the sky, they will be in the same position as those outside the ark when the floodwaters rose. They will watch as the saints are caught up to meet their Savior in the air (1 Thes 4:16–17). Then, just like the wicked at the time of the flood, they will be "taken away." Thus, when Jesus contrasts the one taken with the one left in the next two sentences, the context is clear.

"Then there shall be two men in the field; one will be taken, and one will be left. Two women will be grinding at the mill; one will be taken, and one will be left." (Matt 24:40–41)

---

[7] Tim LaHaye, Jerry Jenkins, *Left Behind* (Wheaton, Il: Tyndale House, 1995), 47–48.

The scene has been set, and the figures of speech prepared. No one is "left behind" to live through a *seven-year* "Great Tribulation." And no one is "taken" to be with God. "Taken" is a Hebrew idiom for being killed,[8] just as the wicked at the flood were killed when they were "taken away." Once the wicked are dead, only the saints will be left (alive).

Consequences of Error

Many have been deceived by the coherent fictional story line of the "Left Behind" books. Their premise sounds plausible, particularly since it has been preached from many pulpits for nearly two centuries. But the mere antiquity of this viewpoint cannot make it correct. After all, Satan has been preaching "the lie" that "you will not surely die" since the Garden of Eden (2 Thes 2:11 NIV, cf. Gen 3:4). This should not be taken to suggest that Tim LaHaye and Jerry Jenkins are not committed Christians. All external evidences suggest that they are. But the great accuser of the people will happily take a misunderstanding of Scripture and turn it into a stumbling block.

When persecutions come upon God's people without them being raptured out of the world, it will be very easy to believe either that God lied or that he doesn't even exist. After all, his word was wrong! A belief in the "scriptural" doctrine of a rapture before the "Great Tribulation" will become evidence of the error of Scripture and may lead to a denial of the cross. Broken faith will create broken lives without hope. Why should anyone endure persecution when there is no salvation at its end? Eyes will turn from the Savior and souls will be lost. We cannot stand idly by when the consequences are so great.

His "Appearing"

The second coming is described in Greek by the words *parousia*,[9] *epiphaneia*,[10] *phaneroo*,[11] *apokalupsis*,[12] and *er-*

---

[8] See also Jesus' story of the bridegroom in Mark 2:18–20.

[9] *Parousia* is used in reference to the second coming in Matt 24:3, 27, 39; 1 Cor 15:23; 1 Thes 2:19; 3:13; 4:15; 5:23; 2 Thes 2:1, 8, 9; James 5:7–8; 2 Pet 3:12; 1 John 2:28.

chomai.[13] *Parousia* is drawn from *pareimi*, which means to be near. Depending on specific usage, it refers to "coming" or "presence." *Epiphaneia* was commonly used by pagan Greeks to describe the visible form of a divine being. *Phaneroo* means to show or reveal oneself. *Apokalupsis* means to "take off the cover" or to reveal. *Erchomai* simply means "coming."

In general, these words are used interchangeably to describe Jesus' return. The saints are told to wait and hope for the *apokalupsis*[14] and the *epiphaneia*[15] and be patient until the *parousia.*[16] The "Day of the Lord" is described as both the *apokalupsis* and the *parousia.*[17] The words *apokalupsis, epiphaneia, erchomai,* and *parousia* are all used to describe Christ's coming to judge the wicked.[18] Christ's *erchomai,* his *parousia,* and the Day of the Lord all refer to the future judgment that will "come like a thief" on the wicked.[19] Saints are exhorted to pursue blamelessness and holiness in expectation of the *epiphaneia* and *parousia* of Christ.[20] Believers will be gathered together to be with Christ when he comes (*erchomai*) and at his *parousia.*[21]

When considered together, the use of these Greek terms to describe a single event makes it clear that the second coming will be visible and physical. Jesus will be revealed at that time.

> Therefore, gird your minds for action, keep sober in spirit, fix your hope completely on the grace to be brought to you at the revelation [*apokalupsis*] of Jesus Christ. (1 Peter 1:13)

---

[10] *Epiphaneia* is used in reference to the second coming in 2 Thes 2:8; 1 Tim 6:14; 2 Tim 1:10; 4:1, 8; Titus 2:13.

[11] *Phaneroo* is used in reference to the second coming in Col 3:4; 1 Pet 5:4; 1 John 2:28; 3:2.

[12] *Apokalupsis* is used in reference to the second coming in Luke 17:30 and 1 Peter 5:1.

[13] *Erchomai* is used nearly 650 times in the New Testament.

[14] 1 Cor 1:7; 1 Pet 1:13.

[15] Titus 2:13.

[16] James 5:7–8.

[17] 1 Cor 1:7; 2 Thes 2:1; 2 Pet 3:4, 9–12.

[18] Matt 24:50–51; 25:31–46; 2 Thes 1:7–10; 2:8.

[19] Matt 24:42–44; Luke 12:38–40; 1 Thes 5:1–4; 2 Pet 3:10; 1 John 2:28.

[20] 1 Thes 3:13; 5:23; 1 Tim 6:11–14; 2 Tim 4:1–5; 2 Pet 3:9–12; 1 John 2:28.

[21] Matt 24:31; 1 Thes 4:16–17; 2 Thes 2:1.

His coming will be the time when he is revealed to the entire world, and it is also the time when the saints receive the full measure of grace by being removed from this sinful world. Scripture does not even require a study of Greek to fill out this picture. Jesus' own ascension provides the model.

> And after He had said these things, He was lifted up while they were looking on, and a cloud received Him out of their sight. And as they were gazing intently into the sky while He was departing, behold, two men in white clothing stood beside them; and they also said, "Men of Galilee, why do you stand looking into the sky? This Jesus, who has been taken up from you into heaven, will come in just the same way as you have watched Him go into heaven." (Acts 1:9–11)

Jesus rose from the earth and then went into the clouds. He will return "in just the same way." His return will be "on the clouds" (Matt 24:30). It will be visible, exactly as His departure was visible. In Tim LaHaye's words, it will be sudden, but it will not be in any way secret, since it will flash from horizon to horizon like a bolt of lightning (Matt 24:27). In fact, "every eye shall see him' (Rev 1:7). There will be no newscasts, because God will make the return so obvious that it cannot be missed in any part of the earth. It will be not only the brightest event in history, it will be the loudest. The rapture will begin with a "shout" from the archangel and the "trumpet of God." Since the dead will hear his voice (John 5:25), certainly no living person will be able to miss it. All of the saints, living and dead, will be changed instantly into immortal, perfect beings (1 Cor 15:51–52) who will rise above the earth to join our Savior in the clouds (1 Thes 4:16–17).

We must pause momentarily to consider the language used by Paul. In 1 Corinthians 15:52 he says the resurrection will be "at the last trumpet." In 1 Thessalonians 4:16 (cf. Matt 24:31) he calls it "the trumpet of God." Trumpets are not an ordinary element of Christian worship, but they are an integral part of the ancient Hebrew worship. Trumpets were used to announce a wide variety of things which had the common thread of calling the people together. If "the last trumpet" refers to the rapture of the church before a seven-year Tribulation, then we have a Jewish scene which excludes Jews. But, if Israel truly means all the people of

God over all the history of the earth, then this imagery is a perfect match for the event. Further, God only blows the trumpet twice in all of Scripture. The first time was at Sinai when all the sons of Israel were gathered to him to receive the Law. The last time will be when all the sons of Israel are gathered to him to receive grace.

The Feast of the Birds

As the saints leave the earth, the wicked will be destroyed. Jesus notes this both in his story of the time of Noah and in a statement which has caused interpreters much grief.

> "For just as the lightning comes from the east, and flashes even to the west, so shall the coming of the Son of Man be. Wherever the corpse is, there the vultures will gather." (Matt 24:27–28)[22]

The reference to vultures here is amplified by John.

> And I saw an angel standing in the sun; and he cried out with a loud voice, saying to all the birds which fly in midheaven, "Come, assemble for the great supper of God; in order that you may eat the flesh of kings and the flesh of commanders and the flesh of mighty men and the flesh of horses and of those who sit on them and the flesh of all men, both free men and slaves, and small and great." And I saw the beast and the kings of the earth and their armies, assembled to make war against Him who sat upon the horse, and against His army. And the beast was seized, and with him the false prophet who performed the signs in his presence, by which he deceived those who had received the mark of the beast and those who worshiped his image; these two were thrown alive into the lake of fire which burns with brimstone. And the rest were killed with the sword which came from the mouth of Him who sat upon the horse, and all the birds were filled with their flesh. (Rev 19:17–21)

This scene is taken directly from Ezekiel 39:17–20, where the oracle against Gog and Magog declares that all the people of Gog will become food for predatory birds. The image that a Jew of the first century would see was that Israel's external enemies would

---

[22] Some preachers in Shakespeare's England actually taught that the corpse symbolizes Jesus and the gathering vultures believers! The correct meaning can be determined by examining Isa 18:6; Jer 7:33; 15:30; 16:4; 19:7; 34:20; and Ezek 32:4.

be destroyed and fed to predators. This must be contrasted with a normal expectation at death. When a Jew died, there was a specific burial ritual. Leaving a dead body unburied was an abomination and a sign of being cursed (2 Kings 9:10; Prov 30:17; Jer 16:4). Thus, the feast of the birds is not so much a view of literal events as an expression of the evil nature of Israel's enemies and the curse of judgment on them extending beyond death. Such a view is also reflected in the non-canonical Jewish literature.[23]

The result of the destruction of the wicked will be a world uninhabited by humans. Into such a place the scapegoat was taken (Lev 16:22 KJV). And this is the only part of the Day of Atonement remaining to be explored.

Summary

The return of Christ will be the most greatly anticipated event in Christian circles. But the wicked will be blissfully unconcerned. They will "keep on keepin' on" until the "great and dreadful Day of the Lord" (Mal 4:5 NIV) overtakes them like a thief. There will be no warning of ultimate doom in the form of a rapture of the saints before a "Great Tribulation." Such an event is unimagined in Scripture. An event of this character would allow the wicked to set a "prophetic clock" running to tell them exactly when to align themselves with God. Prepared Christians will see the signs of the times, even though they won't know the exact day and hour of Christ's return. A detailed calendar will be unnecessary for them. Faith in God is all that will be needed.

> Now as to the times and the epochs, brethren, you have no need of anything to be written to you. For you yourselves know full well that the day of the Lord will come just like a thief in the night. While they are saying, "Peace and safety!" then destruction will come upon them suddenly like birth pangs upon a woman with child; and they shall not escape. But you, brethren, are not in darkness, that the day should overtake you like a thief; for you are all sons of light and sons of day. (1 Thes 5:1–5)

---

[23] Sibylline Oracles, Book 3:697.

Here Paul declares explicitly that the Day of the Lord *will not* come "just like a thief in the night" for God's people, though it will for everyone else. When Christ returns, He will gather His saints from the four winds, and remove them from the world. (This is what is meant by being "caught up" in 1 Thessalonians 4:17, but it is not what Jesus means by "taken" in Matthew 24:39–41, where it means, "taken in death." Those "left behind" are those untouched by God's wrath against those who are hurting his children.) Then the wicked, who have become express enemies of God (Rev 13), will all be killed. This is described as the Feast of the Birds.

Jesus' coming will be sudden, visible, and the loudest event in history. No one will be unaware of it. And no one will be left on earth after it. It is both the Blessed Hope of the saints and the wrath of God upon the wicked. In one glorious moment everything on this wicked earth will be finished.

CHAPTER EIGHT:

A THOUSAND YEARS OF PEACE

> Such a [millennial] reign of Christ will bring righteousness
> to a wicked world, peace to a war torn world, prosperity to
> an economically disabled world, new standards of spiritual
> and social life, and a renovated earth suited for the millen-
> nial kingdom. (Pentecost, 390)

Scripture speaks directly of the millennium in exactly one place: Revelation 20. This means that almost all other discussion of the millennium relies on inferences from other parts of the Bible, primarily from the Old Testament. As we examine the suggestions that are made about the millennium, it will become clear that many inferences may charitably be described as speculation.

A few of the many ideas proposed include:

- Jesus Christ rules in person on a literal throne in Jerusalem.[1]
- His throne is located within a rebuilt temple as described in the book of Ezekiel (395).
- Some of the people sin (398, 401).
- Some saints die (408–409).
- The Jews possess the lands promised to Abraham (403).

It would be possible to continue along these lines for some time, but space does not permit us to explore every proposed manifestation of the Futurist plan. However, based on the foundation which has been prepared so far and an examination of Revelation 20, we will attempt to outline just what God has planned for the millennium.

---

[1] John Walvoord, *Major Bible Prophecies* (Grand Rapids: Zondervan, 1991), 390.

The Abyss

> And I saw an angel coming down from heaven, having the key of the abyss and a great chain in his hand. And he laid hold of the dragon, the serpent of old, who is the devil and Satan, and bound him for a thousand years, and threw him into the abyss, and shut it and sealed it over him, so that he should not deceive the nations any longer, until the thousand years were completed; after these things he must be released for a short time. (Rev 20:1–3)

The key word in this opening millennial passage is "abyss," or bottomless pit. In the trumpets (Rev 9:1, 2, 11), *abussos* describes the home of Satan and evil spirits. In Revelation 11:7 and 17:8 a beast comes from the abyss. By inference, this citation also refers to the home of Satan. Thus, from the evidence in Revelation alone, Satan will be bound in his home. Since he is the prince of the earth (John 12:31; 16:11), his home is the earth, and this is where he will be bound.

Paul describes the abyss as the place of the dead (Rom 10:7). This suggests that Satan will be chained in the graveyard of the wicked. Since Christ will destroy the wicked at his second coming, there will be no one left alive on the earth. This is where Isaiah places Satan in the oracle against the King of Babylon.

> "All the kings of the nations lie in glory,
> Each in his own tomb.
> But you have been cast out of your tomb like a rejected branch,
> Clothed with the slain who are pierced with a sword,
> Who go down to the stones of the pit,
> Like a trampled corpse.
> You will not be united with them in burial,
> Because you have ruined your country,
> You have slain your people." (Isa 14:18–20)[2]

---

[2] On the surface this chapter seems to be talking about a human, but some of the details don't fit any human, and for centuries most scholars have believed the chapter is speaking in a guarded way of our adversary. Given this covert language and the metaphorical nature of prophetic speech, it's not surprising that some of the statements in the chapter are rather peculiar.

Satan is responsible for the death of the wicked, since he led them to sin. He will be trapped with them ("clothed with them"), but he will not have the luxury of death himself. Because of his guilt, his own grave will be empty, and he will have no one to tempt.

The greatest impact of *abussos* is found in the Septuagint. Genesis 1:2 portrays the earth before creation as "formless and void [Heb. *tohu wabohu*]," with "darkness on the face of the deep." *Bohu* means emptiness or an undistinguishable ruin and is translated by the LXX as *abussos*. Thus, the place where Satan will be bound is the earth in a state like that before creation: formless, empty, uninhabited, and dark. Jeremiah seems to describe the condition of the earth after the wrath of God is poured out on the Day of the Lord.

> I looked on the earth, and behold, it was formless and void [*tohu wabohu / abussos*];
> And to the heavens, and they had no light.
> I looked on the mountains, and behold, they were quaking,
> And all the hills moved to and fro.
> I looked, and behold, there was no man,
> And all the birds of the heavens had fled.
> I looked, and behold, the fruitful land was a wilderness,
> And all its cities were pulled down
> Before the LORD, before His fierce anger. (Jer 4:23–26)

Jeremiah's description of the earth after the Day of the Lord quotes Genesis 1:2's *tohu wabohu* language exactly. It is of particular interest that this is the *only* place in the Hebrew scriptures where that quotation is made. This suggests that the reference is intentional, and specifically describes the exact condition of the earth during the millennium.

Isaiah uses similar language (Isa 34:8–11) in his description of the post–wrath earth. In both of these passages the result of God's wrath is a state like that before creation. The Day of the Lord will sweep the earth clean, leaving Satan's realm completely dark and formless. And in this place Satan will be "chained" for a thousand years. He will be completely isolated from the universe and will have no one alive to tempt.

The phrase "a thousand years" in Revelation 20:2 strongly suggests that this will be the literal span of Satan's imprisonment. In this we have no disagreement with the Futurists. But we should note that the nature of the earth after the second coming as suggested by Futurists is radically different from what the Scriptures indicate. In order for their suggested millennial kingdom of peace to exist on the earth, it will be necessary for the earth to be habitable at that time. To say that the condition described by Jeremiah is incompatible with a kingdom of peace on earth would be to understate the obvious.

The Scapegoat

In the pattern of the Yom Kippur temple service, only the discussion of the scapegoat remains. The trumpets announce the coming judgment, and then the heavenly original of the earthly Holy of Holies entered only on the Day of Atonement services is seen in the seventh seal, trumpet, and bowl (8:1, 3–5; 11:19; 16:18). With the announcement "It is done," God decrees that the righteous are to be reckoned forever clean, ready for the harvest. The wicked have forever rejected their opportunity for salvation and so are likewise ready to be reaped. When the high priest leaves the temple, both harvests are made.

At the beginning of the Old Testament Atonement ceremony, lots were cast over two goats. One was chosen for the Lord and the other "for Azazel" (Lev 16:7–8). The apparently opposite designation of these two goats indicates that "Azazel" probably refers to Satan.[3] Some have suggested that Satan cleanses the sanctuary by bearing all of the sins of the people away from it. But this would make Satan our sin-bearer, and Scripture clearly indicates that Jesus bore our sins (Isa 53:6, 10, 12; John 1:29). The scapegoat is not sacrificed, so it atones for nothing. It simply carries away the record of already forgiven sins to the wilderness.

---

[3] Other indications may be noted. The goat for Yahweh was sacrificed, while the goat for Azazel was not. Sins were confessed over the goat for Azazel—and so transferred to it—but not over the Lord's goat.

There are two parts to any sin. The sinner is obviously responsible for his own actions. But Satan is also responsible, since he is the originator of all sin. Thus he had a part in every sin brought into the sanctuary. The confession of sins brought the record of them into the sanctuary and away from the sinner. The cleansing atonement was complete by the time the scapegoat was offered, so the sins of the people were "covered over." The sinner was "washed in the blood" (Rev 7:14), rendering him clean (Lev 16:30). It is "the Lord's goat" whose blood is shed, and that goat points to Christ's sacrifice on the cross.

The only liability remaining was Satan's. The confession of the sins that had been brought into the sanctuary transferred the record of those sins to the scapegoat. (Since the sins of the wicked were never brought to the sanctuary, there was no atonement to be made for them.) The scapegoat then carried the record of Satan's culpability for those sins away into "a place not inhabited" (16:22 KJV).

The language of the atonement ceremony could not be a more perfect match for the conditions in the millennium. Satan, whose guilt in every sin is unquestionable, will bear that guilt with him to a "place not inhabited." The earth at that time will be desolate and lifeless.

The scapegoat in the original ceremony was driven into the wilderness.[4] It might live there for a number of years, but it would eventually die. In an identical manner Satan will live in the wilderness for a thousand years, then will be destroyed in the lake of fire. The pattern of the sanctuary will be fulfilled exactly as the great controversy between Christ and Satan (Rev 13:7) comes to its end.

Reigning with Christ

The next paragraph of Revelation 20 clearly follows in chronological order after the binding of Satan in the abyss.

And I saw thrones, and they sat upon them, and judgment was given to them. And I saw the souls of those who had been beheaded be-

---

[4] In later Jewish practices the scapegoat was pushed over a cliff to its death. There was no scriptural warrant for this practice.

cause of the testimony of Jesus and because of the word of God, and those who had not worshiped the beast or his image, and had not received the mark upon their forehead and upon their hand; and they came to life and reigned with Christ for a thousand years. The rest of the dead did not come to life until the thousand years were completed. This is the first resurrection. Blessed and holy is the one who has a part in the first resurrection; over these the second death has no power, but they will be priests of God and of Christ and will reign with Him for a thousand years. (Rev 20:4–6)

The people in view in this paragraph are initially called "they," looking back to the introductory scene in heaven (19:1–8). There, John heard the voice of a "great multitude" singing praises to God. In the scene of the sealing of the saints this group represents all who have been redeemed by the blood of the Lamb (7:9–10). There also seems to be a second group in view. It is made up of martyrs and those who did not receive the mark of the Beast. This is the description of the saints in 7:14, the same group described by "they" in the sentence before. Therefore, there is actually only one group of people in this scene. This is confirmed by the fact that there are only two resurrections in Scripture, that of the righteous and that of the wicked.[5]

In the first description "they" are given the task of judgment. In the second the saints are to be priests who reign with Christ. Deuteronomy 17:8–13 and 19:16–18 define judgment of difficult cases as one of the tasks of a priest. This indicates that reigning and judgment are the same activity.

The subject of the judgment seems to be "the world" and "angels" (1 Cor 6:2–3). But since Jesus will have already judged them all, a proceeding to determine guilt would be both redundant and futile. The destiny of all has been sealed before the saints even reach heaven. So why is there any need for further judgment? Paul gives us the key.

---

[5] We must note for the sake of accuracy that there will be only two eschatological mass resurrections. The first is the resurrection of the just and the second the resurrection of the wicked. Certain past individual resurrections include Jesus, Jairus' daughter, Lazarus, the son of the widow of Nain, and the saints who came to life at the time of the cross. The disciples and apostles also brought back to life individuals who are not named in Scripture. The martyrs mentioned here represent all God's faithful people, whether or not they were actually martyred. If they were truly faithful, they would have died for God had they been called to do so.

What then? If some did not believe, their unbelief will not nullify the faithfulness of God, will it? May it never be! Rather, let God be found true, though every man be found a liar, as it is written, THAT THOU MIGHTEST BE JUSTIFIED IN THY WORDS, AND MIGHTEST PREVAIL WHEN THOU ART JUDGED. But if our unrighteousness demonstrates the righteousness of God, what shall we say? The God who inflicts wrath is not unrighteous, is He? (I am speaking in human terms.) May it never be! For otherwise how will God judge the world? (Rom 3:3–6)

God is on trial! Satan's fundamental accusation is that God is unjust. He's been accusing God of that at least since Genesis 3:1. In tempting Jesus in the wilderness (Matt 4), he had hoped to demonstrate that God's laws could not be kept. Instead, Jesus triumphed over Satan, becoming the perfect sacrifice and the perfect high priest (Heb 4:15). So Satan shifted his attack to the tabernacle (Dan 8:11; Zech 3:1–2; 2 Thes 2:4),[6] which is the center of worship. Throughout history it has also been the seat of judgment (Num 16:19).[7] It is not too strong to say that God's right to rule is at issue, since Satan is said to claim that right for himself (2 Thes 2:4; cf. Ezek 28:2).

Paul explicitly states that God's justice, and therefore His right to rule, will be revealed at this trial.

To me, the very least of all saints, this grace was given, to preach to the Gentiles the unfathomable riches of Christ, and to bring to light what is the administration of the mystery which for ages has been hidden in God, who created all things; in order that the manifold wisdom of God might now be made known through the church to the rulers and the authorities in the heavenly *places*. (Eph 3:8–10)

Paul was given the task of preaching the gospel so that God's "administration of the mystery [of the gospel]" would be exposed for the benefit of "the rulers and the authorities in the heavenly *places.*" The question to be answered is simply: "Was God fair and just in saving those he saved and similarly fair and just in pouring

---

[6] Richard M. Davidson, "Cosmic Metanarrative for the Coming Millennium," *Journal of the Adventist Theological Society* 11:1–2 (Spring-Autumn, 2000): 102–119.
[7] Ibid.

out curses on the wicked?" The first parties who must be convinced of the answer are the angels and inhabitants of unfallen worlds (1 Pet 1:12).[8] And the saints will have questions. "Why wasn't _____ saved?" "Was God truly fair?"

Finally, this verdict cannot be carried out prior to the completion of God's determination of judgment. To do so would preempt the completion of the administration of the mystery. Paul explained that the proper time would come.

> Therefore do not go on passing judgment before the time, *but wait* until the Lord comes who will both bring to light the things hidden in the darkness and disclose the motives of *men's* hearts; and then each man's praise will come to him from God. (1 Cor 4:5)

When all have had a chance to respond to the gospel message, God will complete His judgment on mankind. Then the Lord will come. *After* the second coming will be the time for a review of the hidden things of men's hearts. The priestly task of the saints during the millennium will be to open the books and consider the facts contained in them. They will see and declare the justice with which God judged sinful mankind. This is necessary because man cannot look into a man's heart the way the Lord can (1 Sam 16:7). In fact, man does not even truly know his own heart (Jer 17:9). An exploration of the records is the only way all God's people can see as fact what they already believe by faith: that God has judged righteously. And this is exactly the verdict that will be rendered after they review the endless examples of God's providence, longsuffering, and pleading with sinners to repent and return to him.

> And I heard the angel of the waters saying, "Righteous art Thou, who art and who wast, O Holy One, **because Thou didst judge these things**; for they poured out the blood of saints and prophets, and Thou hast given them blood to drink. They deserve it." (Rev 16:5–6; emphasis added)

---

[8] A full discussion of the existence of unfallen worlds is beyond the scope of this book. Job 1:6 strongly suggests that there are such worlds, since no fallen person could come to present himself to God, and no unfallen person existed on earth at the time of Job.

"Hallelujah! Salvation and glory and power belong to our God; **because His judgments are true and righteous**; for He has judged the great harlot who was corrupting the earth with her immorality, and He has avenged the blood of His bond-servants on her." (Rev 19:1–2; emphasis added)

The Millennium in the Old Testament

The millennium itself was prophesied in figurative terms in Ezekiel 38. The prophet was given an oracle against "Gog, the chief prince of Meshech and Tubal" (lit. trans.). This is a symbolic oracle against Satan, similar to the oracle against the King of Tyre (Ezek 28) and the King of Babylon (Isa 14). The specific parties listed are sons of Japheth, the son of Noah who settled to the north (Gen 10:2).[9] This was the direction from which conquests of Palestine came, whether from Assyria, Babylon, or Rome. Thus, these names are symbolic of pagan enemies of God. Gog, as the chief prince (cf. Dan 10:13), can be none other than Satan.

Ezekiel 38:4–6 describes the fact that God will "put hooks in [Gog's] jaws" which will prevent him from carrying out his plans to make war against God. Then "after many days [he] will be summoned" (38:8). This interval suggests the millennium, after which Gog will lead an assault on "My people Israel" (38:14). He is pictured as coming out of the north with a great assembly and a mighty army (38:15) "like a cloud" (38:15). The final end of Gog prefigures Revelation 20:9.

"Thus says the Lord GOD, "Are you the one of whom I spoke in former days through My servants the prophets of Israel, who prophesied in those days for many years that I would bring you against them? And it will come about on that day, when Gog comes against the land of Israel," declares the Lord GOD, "that My fury will mount up in My anger. And in My zeal and in My blazing wrath I declare that on that day there will surely be a great earthquake in the land of Israel. And the fish of the sea, the birds of the heavens, the beasts of the field, all the creeping things that creep on the earth, and all the men who are on the face of the earth will shake at My presence; the mountains also will be thrown down, the steep pathways

---

[9] Once again the individual names are used *pars pro toto*.

will collapse, and every wall will fall to the ground. And I shall call for a sword against him on all My mountains," declares the Lord GOD. "Every man's sword will be against his brother. And with pestilence and with blood I shall enter into judgment with him; and I shall rain on him, and on his troops, and on the many peoples who are with him, a torrential rain, with hailstones, fire, and brimstone. And I shall magnify Myself, sanctify Myself, and make Myself known in the sight of many nations; and they will know that I am the LORD."' (Ezek 38:17–23)

In the language of ancient Israel the end of Satan and the wicked was pictured by Ezekiel.[10] And just as John expanded other parts of Ezekiel's prophecies, new details are given in Revelation 20. But no prophet ever indicated that there would be a millennial kingdom on the earth. The prophets repeatedly presented the fact that at the end of *all things* [11] God would be glorified and all people would come to praise him. "Zion" or "Jerusalem" was indicated as God's home, since that was the usual way in which the final hope of Israel was expressed. And the character of this time would be peace.

And when the thousand years are completed, Satan will be released from his prison, and will come out to deceive the nations which are in the four corners of the earth, Gog and Magog, to gather them together for the war; the number of them is like the sand of the seashore. And they came up on the broad plain of the earth and surrounded the camp of the saints and the beloved city, and fire came down from heaven and devoured them. And the devil who deceived them was thrown into the lake of fire and brimstone, where the beast and the false prophet are also; and they will be tormented day and night forever and ever. (Rev 20:7–10)

At the end of the millennium, the wicked will be resurrected. Satan will again be able to tempt them, and they will surround the

---

[10] This passage describes the sword of brother against brother. This scene was repeated throughout Hebrew history, including the victory of Gideon over the Philistines (Judg 7:22), Jonathan's victory over the Philistines (1 Sam 14:20), the delivery of Judah in the days of Jehoshaphat (2 Chron 20:23), etc.

[11] The end of all things on earth is to be distinguished from the end of the era before the millennium. Because Satan and the wicked will be released to attack God's people after the New Jerusalem descends, "the end of all things" refers to the time when Satan and the wicked will be destroyed.

camp of the saints. Since the wicked are on earth, this requires that the saints will have returned to earth from heaven.[12] Fire will come from heaven and destroy the wicked (Rev 20:9). This is described in the great white throne judgment scene as being cast into the lake of fire.

One may ask just what God's point is in allowing this attack on the New Jerusalem. While Scripture does not speak to the issue directly, there is a reasonable premise we may consider. The white throne judgment allows all creation to see the recorded evil of every lost person. But this is not the same as seeing it firsthand. I may think of my grandmother as wonderful and have a hard time accepting that she is not among the saints, even after reviewing the record. This emotional tie will be severed when I see her assault the camp of the saints with satanic hatred on her face. I will then be fully convinced of the justice and mercy of God.[13]

The Great White Throne

And I saw a great white throne and Him who sat upon it, from whose presence earth and heaven fled away, and no place was found for them. And I saw the dead, the great and the small, standing before the throne, and books were opened; and another book was opened, which is the book of life; and the dead were judged from the things which were written in the books, according to their deeds. And the sea gave up the dead which were in it, and death and Hades gave up the dead which were in them; and they were judged, every one of them according to their deeds. And death and Hades were thrown into the lake of fire. This is the second death, the lake of fire. And if anyone's name was not found written in the book of life, he was thrown into the lake of fire. (Rev 20:11–15)

It will be immediately argued by Futurists that this event takes place after the millennium, since it is recorded in vision after Sa-

---

[12] The return of the saints is the descent of the New Jerusalem described in Revelation 21–22. As with so many of the visions in the apocalypse, each one presents a specific perspective, often leaving out facts which must be gleaned from other visions.

[13] This example is not intended to suggest that my grandmother will not be in the kingdom. I have no way of knowing absolutely whether she will or will not. It was chosen strictly for verbal simplicity.

tan is released from his millennial bondage (20:7). On this point
we can agree. But on the details of the judgment the Bible presents a different picture from that of the Futurists.

The Futurist approach parades the wicked before the throne
of Jesus in a literal Jerusalem at the end of the millennial period
of peace on earth. And in a perverse coincidence they are almost
right. The throne will be on earth, as will be seen in chapter nine,
but as we have already seen, it will not be after a peaceful and
prosperous thousand years on earth. Instead, it will be a part of
the New Jerusalem which has descended from heaven for the
final scene in the drama of sin.

All determination of guilt or innocence will have been completed by this time. The mere fact that the wicked are not part of
the first resurrection indicates that they have already been condemned by God. The reiteration of this in the absence of their
names from the Book of Life (20:15) confirms that there will be
no fact-finding to do at this time. The judgment by the saints will
be similarly complete, since they will have already spent a millennium with God. The final "judgment" at the great white throne
will not be a determination of guilt, but a pronouncement of the
sentence.

The word translated "judged" in v. 12 is *ekrithesan*. It is a form
of *krino*, a word with multiple uses. In Col 2:16 it refers to the
power to legislate. In John 5:22 it refers to the process of fact-
finding. In John 3:18, it speaks of declaration of guilt. And it is
this third application of the word which is in view. There will be
no laws left to create, and no guilt to determine. Those processes
will have been completed. All that will remain will be the pronouncement of the verdict, which will certainly not come as a
surprise.

Ultimate justice requires that all participants agree that the
verdict is just. This is the purpose of the covenant lawsuit form
seen over thirty times in scripture.[14] God has set aside the millennium for the entire living universe to examine and understand the
righteousness of His judgments. Only Satan and the wicked will
have been isolated from this process. Thus, when God descends

---

[14] We reviewed this form in chapter three in the covenant lawsuit brought by
Stephen that ended the seventy weeks of probation for the Jews.

with the saints and the wicked are resurrected, they must be made
aware of the grounds on which they have been condemned.
When the attack on the camp of the saints is arrested by God,
perhaps they will all see a sort of replay of the grounds for their
condemnation. In any case, their blame will be immediately clear.
No millennium is reserved for this process. It will happen in a
moment.

When the wicked are convicted of their own evil and of
God's righteousness in passing judgment, they will all cry out
with the scribes, Pharisees, and hypocrites, "Blessed is He who
comes in the name of the Lord" (Matt 23:39; cf. Phil 2:11). This
is not a plea for mercy, but an admission of the correctness of the
sentence that the judge announces. The universe will be unanimous in proclaiming God's praise. But it will be too late for the
wicked. They had a chance to repent, but did not. Their end will
be in the lake of fire.

The Kingdom

Daniel 2 presents the clearest outline in Scripture of the future history of the world. And since clear Scripture must always
be allowed to illuminate the less clear, this is where we should
start to gain an understanding of God's kingdom.

Nebuchadnezzar dreamed of a statue symbolic of four kingdoms (Dan 2:37–40). These are generally recognized to be Babylon, Medo-Persia, Greece, and Rome. Of particular interest is the
fact that the fourth kingdom began strong but became a broken
kingdom (2:40–43). Speaking of the fragmented state, Daniel
says:

> "And **in the days of those kings** the God of heaven will set up a
> kingdom which will never be destroyed, and *that* kingdom will not be
> left for another people; it will crush and put an end to all these king-
> doms, but it will itself endure forever. (Dan 2:44; emphasis added)

In the time of fragmentation, God will set up His eternal
kingdom. It is a once-for-all-time kingdom. Just as Jesus' sacrifice
on the cross will never be repeated, God's eternal kingdom is not
two successive kingdoms. There is no "millennial kingdom of

peace" to be followed by the final kingdom where all sin is abolished.

As we have discovered from an investigation of other scriptures, history sweeps forward toward a single end time for all people. There is no second plan for the Jews involving a one-world government under an "Antichrist" character. That would require that the fragments of the Roman Empire coalesce. God has decreed that they "**will not** adhere to one another" (2:43 emphasis added).

Daniel's prophecy will be fulfilled. All the earth will remain fragmented politically until the second coming of Christ. That return in power and glory will destroy all the kingdoms of the earth. They will become like dust to be blown away without a trace (2:35). At that moment the kingdom will be given to the saints (7:22), who will possess it forever. During the millennium they will reside in heaven[15] as the books are opened in the final examination of God's administration of the gospel. Then the saints return to the earth. In a brief moment after the second resurrection the wicked will try to assault the New Jerusalem, but they will be destroyed. Sin will have been finally eliminated. The earth can be made new (Rev 21:5), and peace will reign forever.

A Millennial Kingdom of Peace?

In the Futurist model, the millennium is a time of peace on earth. We must admit that there will be no strife in a formless and empty world, but this is not quite what they have in mind. Rather, Jesus is expected to reign over a peaceful world from a temple in

---

[15] Where will they reside? Perhaps in the "place" Christ says he goes to prepare for us (John 14:1–3). And perhaps that place is a sort of new subdivision or housing project called New Jerusalem. And perhaps it is this New Jerusalem Christ has prepared that descends to earth after the millennium. Jesus says, "I **go** to prepare a place for you" because that place is now in heaven, where we will live during the millennium. He says, "And if I **go**...I will **come again** and **receive you** unto **myself**, that **where I am** there ye may be also." He doesn't say "that where **you** are there **I** may be," but "that where **I** am there **you** may be." Where we are is on earth, and where he is, heaven. Thus, clearly, he **returns** for us, then takes us to where he has been. There we spend the millennium. Then we return to earth for the final judgment and destruction of sin. Then, it seems, the "camp of the saints" is pulled back into the air while God recreates the world, and finally the New Jerusalem comes down from the sky and lands on earth, where it will be forever.

Jerusalem. David will be resurrected to serve as Christ's regent (Walvoord, *Prophecies*, 393). While the general climate is one of peace, sin will not have been abolished.

> "As the Millennium progresses, there will be an element of false profession due to the abundance of knowledge of the Lord (Jer 31:34), but it would be reasonable to assume that more people will be saved than in our present world situation" (398)

> ". . . the rule of death and sin will still be present in the millennial kingdom . . ." (401)

LaHaye and Jenkins suggest that as the millennium begins, millions will have concealed their true spiritual allegiance. Disregarding the fact that it is impossible to conceal anything from God, they go on to say,

> We believe . . . that the unregenerate will be given one hundred years to repent and accept Christ as their Lord; if they refuse to do so, they will die . . . We believe this rebellion will essentially be a youth movement, since people in the Millennium will be given a hundred years to make a decision for the Savior.[16]

> The Millennium will prove that even the best of conditions—a thousand years of peace, prosperity, safety, long life, abundance—cannot change the wickedness of the unredeemed human heart (*End Times*, 245)

They go on to point out that rebellious sinners will become "as the sand of the sea." We must consider just how this situation could be possible. After all, even they admit that Satan will be bound so that he cannot tempt the nations. Without a tempter, just how is sin supposed to manifest itself? Even in the Futurist

---

[16] LaHaye and Jenkins, *End Times*, 240–241; contradicted in Isa 60:18. These speculations are based on a literal reading of Isa 65:20, which reads, "For the youth will die at the age of one hundred and the one who does not reach the age of one hundred will be *thought* accursed." If this is literal, however, it contradicts the previous verse, which promises no more weeping (would no one weep when the young man died?). Also, this is a "new heavens and a new earth" passage (see v. 17), parallel with Rev 21, which is set after the millennium. Is there then sin and death after God destroys the wicked? It seems much more likely that in this passage God is using language understandable to Isaiah's original audience, at a time when the idea of eternal life was very uncommon.

model Christ will kill all the wicked at the Glorious Appearing, which is supposedly to ring in the millennial kingdom. Thus, without sin and with no tempter to introduce it, the Futurist model requires that mankind fall a second time, this time without help from a serpent. And if it is possible to fall a second time, how is it that man will not fall a third time, a fourth time, and so on?

Satan's fundamental accusation is based on the idea that no one can keep God's law. If sin will be present in the millennial kingdom, then Satan's accusation is true and God is a liar. And if man can sin in a kingdom where God incarnate is present and Satan is not, how can God ever guarantee an end of sin? The awfulness of this thought is beyond comprehension.

Sir Robert Anderson comments:

> The fulfillment to Judah of the blessings specified in Dan. ix. 24 is all that Scripture expressly states will mark the close of the seventieth week (Anderson, 184)

The first three conditions listed in Daniel 9:24 are "to finish the transgression, to make an end of sin, [and] to make atonement for iniquity." These three descriptions of sin sum up the entire Hebrew universe of sin. If this is a list of the blessings that end the seventieth week and therefore begin the millennial kingdom, then there will be no sin whatever in the millennial kingdom.

A second difficulty arises from the presence of sin in the millennial kingdom. Every time someone sins, it will disturb the peace. Conflict will become a prominent feature, just as it is today. Walvoord even describes a rebellion in the millennial kingdom (*Prophecies*, 404ff). Thus, it will be impossible for a kingdom of peace to exist without a functional police state. To describe that as peaceful is to strain the imagination. Therefore the conditions proposed for the millennial kingdom are internally inconsistent.

Third, such a kingdom is inherently different from the final kingdom of God. There the consequences of sin are absent, so that there are "no more tears" (Rev 7:17; 21:4). Death, which Walvoord indicates will be present in the millennial kingdom, will cause the living to grieve. Because the two are different, this is not the eternal kingdom of God. God revealed the truth about this to Daniel.

> And in the days of those kings the God of heaven will set up a kingdom which will never be destroyed, and that kingdom will not be left for another people; it will crush and put an end to all these kingdoms, but it will itself endure forever. (Dan 2:44)

The kingdom God will set up in the days of the fragments left from the Roman Empire will last forever. This leaves no place for a millennial kingdom followed by a kingdom in which all sin is finally abolished. The Futurist plan has *two* kingdoms following the Glorious Appearing, not one. But since God speaks the truth, only one kingdom will be established.

David the Prince

Based on several passages in Ezekiel, Futurists insist that David will be resurrected to be co-regent with Christ in the millennial kingdom. The language appears to be literal, so there seems to be *prima facie* support for this premise. But once again, the Futurist interpretation is not consistent with other Scripture.

Psalm 22 is a well-recognized Messianic Psalm. It was written by David and presents a poetic lament in first person voice. That is, David speaks as if he is himself the sufferer. Charles Briggs comments.

> **These sufferings transcend those of any historical sufferer**, with the single exception of Jesus Christ. They find their exact counterpart in the sufferings on the cross. They are more vivid in their realization of that dreadful scene than the story of the Gospels. The most striking features of these sufferings are seen there, in the piercing of the hands and feet, the body stretched upon the cross, the intense thirst, and the division of the garments.[17]

---

[17] Charles A. Briggs, *Messianic Prophecy* (Scribner's: New York, 1889), 326 (emphasis added).

While David laments about the events that "have" happened to him, it is hard to dispute that the Psalm actually speaks prophetically about Christ. Therefore, "David" in this context is Christ. In Psalm 16, David again speaks in first person about events which do not pertain to him, but do happen to Christ. In this case, Peter's sermon on the Day of Pentecost quotes verse 10 (Acts 2:27), supplying us with inspired proof that "David" in this Psalm is actually Christ, just as in Psalm 22.

Because Scripture does identify "David" as the Messiah in these Psalms, it is improper to require that King David be resurrected to serve as regent with Christ in a millennial kingdom. The concept of corporate identity permeates Hebrew thought. Just as "Jacob" stands *pars pro toto* in place of all of his descendants, "David" stands as the typological identity of the Messiah.

> For a child will be born to us, a son will be given to us;
> And the government will rest on His shoulders;
> And His name will be called Wonderful Counselor, Mighty God,
> Eternal Father, Prince of Peace.
> There will be no end to the increase of His government or of peace,
> On the throne of David and over his kingdom,
> To establish it and to uphold it with justice and righteousness
> From then on and forevermore.
> The zeal of the LORD of hosts will accomplish this.
> (Isa 9:6–7; emphasis added)

In this passage Isaiah identifies the place from which the Messiah will reign as David's throne.[18] Other passages link Him in other ways to David. Is it any surprise that Ezekiel would blend all of these expectations into a single idea and refer to the Messiah as David?

The Promised Land

Throughout all Futurist interpretation of prophecy sounds the constant drumbeat that the promise of Palestine to Abraham

---

[18] It should also be noted that this prophecy again identifies the Messianic kingdom as being without end. The prophets are united in declaring that the eschatological expectation is a single kingdom of peace, not a Futurist thousand year reich terminating with another judgment and resurrection before the final divine kingdom is established.

was unconditional. The creation of the secular state of Israel in 1948 is widely regarded as being of extreme importance in the ultimate fulfillment of this promise. While a discussion of the details of the covenant is beyond the scope of this book, we may make a few observations.

First, as we discussed in chapter two, the promises given to Abraham were passed to his descendants *by faith*. Genetics were not involved. If Abraham had been unfaithful, the promise would have become null and void. Similarly, if Isaac or Jacob had been unfaithful, the chain would have been broken. This birthright blessing continued on because there was a faithful remnant in every generation. Eventually, though, God had had enough. Through Daniel God set a time limit of 490 years (Dan 9:24) for the Hebrew people to come into compliance with his covenant. Jesus declared that their failure to meet the conditions of their probation would cause their heritage to become desolate (Matt 23:38). And in 34 AD, Stephen brought God's covenant lawsuit against them. The guilty verdict ended the Jewish birthright blessings. The promise of possession of the land became forever void due to their unfaithfulness.

Second, the promise of land given to Abraham was of a relatively small area (though much larger than the present country of Israel). It was the crossroads of the earth, "the center of the nations" (Ezek 5:5), in order to allow Abraham's descendants to fulfill their missionary task.[19] David expanded the promise to "the land" in Psalm 37:11. But he qualified it by saying that the humble would be the heirs, not the Jews.[20] Jesus universalized this promise to the entire earth in the Sermon on the Mount (Matt 5:5). Paul identified that the promise to Abraham had been that he would inherit not just Palestine, but the entire world (Rom 4:13). Thus, a claim to a limited inheritance in Palestine is myopic. It is also arrogant, since this birthright blessing was revoked prophetically during Jesus' ministry and in judicial fact at the covenant lawsuit prosecuted by Stephen.

---

[19] Walter C. Kaiser, *Mission in the Old Testament: Israel as a Light to the Nations*, (Grand Rapids: Baker, 2000)

[20] Other Old Testament prophecies expand the Promised Land as well. (Ps 25:13; 37:9, 11, 22, 29, 34; Isa 60:21).

The Millennial Temple

The centerpiece of Futurist millennial thought is the temple described in Ezekiel 40–46. In 573 BC, the prophet was given a very detailed vision of a great temple. This temple was quite different from either Solomon's temple or the temple later built by Zerubbabel. Because of this, the assumption is made that this temple is to be built in the future. In this, the Futurists are not alone. The great Rabbi Maimonides clearly stated that this third temple would be built by man.[21] Since events seem to be proceeding rapidly toward end times, it is proposed that this temple will be built soon. A number of difficulties arise from this premise.

The site of the proposed temple is Mount Zion, the site of the previous two temples. This literalistic assertion is based on an interpretation of the Old Testament that ignores the New Testament. Since the apostolic New Testament writers are inspired by the same Holy Spirit inspiring the Old Testament writers, their statements are of equal authority. Paul presents the definitive interpretation for us.

> For you have not come to a *mountain* that may be touched and to a blazing fire, and to darkness and gloom and whirlwind, and to the blast of a trumpet and the sound of words which *sound was such that* those who heard begged that no further word should be spoken to them. . . . But you have come to Mount Zion and to the city of the living God, the heavenly Jerusalem, and to myriads of angels, to the general assembly and church of the first-born who are enrolled in heaven, and to God, the Judge of all, and to the spirits of righteous men made perfect, and to Jesus, the mediator of a new covenant, and to the sprinkled blood, which speaks better than *the blood* of Abel. (Heb 12:18–19, 22–24)

New converts *have come to Mount Zion!* They have joined as citizens of the heavenly Jerusalem by accepting Christ. Now that Christ lives in them, they are at Mount Zion. Jesus is not found by locating Mount Zion. Mount Zion is found by locating Jesus! The Old Testament meets its definitive interpretation in the New Testament.

---

[21] Maimonides, *Introduction to Mishna Tractate* Middot.

The first temple of Israel was built by Solomon, then destroyed by Nebuchadnezzar in 586BC. The second temple was completed by Zerubbabel in 516 BC. The scriptural record of this event is instructive.

> And the elders of the Jews were successful in building through the prophesying of Haggai the prophet and Zechariah the son of Iddo. And they finished building **according to the command of the God of Israel** and the decree of Cyrus, Darius, and Artaxerxes king of Persia. And this temple was completed on the third day of the month Adar; it was the sixth year of the reign of King Darius. (Ezra 6:14–15; emphasis added)

The temple was completed *as commanded by God* through the voices of the prophets Haggai and Zechariah. All temple construction was done *after* Ezekiel received his vision. If God intended that this temple should be built, why would He instruct his prophets that a different temple be constructed? Futurists suggest that this means that the temple belongs in the millennium. A more likely answer is that God did not intend for this temple to be built, but rather to be instruction for wayward Israel.

The description of the millennium in Ezekiel 38 immediately precedes the temple vision. Since the book generally proceeds from the departure of the presence of God toward its return, it is only logical to expect that the millennium is in chronological sequence before the temple vision. This would suggest that the temple, if it is to have a literal physical expression, will not be in the millennium, but will be part of the kingdom *after* the millennium.[22]

The sequence of events in Ezekiel also includes a considerable number of curious scenes. Many of them are obviously symbolic. The prophet is told to eat a scroll (Ezek 2:8–3:3), which is actually a reference to being given a message. He lays siege to a brick (4:1–3). He lies on his side for extended periods (4:4–8). His diet is to be bizarre (4:9–17). His hair is to be shaved, divided, and manipulated as a sign (5:1–4ff). He is to prepare his baggage and dig a hole in the wall of his house through which to

---

[22] But of course, there will be no physical temple after the millennium, either. This will be discussed in chapter nine.

carry it (12:2–6ff). In all this he is to be a "sign" to the house of Israel. He is to eat his meals with fear and trembling (12:18). As the book proceeds, a number of symbolic oracles unfold. In fact, the largest volume of the book is unquestionably symbolic. But when the temple vision is presented, this distinction is not immediately obvious. This allows Futurists to insist that the vision must be literal and physical in intent. But before Ezekiel is given the contents of the vision, he is told to "Declare to the house of Israel all that you see" (40:4b). The vision's purpose will be fulfilled in telling the Hebrews all that is seen. If its purpose were physical, the direction would have been to give instructions to build the temple. But the evidence so far suggests that the vision was intended to be symbolic.

The next hint as to the purpose of the vision comes when Ezekiel is brought in vision to the inner court.

> And the Spirit lifted me up and brought me into the inner court; and behold, the glory of the LORD filled the house. Then I heard one speaking to me from the house, while a man was standing beside me. And He said to me, "Son of man, this is the place of My throne and the place of the soles of My feet, where I will dwell among the sons of Israel forever. (Ezek 43:5–7)

The inner court is where God will "dwell among the sons of Israel forever." If this is to be true in a literal physical sense according to the Futurist ethnic definition of Israel, then God will not dwell with the Gentiles. That forces this vision into conflict with John's apocalypse, where God is said to dwell with "men" in the earth made new (Rev 21:3), not "Jews." On the other hand, if "Israel" describes the faithful, then there is no contradiction. Next, if the temple is to be a literal physical temple "forever," then it is again in conflict with John's apocalypse, since there will be no temple in the New Jerusalem because "the Lord God, the Almighty, and the Lamb" are its temple (21:22). But if Ezekiel's temple is symbolic, this contradiction is resolved as well.

The priestly rites in this temple are clearly levitical in nature. And this brings us to an impossible problem for the Futurist view. The levitical priesthood was established by a series of regulations at Sinai. These included various washings, offerings, sacrifices, and ceremonial sabbaths. Paul describes them as a "tutor" to bring us to Christ (Gal 3:24–25), since they were all object lessons pointing to the Messiah. But now that the Messiah has come, they are "obsolete" (Heb 8:13). The theme of Hebrews is that Christ is now our better high priest, in a better temple, offering a better sacrifice.

Jesus was from the tribe of Judah (7:14), not the tribe of Levi. Therefore, under the levitical rules, he could not be a priest at all. There must have been a change in the law (7:12) to allow Jesus to become a priest. Since he *is* our high priest according to the order of Melchizedek (7:17), the levitical laws *have* been set aside (7:18, 19, 28; 8:4, 9:19, 22; 10:1, 8). Since Jesus is a high priest *forever* (7:17), the change in the law which allows Him to be a priest is *permanent*. There will never be another levitical priest in the divine economy.

Pentecost suggests that there might be a new priestly order different from the levitical (*Prophecies*, 518ff). But Ezekiel's temple has hereditary "levitical" priests (Ezek 43:19; 44:15, 25–27). Hebrews makes it quite clear that the Melchizedek priesthood is not based on heredity (Heb 7:3). Therefore a reversionary change in the law of the priesthood would have to take place to allow this temple to operate. And as we have just seen, the change to the Melchizedek priesthood is *permanent*. Scripture absolutely precludes the legitimate future operation of this priesthood. Without its priests, the temple cannot operate.

One other feature of the temple is problematic. It is described as having daily sacrifices (Ezek 46:13). Christ's death on the cross is clearly the one final sacrifice for all time (Heb 9:26). There are no other sacrifices in the divine plan. Futurists must find a way around this clear scriptural difficulty. Pentecost suggests that the "sacrifices *will have no relation to the question of expiation*" (524; emphasis in the original). In other words, they have no effect in taking away sins. Instead, "the sacrifices *will be memorial in character*" (525; emphasis in the original). "Interpreted in the light of the New Testament, with its teaching on the value of the death of Christ, they [the sacrifices] must be memorials of that death" (525). But no Scripture is offered to support this position. And once again, Futurists run headlong into a dilemma.

There is no scriptural example of a sacrifice that was exclusively memorial in character.[23] To suggest now that there should be in the future is to step outside the realm of interpretation into the forbidden practice of adding to Scripture (Deut 4:2; Prov 30:6; Rev 22:18). Futurists must find a way for their construct to appear scriptural, so a memorial is called upon. To the modern mind, it seems reasonable, but it is not biblical. And it also violates a divine command.

The sacrifices in the Old Testament temple were an acted-out prophecy of the cross. When Jesus died, they were abolished (Dan 9:27; Matt 27:51). In their place our Lord instituted a very specific memorial of His death, the Lord's Supper (1 Cor 11:23–26). It is the *only* memorial of this type in Scripture. The suggestion of memorial sacrifices in a millennial temple is a substitution of the traditions of men for the law of God (Mark 7:13). If actually implemented, they would be nothing less than idolatry.

If the temple in Ezekiel were to be a literal physical building with literal physical levitical services, this would place it in conflict with the book of Hebrews. Thus, if a temple should be built, and Levites are called to service, it will not be with God's approval. Therefore we must consider the true import of Ezekiel's vision.

God's Purpose for Ezekiel's Vision

A careful reading of the book of Ezekiel reveals that God made the purpose of the vision quite explicit. Before giving Ezekiel the vision, God told him that he should make the vision known to the house of Israel (Ezek 40:4). After the extensive measurement of the temple, a more detailed instruction was given.

---

[23] At this point, it would be tempting to suggest that the Passover sacrifice was such a memorial (Deut 16:1). But the Passover was initiated as a means of demonstrating the faith of the individual while in Egypt, before the destroying angel passed over (Exod 12:3-14). Later generations were to be instructed in the Passover as a memorial (Exod 12:27). The Passover's greater function was to be a type pointing forward to Christ (1 Cor 5:7). Indeed, the Passover has again become a memorial for us, since its bread and wine are the model for the Lord's Supper.

"As for you, son of man, describe the temple to the house of Israel, that they may be ashamed of their iniquities; and let them measure the plan. And if they are ashamed of all that they have done, make known to them the design of the house, its structure, its exits, its entrances, all its designs, all its statutes, and all its laws. And write it in their sight, so that they may observe its whole design and all its statutes, and do them. (Ezek 43:10–11)

Ezekiel was instructed to "describe" the temple to the "rebellious people" (44:6). In doing so, the people were to "measure the plan." It was intended that the plan of the temple would cause the apostates to become ashamed of what they had done. If the intent was that the construction diagrams were to cause shame among the house of Israel, that would be very surprising. But if the word "plan" describes the plan of salvation offered in the temple, everything fits. The people would see that the temple pointed in every way toward an ultimate salvation to be provided for them by a loving God. He would even provide the sacrifice (45:17)!

This message was not to be presented to faithful Jews. It was only to be given to the rebellious ones! If they would become ashamed when they saw God's plan, they would repent of their wickedness. Only then would the laws of the temple be explained. Once the statutes were understood, they could be observed. There was no hint of construction. It was designed to be an object lesson by which the evil in the hearts of apostate Israel could be turned back to the Lord, so that they could understand His laws to "observe . . . and do them."

There was one part of the temple which was to be built: the altar (43:18). And we know that it was built, since Jeshua the son of Jazodek and Zerubbabel the son of Shealtiel offered burnt offerings on it immediately after the exiles returned after the decree of Cyrus (Ezra 3:2–3).

The temple shown to Ezekiel was an outline of the plan of salvation, drawn in bricks and mortar. It was intended to bring the apostates back to Yahweh. It also gives us a glance at God's plan for the end times, written on the tapestry of the Old Testament sanctuary.

"Israel" in Ezekiel

Futurists have proposed the temple vision as a guarantee for the future of the Jews in the millennium. From a number of angles we have seen how this notion is incorrect. The millennium will find the earth uninhabitable, so no kingdom of peace will be possible on earth. The saints will all be in heaven, reviewing the books which record God's management of the gospel. And the temple is a symbolic vision, identified as such by both the vision and history.

Ethnic Jews are offered no special position even in Ezekiel's prophecies. God makes this quite clear.

> Then the word of the LORD came to me, saying, "Son of man, your brothers, your relatives, your fellow exiles, and the whole house of Israel, all of them, are those to whom the inhabitants of Jerusalem have said, 'Go far from the LORD; this land has been given us as a possession.' (Ezek 11:14–15)

Two groups of people are in view here, "the whole house of Israel" and "the inhabitants of Jerusalem." At the time of this oracle (592 BC), Jerusalem had not been destroyed and was inhabited by Jews. Yet these people are distinguished from the house of Israel by the fact that they incited apostasy and claimed the land promises as if they were unconditional. The house of Israel, on the other hand, had not apostatized, or the Jews in Jerusalem would not be telling them to do so. Thus, God explicitly identifies "the house of Israel" as the body of believers, a group not identified by ethnicity.

> "Therefore say, 'Thus says the Lord GOD, "Though I had removed them far away among the nations, and though I had scattered them among the countries, yet I was a sanctuary for them a little while in the countries where they had gone. Therefore say, "Thus says the Lord GOD, I shall gather you from the peoples and assemble you out of the countries among which you have been scattered, and I shall give you the land of Israel."" (Ezek 11:16–17)

This promise of restoration was given *only* to the faithful. It was not given to ethnic Jews, regardless of the use of the word "Israel." Since the primary purpose of the book of Ezekiel was to bring the apostates back to Yahweh, any interpretation centered on ethnic Jewish restoration violates the intent of the book. God's purpose was then, as always, redemptive, not political. "Israel" in Ezekiel has a root meaning of the faithful. When apostasy was present, then Israel may have been the name used, but it then described a formerly faithful group.

> "When they come there, they will remove all its detestable things and all its abominations from it. And I shall give them one heart, and shall put a new spirit within them. And I shall take the heart of stone out of their flesh and give them a heart of flesh, that they may walk in My statutes and keep My ordinances, and do them. Then they will be My people, and I shall be their God. (Ezek 11:18–20)

Once the believers have been restored, God will add extra blessings to them. But those who do not repent have another fate.

> "But as for those whose hearts go after their detestable things and abominations, I shall bring their conduct down on their heads," declares the Lord GOD. (Ezek 11:21)

The punishment of the wicked will not be mitigated by membership in any ethnic group. Only belief or unbelief will be in view when God distributes blessings and curses. Israel will be blessed. Therefore, just as we found in chapter two, Israel is primarily identified in Ezekiel as the body of believers.

Summary

Direct scriptural material regarding the millennium is relatively sparse. But when Revelation 20 is combined with other prophecies a clear picture can be painted. When Christ returns for His people, all saints of all ages without reference to ethnicity will rise to meet Him in the air. They will then be conducted to heaven. The wicked on earth will be killed, and the earth will be transformed into a lifeless, chaotic, formless ball. John describes it as the "abyss," or "bottomless pit." Satan will be unable to leave the earth.

For a thousand years the saints will review the records of all who were not saved, noting God's proper administration of the gospel. The end of this process will be a resounding cry throughout heaven of "Holy, Holy, Holy, art Thou, for Thy judgments are righteous and true!" The rulers and authorities in the heavenly places will be fully satisfied with the mercy and justice of God. When this is completed, it will be time to bring the saints back to earth in the New Jerusalem.

There will be no millennial kingdom of peace on the earth. Nor will there be a great temple on earth, because the earth will be formless and lifeless. There will be no activity at all on earth. It will be a dead world. Its sole purpose will be to function as a prison for Satan.

The extreme literalistic straightjacket of the Futurists forces them to ignore great volumes of Scripture. If they would allow Scripture to interpret itself, they would be able to recognize the great truths contained within it. But because they insist on a literalistic interpretation whenever possible, they are blinded to the fact that literal-sounding statements are often greater truths of God painted symbolically on a physical canvas. We must be open to hear all that God has to say, not what men would like Him to say.

CHAPTER NINE:

THE NEW JERUSALEM

"Though the Bible does not comment on this, it is possible that the New Jerusalem will be a satellite city in relation to the millennial earth, and that those with resurrected bodies, as well as the holy angels, will occupy the New Jerusalem during the thousand year reign. They will be able to commute to earth, much as people go from the country to their city offices and participate in earthly functions without necessarily living in the city."
(Walvoord, *Prophecies*, 414)

The Final Rebellion

When the saints have completed their examination of the books at the end of the millennium, only one scene in the drama of salvation will remain to be played. It will be time for the final demonstration of the evil character of sin.

And when the thousand years are completed, Satan will be released from his prison, and will come out to deceive the nations which are in the four corners of the earth, Gog and Magog, to gather them together for the war; the number of them is like the sand of the seashore. And they came up on the broad plain of the earth and surrounded the camp of the saints and the beloved city, and fire came down from heaven and devoured them. And the devil who deceived them was thrown into the lake of fire and brimstone, where the beast and the false prophet are also; and they will be tormented day and night forever and ever. (Rev 20:7–10)

Satan will have been held captive in the formless earth for a thousand years. The saints will have been in heaven, and the wicked will have been in *Hades*, the place of the dead.[1] When the

---

[1] *Hades* is the Greek equivalent of the Hebrew *Sheol*. Ecclesiastes 9:10 states that "there is no activity or planning or knowledge or wisdom in Sheol." This indicates that

saints return to the earth, they will be greeted by a wasteland. At that moment, however, the wicked will be resurrected. This time no influence of God will moderate their actions. Satan will be totally unopposed, and the father of lies will deceive one final time.

> "And you will go up, you will come like a storm; you will be like a cloud covering the land, you and all your troops, and many peoples with you."
>
> 'Thus says the Lord GOD, "It will come about on that day, that thoughts will come into your mind, and you will devise an evil plan, and you will say, 'I will go up against the land of unwalled villages. I will go against those who are at rest, that live securely, all of them living without walls, and having no bars or gates.
>
> "And you will come from your place out of the remote parts of the north, you and many peoples with you, all of them riding on horses, a great assembly and a mighty army; and you will come up against My people Israel like a cloud to cover the land. It will come about in the last days that I shall bring you against My land, in order that the nations may know Me when I shall be sanctified through you before their eyes, O Gog."
>
> "And it will come about on that day, when Gog comes against the land of Israel," declares the Lord GOD, "that My fury will mount up in My anger.
>
> "And I shall call for a sword against him on all My mountains," declares the Lord GOD. "Every man's sword will be against his brother. (Ezek 38:9–11, 15–16, 18, 21)

Satan will tell his people that the saints are unguarded (this may be why their "camp" is referred to in Rev 20, suggesting that it is unwalled at this point, more like an army than a city).[2] If

---

the dead will be unaware during the millennium. While a complete discussion of the state of the dead is beyond this book, we may confidently state that in effect the unsaved dead have slept away the millennium and will be wakened for this final scene prior to their ultimate destruction. The biblical support for this destruction can be found in the Appendix.

[2] Gog is another name for Satan, as we found in chapter 6. A person reading the above verses could easily think, because of the references to horses and unwalled villages, that Ezekiel 38 was fulfilled in Old Testament times, perhaps even by Nebuchad-

they attack at once, they can win the final battle after all. He knows the saints will be protected by God, but as the greatest liar of all he will delude the people about their chances. They will attack with a fury never imagined. And in this, God will be "sanctified through [Satan] before [the saints'] eyes." (cf. Ezek 38:23)

No examination of records done by the saints can ever be as dramatic as witnessing "the real thing." This is demonstrated today by the fact that even watching a live event such as the destruction of the World Trade Center in real time on television has a surreal quality. But visiting the site and seeing the destruction first-hand has an impact which cannot be equaled. In the same way, a saint witnessing the awful wickedness of undiluted sin will have all doubts erased forever. The unrepentant loved one will be seen clearly as the servant of evil he is. Before any harm can come to any saint, God will end the battle.

We must be cautious in ascribing complete literalness to the specific words of this prophecy. For example, in Ezekiel's rendering, the attack comes from the North. This is the direction from which the great conquests of Jerusalem came and is the natural expression for the approach of another conqueror. In Revelation the attacking forces surround the camp, indicating an approach from all directions. The variations in the descriptions come from the fact that while both prophecies portray the same literal event, they are described in symbolic language. And if an examination of the various prophecies is made, one will discover that the symbolic terms vary from prophet to prophet. Such fluidity of language should caution us against requiring a literal fulfillment of every word. The scenes that the prophecies describe are quite real and will take place, but they may not take place in a literalistic word-for-word fashion.

In the same way, we must be cautious when considering the manner in which the destruction of the wicked comes about. In Ezekiel, the wicked destroy each other (Ezek 38:21). The image of man against man recalls Old Testament victories (Judg

---

nezzar's destruction of Jerusalem. However, the unexpected reference to Gog and Magog in Rev 20 sends the alert reader back to Ezek 38 and suggests either a fuller fulfillment, an antitypical fulfillment, or an important allusion meant for "those who have ears" and know the Scriptures well. We must always bear in mind that the message of prophecy is usually embedded in symbols.

7:22; 1 Sam 14:20; 2 Chron 20:23) where the Lord fought the battle (1 Sam 17:47; 2 Chron 20:15). In Revelation 19, the wicked are destroyed by the sharp sword that comes from the mouth of the rider on the white horse, who is called "the Word of God." This is before the millennium, and the result is death (Rev 19:15, 21).[3] This figure portrays a blend of the Word of God who spoke the world into existence (John 1:3) with a conquering hero. In Revelation 20:9, after the millennium and the resurrection of the wicked, the wicked are "devoured" by fire that comes down from God out of heaven. "Devoured" points with certainly to death— it simply cannot point to eternal torment, as that is not how the word is used in the Bible. If it is symbolic, it symbolizes death. In v. 15, however, the wicked are cast into the lake of fire, where the devil is cast in v. 10. This brings to mind God's judgment on Sodom and Gomorrah, where "eternal fire" (Jude 7) destroyed them "as an example." All three of these descriptions can legitimately be taken as describing the end of the wicked. But the three cannot all be physically exact, for if they were, the wicked would suffer three second deaths.

If we recognize the fluidity of symbolism, then a more complete picture can be understood. After their continuing wickedness is demonstrated, Satan and all of his followers will be destroyed.[4] That the attack on the city will be stopped is not in

---

[3] It is impossible not to comment on the speculative way in which LaHaye and Jenkins interpret Revelation 19:11–16. (LaHaye and Jenkins, *End Times*, 228). "[Jesus] is accompanied by the armies of heaven – but here they are all in white, symbolizing both their purity and Jesus' unconcern that their "uniforms" would be soiled." Such speculation outside of the realm of Scripture (which never refers to uniforms") belittles God's word and diminishes the value of anything else that might be said. Scriptural interpretations focus on the fact that a priest's garments are linen and that the saints are given white robes symbolic of righteousness.

[4] The importance of the utter finality of this event cannot be overstated. If the torment of Satan and the wicked never ends, then God will be unable to put an end to sin. One can even imagine the righteous someday rising up against God and demanding that he cease from his endless torturing of the wicked. If they do that, Satan will have won! Rather, statements such as "their smoke rises forever and ever" (Rev 19:3) must be understood in the language of the time it was written. Hebrew mathematics was poorly developed, and the concept of infinity did not exist. John's intent was to describe a column of smoke rising out of sight. Today his words are generally seen as referring to time rather than space, and as such are misunderstood to refer to eternally burning fire.

doubt. Further, the ultimate physical result will be their complete destruction on the earth.

If the righteous will be rewarded **in the earth,**
How much more the wicked and the sinner! (Prov 11:31; emphasis added)

"For behold, the day is coming, burning like a furnace; and all the arrogant and every evildoer will be chaff; and the day that is coming will set them ablaze," says the LORD of hosts, "so that **it will leave them neither root nor branch."** (Mal 4:1; emphasis added)

Speaking in covert language about Satan, the prophet declares, in God's name,

"By the multitude of your iniquities,
In the unrighteousness of your trade,
You profaned your sanctuaries.
Therefore I have brought fire from the midst of you;
It has consumed you,
And I have turned you to ashes on the earth
In the eyes of all who see you.
"All who know you among the peoples
Are appalled at you;
You have become terrified,
And **you will be no more."** (Ezek 28:18–19; emphasis added)

It is possible to suggest a scenario containing the key elements mentioned by the prophets. First, the attack fizzles when the wicked attackers turn on each other because they cannot trust their neighbors. Then God protects His people by raining fire and brimstone upon the wicked.[5]

---

[5] We are ignoring the discussion of the great white throne judgment depicted in Revelation 20 as occurring at this moment. This is not intended to diminish its importance, but merely to avoid repeating the discussion of it in chapter eight. It's worth noting, however, that vs. 7–15 are not strictly chronological. John's vision has separated the rebellion and punishment from the judgment of the rebellion that leads to the punishment. Chronologically, Satan is released, deceives the nations, and they surround "the camp of the saints" (vs. 7–9a). Then comes the judgment in vs. 11–12. Verse 13 is parenthetical, explaining how the dead happen to be alive. Then, chronologically, we return to v. 9b–10 for the punishment, then to vs. 14–15 for more punishment. Thus, the order of events seems to be as follows: 1) Satan is released and the wicked are resurrected; 2) They lay siege to the "camp of the saints"; 3) God appears for the "great white throne" judgment and judges according to the books; 4) Fire comes from God

Upon the wicked He will rain snares;
Fire and brimstone and burning wind will be the portion of their cup.
(Ps 11:6)

Next flames burst from the rocks.

But the day of the Lord will come like a thief, in which the heavens will pass away with a roar and the elements will be destroyed with intense heat, and the earth and its works will be burned up. Since all these things are to be destroyed in this way, what sort of people ought you to be in holy conduct and godliness, looking for and hastening the coming of the day of God, on account of which the heavens will be destroyed by burning, and the elements will melt with intense heat! (2 Peter 3:10–12)

The surface of the earth becomes a lake of fire in which the wicked will be burned up. It will bring the final vengeance of the Lord on wickedness (Isa 34:8). As Malachi states, that day will leave neither root nor branch. The wicked will be completely destroyed (Matt 10:28), receiving the reward they have earned (Prov 11:31). Even Satan will eventually "be no more" (Ezek 28:19). The final victory over sin will be complete at that moment. Everyone left alive will be fully convinced of the righteousness of God and committed irrevocably to His service. With the destruction of all sinners, the universe will have been sterilized. It will be ready for God to re-create a paradise for His servants. Then they will "inherit the land" (Ps 37:29).

The City

The final home of the saints is described in Revelation as the New Jerusalem. Numerous architectural details are itemized, just as Ezekiel's vision enumerated the specifications of the temple. And just as Ezekiel's vision included sufficient information

---

and devours "the nations" in rebellion; 5) The devil is cast into the lake of fire where the beast and false prophet were cast in 19:20; 6) Death and Hades are cast into the lake of fire. Verse 15 is a summary of these punishments, not additional punishments.

to show its symbolic nature, the major characteristics of the city in Revelation may also be seen to be symbolic.

> And one of the seven angels who had the seven bowls full of the seven last plagues, came and spoke with me, saying, "Come here, I shall show you the bride, the wife of the Lamb." And he carried me away in the Spirit to a great and high mountain, and showed me the holy city, Jerusalem, coming down out of heaven from God, having the glory of God. Her brilliance was like a very costly stone, as a stone of crystal-clear jasper. (Rev 21:9–11)

In this beginning segment, John is told that he will see the bride of Christ, but he is instead shown a great city.[6] That the saints should be identified in this way is not new to John.

> And they will call you the city of the LORD,
> The Zion of the Holy One of Israel. (Isa 60:14b)

Zion was another name for Jerusalem, so this passage in Isaiah's "little apocalypse" identifies the end-time saints as the city of Jerusalem.[7] This is fully in accord with Paul's description of the saints.

> For you have not come to *a mountain* that may be touched and to a blazing fire, and to darkness and gloom and whirlwind, and to the blast of a trumpet and the sound of words which *sound was such that* those who heard begged that no further word should be spoken to them . . . But you have come to Mount Zion and to the city of the living God, the heavenly Jerusalem, and to myriads of angels, to the general assembly and church of the first-born who are enrolled in heaven, and to God, the Judge of all, and to the spirits of righteous men made perfect, and to Jesus, the mediator of a new covenant, and to the sprinkled blood, which speaks better than *the blood* of Abel. (Heb 12:18–19, 22–24)

---

[6] This is reminiscent of chapter 7, where John is told the number of those sealed (the 144,000), but is shown an innumerable multitude.

[7] In several Old Testament passages the name "Zion" is used without reference to the Mount and is equated to Jerusalem (2 Sam 5:7; 1 Kgs 8:1; 1 Chron 11:5; 2 Chron 5:2; Isa 33:20; 52:1; 62:1). In Psalm 48:2 "Mount Zion" is equated with Jerusalem.

"Zion" and "Jerusalem" are therefore no longer necessarily physical places where Jesus will come. Rather, they are names applied to the people Christ indwells. The church is now Zion and Jerusalem.

Another name for the church is "the bride of Christ." (It is true, of course, that when many people dwell together the result is a city, so we are not denying that there will be a physical city, but only suggesting that the description of the New Jerusalem in Revelation may be using symbolic language to imply the nature of God's people, rather than describing how the city actually looks.)

> "Let us rejoice and be glad and give the glory to Him, for the marriage of the Lamb has come and His bride has made herself ready." And it was given to her to clothe herself in fine linen, bright and clean; for the fine linen is the righteous acts of the saints. (Rev 19:7–8)[8]

This name also calls to mind the fact that the saints are truly faithful. Throughout the Old Testament, apostasy was pictured as harlotry. Even in Revelation, the great harlot is repeatedly mentioned, and the image is that of apostate religion. But even more, the image of the bride recalls God's symbolic betrothal to "Jerusalem," recorded by Ezekiel and Isaiah.

> "Then I passed by you and saw you, and behold, you were at the time for love; so I spread My skirt over you and covered your nakedness. I also swore to you and entered into a covenant with you so that you became Mine," declares the Lord GOD. (Ezek 16:8)

> I will rejoice greatly in the LORD,
> My soul will exult in my God;
> For He has clothed me with garments of salvation,
> He has wrapped me with a robe of righteousness,
> As a bridegroom decks himself with a garland,
> And as a bride adorns herself with her jewels. (Isa 61:10)

---

[8] This passage equates "fine linen" and "righteous acts." Again the symbolic use of an object points out the fact that the book of Revelation is built around non-literal—but not unreal—meanings.

No physical city can ever, by an act of conscious will, "make herself ready" (Rev 19:7). Therefore "Jerusalem" is being used here as the corporate identity of those who have trusted in God. They have made themselves ready and have been given fine linen robes (Zech 3:4–5; Rev 3:5, 18). The physical attributes of the city will thus reflect the character of those saved.

John first describes the brilliance of the city as being the result of the presence of the "glory of God" (Rev 21:11). It is like the jasper appearing in the Old Testament on the breastplate of the high priest (Exod 28:20; 39:13) and as part of the "king of Tyre's" "construction" (Ezek 28:13).[9] It also describes the appearance of the Father on the throne in heaven (Rev 4:3). Next John describes the physical structure he is shown.

> It had a great and high wall, with twelve gates, and at the gates twelve angels; and names *were* written on them, which are *those* of the twelve tribes of the sons of Israel. There were three gates on the east and three gates on the north and three gates on the south and three gates on the west. (Rev 21:12–13)

The twelve tribes of Israel provide the entrances. Three gates are arranged on each side of the city in a manner similar to the arrangement of the camp in the wilderness (Num 2:1–31). Throughout the ages, the Israel of God has been the starting place for entry to God. In the wilderness, no one could approach the tabernacle without first passing by one of the tribes. Ethnic Israel also received the oracles of God (Rom 3:2) and was the natural portion of the olive tree (Rom 11:21).

The names of the tribes are given in the account of the sealing of the saints (Rev 7:1–8). Each one suggests what might be an additional meaning that could be added to the description. For example, Reuben was "uncontrolled as water" and an adulterer (Gen 49:4). Those without self-control can receive it from God. Perhaps David, the most famous adulterer, will enter through the gate marked "Reuben." Issachar was one who bore heavy burdens (49:14–15). Christ says that His burden is light (Matt 11:10 KJV). Perhaps those who have been weighed down

---

[9] This oracle, while addressed to the "king of Tyre," is generally understood as referring to Satan while he was the covering angel in heaven.

will enter through the Issachar gate. There will be a gate for everyone who calls on the Lord.

> And the wall of the city had twelve foundation stones, and on them were the twelve names of the twelve apostles of the Lamb. (Rev 21:14)

The church's foundations are the apostles, with Jesus as the chief cornerstone (Eph 2:20). By now it should be clear that the description of the city is largely drawn from prior scriptural material describing the Israel of God. The figurative use of this language strongly suggests that the description of the city is to some extent a symbolic description of the people of God. The next detail firms up this conclusion.

> And the one who spoke with me had a gold measuring rod to measure the city, and its gates and its wall. And the city is laid out as a square, and its length is as great as the width; and he measured the city with the rod, fifteen hundred miles; its length and width and height are equal. (Rev 21:15–16)

The city is described as a cube, 1,500 miles on a side. The physical difficulties such a structure would present are considerable. The space shuttle orbits the earth in hard vacuum at an altitude of about two hundred miles. The upper side of the city would be much further into space. Since God is planning to remake the earth (21:5), and the general descriptions throughout Scripture imagine a new creation similar to Eden, a literal physical city of this size and shape seems greatly out of place. Eden was a relatively flat area with little high ground, almost certainly not exceeding 2,000 feet above sea level.[10] A literal physical structure of the sort John saw would have large effects on rotational mechanics of the earth, as well as requiring pressurization. Such technical wizardry is not characteristic of the God who created an orderly natural world for man.

John continues with his description by including great quantities of precious stones and gold (21:18–21). These again

---

[10] Ted Noel and Ken Noel, "A Scientific Paradigm for the Genesis Flood," *JATS* 12:1 (Spring 2001): 106–138.

recall the gems on the high priest's breastplate, and the great amount of gold in the temple. But there is no temple in the city, since God and the Lamb are the temple (21:22). In the first temple, the Holy of Holies was twenty cubits wide, long, and high (1 Kgs 6:1–17). The New Jerusalem is exactly the same shape, suggesting perhaps that man will once again be freely able to enter the presence of God (Lev 16:2). Jesus opened up a new way into God's presence (Heb 6:19–20) as our forerunner. In the New Jerusalem we will be able to follow in Christ's footsteps into God's presence. Walking on streets of gold to meet with God evokes the image of the Holy of Holies once more, since that chamber was completely covered with gold (1 Kgs 6:21–22).

> And the city has no need of the sun or of the moon to shine upon it, for the glory of God has illumined it, and its lamp is the Lamb. And the nations shall walk by its light, and the kings of the earth shall bring their glory into it. And in the daytime (for there shall be no night there) its gates shall never be closed. (Rev 21:23–25)

Continuing with the constant use of established imagery, John describes the illumination of the city. This passage is almost a quote from Isaiah's apocalypse.

> "No longer will you have the sun for light by day,
> Nor for brightness will the moon give you light;
> But you will have the LORD for an everlasting light,
> And your God for your glory.
> Your sun will set no more,
> Neither will your moon wane;
> For you will have the LORD for an everlasting light,
> And the days of your mourning will be finished." (Isa 60:19–20)

Obeying the commands of God was described as "walking in the light" as early as David (Ps 56:13), and the expression is used throughout New Testament times (John 8:12; Eph 5:8; 1 John 1:7). Since all saints will be fully in compliance with all the commands of God, they will all walk in the light at all times.

We must be careful at this point not to insist on a purely symbolic understanding of the prophecy. While the language lends itself to that type of interpretation, there is a physical precedent as well. The Israelites were led by God in the form of a pillar of fire at night (Exod 13:21–22; cf. Neh 9:12, 19). This provided enough light so that in effect there was no night. Thus, it is entirely possible that there will not be any physical darkness in the earth made new. But it is impossible on scriptural grounds to be dogmatic. It is more likely that such a condition could exist in the New Jerusalem—as the text specifically refers to "the city"—even if not world wide, whatever that city might look like. Indeed, to John, any large modern city today would seem to be lighted day and night, and given that he would not know about electric lights and generating plants, he might well think God provides our light already.

John's description of the city ends with the presence of the River of Life and the Tree of Life (Rev 22:1–2). The river is a recasting of the river which flowed from Ezekiel's temple (Ezek 47:1–11). This stream was a prophetic description of how the gospel would flow from God out to all peoples.[11] In the New Jerusalem it is recalled as a permanent fixture, showing the fact that the gifts which the people receive in the earth made new are all from God. Similarly, the Tree of Life is described using imagery from the same vision for the same purpose (47:12).

We cannot leave the description of the city without noting a few similarities to Eden. After all, God declared that He would make all things new.

- There was a river that flowed from Eden (Gen 2:10). There will be such a river in the new earth (Rev 22:1).

- Out of the ground grew pleasant trees with all kinds of fruit (Gen 2:9). The tree of life in the New Jerusalem is described similarly (Rev 22:2).

- Sorrow came as a result of the curse of sin (Gen 3:15, 17). The curse will be removed in the new earth (Rev 22:3).

- Adam and Eve walked with God in the garden, but no one can see the face of God now (Exod 33:20). The saints will see the face of God in the New Jerusalem (Rev 22:4).

---

[11] Philip Mauro, *The Hope of Israel* (Sterling, VA: Grace Abounding Ministries, 1988), 132–136.

The Feast of Booths (Tabernacles)

And I saw a new heaven and a new earth; for the first heaven and the first earth passed away, and there is no longer *any* sea. And I saw the holy city, new Jerusalem, coming down out of heaven from God, made ready as a bride adorned for her husband. And I heard a loud voice from the throne, saying, "Behold, the tabernacle of God is among men, and He shall dwell among them, and they shall be His people, and God Himself shall be among them, and He shall wipe away every tear from their eyes; and there shall no longer be *any* death; there shall no longer be *any* mourning, or crying, or pain; the first things have passed away. And He who sits on the throne said, "Behold, I am making all things new." (Rev 21:1–5)

The ultimate destiny of the saints will be in a totally new world. Every old thing will have been removed, including sin and death. The pain that sin brings will also have been abolished. A true paradise of unimaginable wonder will be theirs (1 Cor 2:9). And God will dwell among men. The Greek verb used here, *skenoo*, literally means "to pitch a tent" or "erect a temporary shelter [booth]." And this points us toward the final feast of the Levitical year.

The Feast of Tabernacles will be the only element of the entire Mosaic structure that will have not yet met its ultimate antitype. The tabernacle and its sacrifices were types of Christ and met their antitype at the cross. The spring festivals all met their antitypes in the First Advent. The Feast of Trumpets was typical of the trumpet judgments in Revelation and pointed forward to the greater judgment of the antitypical Day of Atonement in heaven, after which would come the Second Advent.

The Feast of Booths (*Sukkot*) began as a memorial of God's protection in the wilderness (Lev 23:43). It was to be an extended joyful celebration.

'On exactly the fifteenth day of the seventh month, when you have gathered in the crops of the land, you shall celebrate the feast of the LORD for seven days, with a rest on the first day and a rest on the eighth day. Now on the first day you shall take for yourselves the foliage of beautiful trees, palm branches and boughs of leafy trees and willows of the brook; and you shall rejoice before the LORD your God for seven days. (Lev 23:39–40)

The language of the command points out the unique nature of this festival. Booths were to be built of the "foliage of beautiful trees." The booths were then decorated. The Hebrews were to "rejoice" because the typical Feast of Booths prefigured the day when God would again live with man. Zechariah predicted that in the day of the Lord's great victory all nations would celebrate it (Zech 14:16–18). In a premonitory fulfillment during His ministry, Jesus "tabernacled" with men (John 1:14).

The rituals of the seven days of *Sukkot* recalled the specifics of God's protection in the wilderness. The shade protected them from the sun and became a symbol of God's protection in all times. Psalm 91:1 describes God's shadow as protection during the woe trumpets and bowl judgments. Hosea 14:7 declares that those who live in His shadow will be greatly blessed. This also recalls the great pillar of cloud by which God protected and guided the Israelites in the wilderness.

The second ritual of *Sukkot* was the water procession, probably devised long after the Babylonian captivity. A priest would use a golden pitcher to draw water from the pool of Siloam. It was brought with songs of rejoicing to the temple. It would then be poured into a silver basin with a hole in the bottom through which it poured out to the base of the altar. It mixed there with wine poured into another basin. This mix flowed down the rocks into the Kidron Valley, following the path of the river from the temple in Ezekiel 47. This water of life ceremony called to remembrance God's miraculous provision of water from the rock in the wilderness (Exod 17:6; cf. 1 Cor 10:4). Jesus may have claimed to be the fulfillment of this type when he declared Himself to be the "living water" (John 7:37–38).[12]

The third ritual was the illumination of the temple, again probably devised after the Babylonian captivity. This recalled the pillar of fire by night in the wilderness (Exod 13:21–22). This pillar provided a way for the people to follow God day and night (cf. Luke 18:7; Rev 7:15). Giant candlesticks were set up so as to light not only the temple, but the entire city (Edersheim, 225).

---

[12] Samuele Bacchiocchi, *God's Festivals in Scripture and History: Part II: The Fall Festivals* (Berrien Springs, MI: Biblical Perspectives, 1996), 250–254.

Jesus may again have declared that He fulfilled this type when he claimed to be the light of the world (John 8:12).

The feast ended with *Shemini Atzaret*,[13] also called the great Sabbath (Lev 23:36, 39). This day was not properly part of the *Sukkot*, but was instead a concluding feast for the Levitical year. The people had lived in booths for a week. On *Shemini Atzaret* they left the temporary shelters and returned to their permanent homes.

The timing of the Feast of Booths, five days after the judgment of the Day of Atonement, is a perfect fit in the plan of end times that the fall festivals provide. Trumpets issued the announcement of impending judgment. This feast meets its antitype in the trumpets of Revelation 8:6ff. Seven days later the harvest was to be complete (Deut 16:13). Jesus refers to the work of saving souls as the harvest (Matt 9:37–38). Thus, shortly before the final Day of Atonement, all those who choose to be saved will be sealed (Rev 7:1–8).

There were two days between the ingathering of the harvest and Yom Kippur. This time is fulfilled in the first two woe trumpets (Rev 9) making the final call to repentance. Then as the time comes for the Day of Atonement to begin, those who have not humbled themselves will be "cut off" from the camp of the Israel of God (Lev 23:29; cf. 1 Pet 5:6). This separation of the saved and the wicked is the antitype of the division between Egypt and Israel during the plagues (Exod 8:23). The bowl judgments on the wicked are the covenant curses pronounced because the wicked will not come to the temple of God for forgiveness.

At the end of the curses, the Holy of Holies ministry of Christ is seen in the seventh Seal, Trumpet, and Bowl. God's people will then be forever clean and ready to join him. The reaping of the harvest of the earth symbolizes His return for them (Rev 14:14–16; cf. 1 Thes 4:13–17). When they have been removed from the earth, the wicked are killed (Rev 14:17–20; cf.

---

[13] The Hebrew phrase means literally "eighth assembly," but functionally means "the assembly on the eighth day." The words occur in Lev 23:36, though not together. This phrase probably came into use many centuries later. On this day, following the Feast of Booths, came a final "holy convocation" before the people dispersed to their own homes across the land.

Matt 24:37–41). The earth will be turned into a wasteland (Jer 4:23) in which Satan, the scapegoat, is chained for a thousand years (Rev 20:2–3).

When the thousand years is finished, it will be time for the Feast of Booths. Jesus will return to the earth with the saints (Rev 21–22). Satan will make his final attack (Rev 20:9). God will erect His booth over the saints to protect them (Rev 7:15). This protection will continue through the time in which the wicked and Satan are finally destroyed in the lake of fire (Rev 20:13–15) in the antitypical fulfillment of the seven days of the feast. Finally, the fulfillment of *Shemini Atzaret* will take place when the saints leave their temporary dwelling in the city for their permanent homes in the earth made new (Isa 65:21–22). There they will partake of the Marriage Supper of the Lamb.

Just as the spring festivals met their antitypical fulfillment in the First Advent of Christ, the fall festivals will meet their's in the Second Advent of Christ. But more than that, the fall festivals provide a detailed calendar for the time of the end. Every prophecy of God—correctly interpreted—will be fulfilled exactly. No excuses will need to be made. Even more, we must note that the calendar for all saints of God is that prescribed in the Torah. No distinction whatever is made between Jew and Gentile. All the types pointed to Christ. And just as the types were "Jewish," Christ was Jewish. But so are the Gentile members of the church the children of Abraham. We are all members of the Israel of God and heirs of the same promises.

The Wedding Feast of the Lamb

Jesus describes the Kingdom in terms of a wedding (Matt 22:2–14; 25:1–13). The first of these parables develops the idea of a wedding feast to which many are invited, though most decline. Following their refusal, the invitation is extended to everyone, and the hall is filled.

In this parable, Christ outlines the story of the gospel. It is first taken to a select group, the Hebrews. When they decline His invitation, they are "destroyed" (22:7). Then the gospel goes to the entire world. All who receive the invitation and accept the righteousness of Christ are given rewards. But the question arises as to the specific character of the gift represented by the wedding feast. LaHaye states that "The Rapture is identified with all the other end-time events: Judgment Seat of Christ, Marriage Supper of the Lamb . . . [etc.]"[14] In other words, the Futurist Marriage Supper is a single event. He places it in heaven during the fictional seven-year "Great Tribulation" on earth. That means the living Jews wouldn't be there for the banquet.

We earlier saw that the Judgment Seat of Christ is not an event in the heavenly kingdom, but a daily request for grace by saints on earth. The repeated failure of Futurists to carefully examine Scripture again leads them to an incorrect understanding of the Marriage Supper. The original covenant promises to Israel were given in Deuteronomy (Deut 28:1–14; 30:1–20). Isaiah's prophecies promised Israel great blessings after repentance and obedience[15] which were linked with the coming of the Messiah[16] and the gathering of the faithful of dispersed Israel back into the land.[17]

And the LORD of hosts will prepare **a lavish banquet** for all peoples on this mountain;
A banquet of aged wine, choice pieces with marrow,
And refined, aged wine.
And on this mountain He will swallow up the covering which is over all peoples,
Even the veil which is stretched over all nations.
He will swallow up death for all time,
And the Lord GOD will wipe tears away from all faces,
And He will remove the reproach of His people from all the earth;
For the LORD has spoken. (Isa 25:6–8; emphasis added)

This passage clearly identifies the time of this feast as the time when death will have been defeated forever and there will be no more tears. We readily recognize this to be the time after the second death of the wicked. The scene is set on earth, not in

---

14 LaHaye, *Rapture*, 185.
15 Isa 1:19; 9:3; 27:2–6, 12–13; 29:17–24; 30:19–29; 32:1–8; 49:6–13; 51:3; 55:1–2.
16 Isa 9:6–7; 24:23; 11:1–5; 42:1–9; 49:6–13.
17 Isa 24:23; 26:1–4, 15–19; 27:6, 13; 27:6, 13; 35:1–10; 43:5–7; 45:20; 49:8–13, 22–23; 51:11–14; 54:7; 60:4–14.

heaven. Isaiah's earlier oracle against Tyre (Isa 23–27) also symbolically presents the destruction of Satan ("Tyre," 23:18) as banquet fare and "choice attire" for Israel. In both cases the "banquet" is a symbolic representation of the blessings coming after the final destruction of sin (Isa 25:2–12). Isaiah further extends the banquet in time (Isa 65) in a prophecy blessing the repentant remnant with flocks, herds, food, and drink. Those who forsake Yahweh will be hungry, thirsty, put to shame, and slaughtered.

Ezekiel visits this same theme. He describes how the unrighteous will be destroyed (Ezek 34:2–10). The righteous remnant will return to the land, where they will be abundantly fed and blessed by the Messiah himself (34:17–30). These blessings will extend to the righteous worshipers of Yahweh from other nations (47:22–23).

The theme of the Messianic banquet is also found in noncanonical works of the intertestamental era. In these works, as in the prophets, the banquet is not an event, but a description of the rich blessings God will bestow on the faithful after the final defeat of Satan. It is a description of the time after the antitypical *Shemini Atzaret* when the faithful live in the earth made new. Had the Futurists examined the Old Testament sources for New Testament statements, they would have discovered this theme. But preconceived ideas have forced them to overlook the interpretive material God provides for them in Scripture (2 Pet 1:20).

Summary

Every event of the Levitical year and every aspect of the Temple service will have met its antitype when the earth is made new. The elements of the sacrificial system were all acted-out prophecies pointing to the cross and became obsolete the moment Christ died. The spring festivals also met their fulfillments in the First Advent. The fall festivals are meeting their antitypes as this is written. The trumpets are sounding. The final step of the Atonement is coming soon, to be followed immediately by the Second Advent. After the millennium will come the final, never ending banquet.

When the saints return to the earth, Satan will have one last hurrah. In that brief instant, the saved will see first-hand the effect of the choice made by everyone who rejected Christ. And then the end of the wicked will come. Christ will then make all things new, re-creating a paradise which this time will never end. Sin will never again rise because every person will be totally convicted of the goodness of God.

The blessings of plenty in the peaceful new world are described in prophecy as a banquet. John combines the Old Testament descriptions into the term "the marriage supper of the Lamb." This is not, as proposed by Futurists, an event in heaven.[18] Instead, it is much bigger. A banquet in heaven would end, but this feast will be eternal. The richness of it is beyond comprehension (1 Cor 2:9).

The description of the New Jerusalem wraps into one great symbolic picture every hope of the sin-sick heart. These are then painted with a Hebrew brush onto a great canvas of joy. May we all be able to join in that great celebration!

---

[18] One must ask just why Futurists would wish to interpret Scripture in such a constricted manner. They take an unending blessing and effectively shorten it into a black tie dinner.

God's Divine Calendar In The Fall Festivals

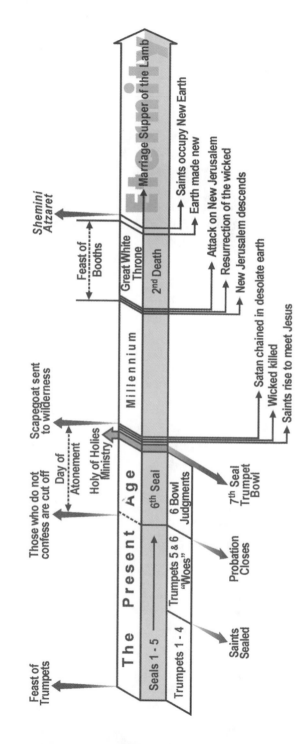

CHAPTER TEN:

THE GREAT DISAPPOINTMENT

For as many as may be the promises of God,
in [Christ] they are yes. (2 Cor 1:20)

In 1816, a New York farmer named William Miller became a Christian. He began to study, using no more sophisticated tools than a King James Bible and a concordance. His studies revealed that the return of Jesus Christ was near. In 1823 he began to discuss his views with friends, and after eight long years they convinced him to begin preaching. So Miller began to give public "lectures."

The message of Miller's lectures was simple. Christ was coming soon. In fact, based on a detailed study of the chronologies in the books of Daniel and Revelation, the Second Advent was due sometime around 1843. Numerous charts were presented to support the date, and a compelling interpretation of Scripture carried the message to the audience.

Miller started with Daniel 8:14, which states that after 2,300 days the sanctuary would be "cleansed" (KJV). He took "cleansing" to be an allusion to the Day of Atonement. The proper starting time of the 2,300 days was determined to be the 457 BC decree of Ezra 7. He concluded that the sanctuary to be cleansed was the earth. The logical extension of this idea was that once the earth was cleansed, all saints would be forever clean, and Jesus would come to claim His own. If his conclusions were correct, there was no time to be lost. Mankind had to commit to the Lord quickly.

Although in 1800 only about seven percent of Americans were church members, Miller preached in an era of religious revival known as the Second Great Awakening. This atmosphere helped his message spread quickly. By early 1843, there were between 300,000 and a million "Second Adventists" from virtually all denominations, eagerly expecting Christ's immediate return.[1] Many of these Millerites carried the word far and wide, and publications made it possible for almost anyone to learn the "truth," whether they could come to meetings or not.

When 1843 passed without the second coming, many were dismayed. But careful study led Miller to accept the idea that his arithmetic had been off by one year. 1844 would bring divine redemption, and it would come on October 22, the Day of Atonement. The message was powerful. Many sold all their possessions to promote the work, convinced that in a very short while they would have no use for them. On October 22 they vainly awaited the divine appearing.

On October 23, the Second Adventists awoke to a great disappointment. In a short time not more than one fifth still believed in Christ's soon return (233). Some returned to their previous churches. Others simply gave up.[2] After all, God had let them down! Why should they care about what the Bible taught when it was so obviously wrong?

The Danger of the Rapture Theory

The secret rapture doctrine has the same potential to destroy lives as the Millerite error. It teaches that the church will be removed from the Earth before tribulation comes. This promises an easy life for wealthy modern Christians. They do not have to worry about hardship, since God will protect them from it! And they are just as deceived as were the Second Adventists. Even today many thousands die each year for their faith.

Our Lord did not promise a deliverance from troubles. In fact, He prophesied that the church would go through terrible

---

[1] George R. Knight, *Millennial Fever* (Boise: Pacific Press, 1993), 213.

[2] It is impossible to determine just how many people fell away from Christianity altogether, since the data to establish this number simply does not exist. However, faced with the apparent failure of God's word, it is almost certain that a substantial number gave up on God. They may have continued to attend church, since the alternative of formal atheism was not generally accepted at that time.

times. They would be worse than anything ever seen on this earth. Many would die, but in His providence, God would cut that time short. What does that mean for a Christian today? We have a lifestyle in the Western World which is beyond the dreams of history. We are "wealthy and have need of nothing" (Rev 3:17). But just as with the church of Laodicea, our security is an illusion. We have become so dependent on ourselves that we are blind to our spiritual poverty. A message telling us we will not have to worry about losing that worldly wealth tickles our ears (2 Tim 4:3). This leads many to accept the theory of the secret rapture. It promises a painless transit from wealth to glory.

Believers in the rapture theory will have a serious decision to make when troubles come. It will be exactly the same decision that faced the Second Adventists. Did God tell the truth in the Bible? If He did, they will ask, why are we experiencing troubles when the Bible said we would be raptured out before the troubles started? And if history is any guide, the vast majority will discard their faith. They will be permanently lost.

With so much at stake, Christians cannot stand idle while their brothers are in danger. Just as our mission requires that we tell others about the gospel, it also demands that we tell them the truths of the Bible on prophetic issues. The simplest place to start is with the passage that LaHaye and Jenkins so terribly misinterpret.

"For the coming of the Son of Man will be just like the days of Noah. For as in those days which were before the flood they were eating and drinking, they were marrying and giving in marriage, until the day that Noah entered the ark, and they did not understand until the flood came and took them all away; so shall the coming of the Son of Man be. Then there shall be two men in the field; one will be taken, and one will be left. Two women will be grinding at the mill; one will be taken, and one will be left." (Matt 24:37–41)

When I ask friends to read this and tell me who is to be taken, not one in five understands Jesus' statement on the first pass. They have been so indoctrinated into the "Left Behind" theory that they cannot see what He actually said. So it becomes necessary to reformulate His statement in a readily understandable way. But before we do this, we need to look at the Hebrew of the flood story.

Genesis 7:23 describes the results of the flood. Every living thing on the land was "blotted out," and only Noah and his family were "left." The Hebrew word for "left" is *sha'ar*, closely related to the words *she'erit* and *she'ar*, which mean "remnant." In other words, only Noah and his family "remained." With this information we may properly paraphrase Jesus' statement.

> When I return, it will be just like Noah's time.
>> Those people kept on living their routine lives until Noah entered the Ark.
>> They did not understand until the flood killed them.
> When I return it will be just like Noah's time.
>> Of two men in the field, one will be killed and the other will remain.
>> Of two women at the mill, one will be killed and the other will remain. (Matt 24:37–41)

To be taken away as people were taken away in the flood is to be killed. Jesus is quite explicit. At his second coming, a remnant will be saved. This remnant will be the group rising to meet him in the air (1 Thes 4:13–17). Those who are not left among this remnant will be killed. Since there are only two groups of people, the saved and the lost, this will leave no one alive on the earth. No other exploration of Scripture is really essential to understand this point. Jesus makes a direct statement LaHaye and Jenkins (like so many other Futurists) contradict in order to maintain their speculations. With this simple bit of study, it is possible to refute the entire secret rapture theory. But simply showing that they are incorrect is a poor way to help out those who have been deluded by the lure of a cheap and easy transit from earth to heaven. We must provide the true outline that Jesus has left for us.

A Key Concept or Two

There are ultimately only two groups of people in view in Scripture: the righteous and the wicked. Heritage has no role in these definitions. God chose the sons of Jacob to be his missionaries. He gave them birthright blessings in the form of his presence. This was manifested as the Shekinah Glory, as well as in miracles and the ministry of prophets. As long as they obeyed, the blessings continued to flow. But eventually those who were evil among this group were so overwhelming in number that God had to completely cut off these birthright blessings. This happened in AD 34, at the end of the seventy weeks of probation.

A remnant who were heirs by faith continued to be blessed. And in this, they carried on the name Israel, since that name had been given to the faithful from the earliest days. The Israel of God continued in an unbroken tradition the work God had given their ancestors in faith. Today we call this group the church, a name which was also applied to the faithful descendants of Jacob in the wilderness. There is no difference between today and then. No group has been substituted for another, as Futurists charge. In fact, the apostolic church was simply the revival of the Mosaic church in the wilderness, as Stephen stated (Acts 7:38).

The attempt to substitute ethnic Jews for Israel is not founded in Scripture, but in a literalistic reading of the Old Testament. Futurists take the Old Testament prophecies that use the name "Israel" and assume that it means ethnic Jews. This is done without an exploration of the use of the name in the Scriptures, and without reading the New Testament. In fact, only if the New Testament is completely ignored can this radical separation between Israel and the church be maintained.

This position is difficult to understand. After all, the New Testament writers are inspired interpreters of the Old Testament and use the Old Testament over a thousand times to support their positions. Jesus never created new doctrine, but always relied on "It is written" to explain his teachings (Luke 24:27, 44). And we are the church that He said he would build up (Matt 16:18).

If the Futurist position is taken at face value, it is the most anti-Semitic teaching that can be imagined. It takes Gentile believers and places them on easy street. No trouble is in their future. Then it takes ethnic Jews and forces them into a tribulation that makes the Nazi Holocaust look like a kindergarten skit. Certainly this cannot be the desire of God for those presented as His "chosen people."

Bible prophecy is Christ-centered (Amos 3:7; John 13:19; 14:29). Thus, we must look for Christ in the focus of every oracle of end times. True Christian exegesis will lead us to Christ. Futurist interpretation forgets this principle and focuses on geopolitical fortune-telling. The utter disregard for Scripture in their discussion of the Seals, Trumpets, and Bowls of the book of Revelation should make this completely clear. And this method should show us that the Futurist approach is not worthy of consideration.

God's Blueprint for End Times

God gave ancient Israel a blueprint for the great controversy between God and Satan. It was presented in the form of acted-out prophecies in the tabernacle and festival calendar. Every part of the tabernacle pointed directly to the ultimate sacrifice that would take away sin. And every part of the festival calendar pointed to the order in which the steps would take place.

The spring festivals were Passover, Firstfruits, and Pentecost. These types were fulfilled in order when Christ died as our Passover. He rose as the Firstfruits from the dead. Then at Pentecost, the feast of the wheat harvest, the first of the harvest of souls were gathered at the great sermon preached by Peter. Thus, the spring festival types all met their antitypes at the First Advent. The first half of the calendar was complete.

But the harvest was not complete. Through the summer, various crops would be raised and harvested. In the same way, the harvest of souls is not complete, and all Christians are called to be workers in the harvest.

Just as ancient Israel apostatized, modern Israel rebels against God. False teachings enter the church, and God is pushed out. This is represented in the Bible as adultery, and the whore of Revelation 17 and 19 is its prophetic image. God is not willing to let these people be lost (2 Pet 3:9), but issues the call for all to "come out of her" (Rev 18:4). This call is issued by means of God's arrows, as seen in the four horsemen of Revelation 6. At the same time, the call to all is made by means of the blowing of trumpets.

The feast of trumpets signaled the nearness of judgment, and this is what the trumpets of Revelation 8 and 9 announce. This call goes to all so that they will know that Yahweh is God, and that time is short. They must come out of spiritual Egypt and Babylon. Throughout this time, Satan is working to keep any more people from accepting salvation. His methods will become more and more devastating, and the cost of faith will seem too great for some as saints are martyred for the glory of God.

Just before the judgment, the harvest will be complete. From this time forward, no saint of God will be harmed. But God will hold the door open a bit longer. Unfortunately, repentance will not come. The time to approach God for forgiveness will end, and those who have rejected Him will have announced their own condemnation. They will be cut off from God and will reap the whirlwind of His wrath. The bowls full of covenant curses will be emptied on their heads.

The final judgment will be made in favor of the saints. The Holy of Holies ministry of the Day of Atonement will cover their sins, and they will be clean. They will become the great harvest taken to heaven, while the wicked are destroyed in the winepress of the wrath of God. Then the scapegoat, Satan, will be chained in the wilderness of the desolate earth for a thousand years.

While in heaven, the saints will review the books. God will reveal completely why he has done what he has done, the strategy he has used in fighting against evil, and he will be judged as to His righteousness in managing the gospel. Then heaven will ring with the verdict "Holy, Holy, Holy, for Thy judgments are righteous and true!" With this complete, God will return to earth with the saints.

As they arrive on the wilderness of earth, Satan will be released from his bondage, and the wicked will be resurrected. They will assault the camp, but Jesus will "erect a booth" over the saints to protect them. And the final feast will meet its antitype. The wicked will be shown the utter depravity of their ways, and then they will be destroyed as the earth becomes a lake of fire to consume them. When Satan and his hosts are similarly destroyed,

God will make all things new. There will be a paradise awaiting every faithful believer.

The saints will then be able to leave their temporary protective booth and return to their home, in fulfillment of the great sabbath of the Feast of Booths. The blessings that follow in the earth made new will be the never-ending Marriage Supper of the Lamb.

Every type will meet its antitype. The divine calendar revealed at Sinai will be followed to the letter. Truly, "For as many as may be the promises of God, in [Christ] they are yes."

A Plea

The true understanding of end times always focuses on the Savior. Certainly we have not exhausted the details of any prophecy. But we have explored the unity of design and purpose which ties the Scriptures into a unified whole. Christ is the center of every part of the word of God. He has provided the way of escape from sin. The cross is the payment, and the prophecies are the roadmap.

Let us fix our eyes on the Savior. He has promised the victory, even though the way today may be rocky. We may even be called upon to give up our lives, but it will all be ultimately for His glory.

The Futurist approach to prophecy is a snare that must be avoided. It tempts a complacent Laodicean church (cf. Rev 3:14-22) with the promise of easy passage. And when hard times come, the great majority may give up their faith rather than face the music. And a great tragedy will overcome them. Such terrible loss is not necessary.

The Bible is understandable for anyone willing to study and allow God to lead. Open the book. Gather whatever tools and helps you can find, and read what God has said. Write down questions. Compare passage with passage, and allow Scripture to interpret itself. Do not accept anyone's representations as truth until they have been fully investigated, not even those in this book. And never take your eyes off of Christ.

Tim LaHaye and Jerry Jenkins may want to be taken, but

I Want To Be Left Behind.

APPENDIX:
THE FATE OF THE WICKED: DO WORDS
MEAN WHAT THEY SAY?[1]

"When *I* use a word," Humpty Dumpty said, in rather a scornful tone, "it means just what I choose it to mean—neither more nor less."

"The question is," said Alice, "whether you *can* make words mean so many different things."

"The question is," said Humpty Dumpty, "which is to be master—that's all."

–Lewis Carroll, *Through the Looking Glass*

Evangelicals have long prided themselves on basing their beliefs on Scripture alone. In fact, however, we may argue *sola scriptura* when disproving the unbiblical beliefs of other denominations, yet when it comes to our own dearly held views, we are not above ignoring biblical evidence that contradicts us. Should Evangelicals ever argue from tradition rather than Scripture, though? Should Evangelicals base their teachings on ambiguous texts viewed by the light of traditional understandings, while ignoring clear texts that point to the opposite conclusion? Who among us would say yes?

It seems to me that like Humpty Dumpty, those arguing for the eternal torment of the wicked often assign arbitrary and contradictory meanings to words already perfectly clear in English, Hebrew, and Greek—words like "destroy," "consume," "dead," and "devoured."[2] It is true that these words, as used in Scripture, may refer to several areas of experience, and it is also true that they are often used metaphorically. However, **when metaphors are used, they always allude to the established meanings of words, not to their opposites.**

---

[1] This appendix was written by Ed Christian, Assistant Professor of English & Bible, Kutztown University of Pennsylvania. This is, essentially, the text of the overhead transparencies used in a talk he gave on this topic at the 2001 annual meeting of the Evangelical Theological Society, held in Colorado Springs. It was originally published in *JATS*, 12:1 (Autumn 2001): 219–224. Copyright © 2001 by Ed Christian; used with permission.

[2] Rather than give instances that cause embarrassment to scholars, I will leave it to readers to consider what they've read and remember such instances. There have been many.

What follows is not a formal paper, but a collection of texts with a few words of commentary. My hope is that they will spark thought, discussion, and study.

What Does "Eternal" Mean?

Eternal Judgment (*krímatos aiōníou*): **Heb 6:2** "of the doctrine of baptisms, of laying on of hands, of resurrection of the dead, and of **eternal judgment**." [The period of **judging** or **judgment** is **limited** in duration, but the **verdict** will **never** be reversed, so the **judgment is eternal.**]

Eternal Redemption (*aiōnían lútrōsin*): **Heb 9:12** "Not with the blood of goats and calves, but with His own blood He entered the Most Holy Place **once for all** having obtained **eternal redemption.**" [Jesus redeemed us "**once for all,**" but the **effect** of that redemption is **eternal.**]

Eternal Salvation (*sōtērias aiōníou*): **Heb 5:9** "And having been perfected, He became the author of **eternal salvation** to all who obey Him." [Jesus saved us by a "**once for all**" act, called salvation, but the **effect** of that salvation is **eternal.**]

Eternal Sin (*aiōníou hamartēmatos*): **Mark 3:29** "but He who blasphemes against the Holy Spirit will never be forgiven, but is guilty of an **eternal sin.**" [The sin occurs during a **finite lifetime**, but its **effect** is eternal.]

Eternal Destruction (*ólethron aiōníon*): **2 Thes 1:9** "These shall be punished with **everlasting destruction** from the presence of the Lord and from the glory of His power." [**Destroyed once**, but the **effect** of that destruction is **eternal.**]

Eternal Punishment (*kólasin aiōníon / zōèn aiōníon*): **Matt 25:46** "And these will go away into **everlasting punishment**, but the righteous into **everlasting life.**" [**Resurrection** to life happens "**in a twinkling of an eye,**" but the **effect** is **eternal. Execution** is an event **completed only by death**, and **it has not occurred unless death results**, but it is an **eternal punishment** because it is **irreversible.**]

Eternal Fire (*puròs aiōníou*): **Jude 7** "as Sodom and Gomorrah, and the cities around them in a similar manner to these, having given themselves over to sexual immorality and gone after strange flesh, are set forth as **an example** [*deigma*, a specimen], **suffering the vengeance of eternal fire.**" [The clear statement here is that Sodom and Gomorrah were destroyed by "**eternal fire,**" yet **that fire is not still burning.** The **effect** of the fire is **permanent**, but the fire burned until the fuel was consumed, then went out. Genesis 19:24–29 tells us the cities were "destroyed," and 2 Pet 2:6 tells us they were turned to "ashes." We may think we know what Jesus means by "eternal fire" in Matt 18:8 and 25:41, but the Bible provides its own answer.][3]

---

[3] The word most frequently used with "eternal" is of course "life." It begins at the resurrection (1 Cor 15:42–43). The resurrection to life is a single event with eternal effects the Bible calls "eternal life." Similarly, "eternal destruction" is a single event with eternal effects the Bible calls "death" (Rom 6:23). "Eternal life" is lived in the presence of the "eternal glory" of the "eternal

What Do the "Worms and Unquenchable Fire" Verses Mean?

Mark 9:44, 46, 48 "**Their worm does not die**, and the **fire is not quenched.**" Jesus is quoting Isa 66:24 "And they shall go forth and look upon the **corpses** [*peger*; corpse/carcass] of the men who have transgressed against Me. For **their worm does not die, and their fire is not quenched.** They shall be an abhorrence to all flesh." [The correct understanding of Jesus' meaning must take into account the following points: 1) One is not a **corpse** until one is **dead**; 2) **Maggots eat only dead flesh, but fire kills maggots**; 3) Thus, this is a mixed metaphor, and literal fulfillment is impossible; 4) But, the metaphors point to **an irreversible process of destruction following death.**]

Ezek 20:47–48 "And say to the forest of the South, 'Hear the word of the LORD! Thus says the Lord GOD: "Behold, **I will kindle a fire in you**, and **it shall devour** every green tree and every dry tree in you; the **blazing flame shall not be quenched**, and all faces from the south to the north shall be scorched by it. All flesh shall see that I, the LORD, have kindled it; **it shall not be quenched.**"'" [This metaphorical language refers to the destruction of Jerusalem and Judah, using the image of "**unquenchable fire**" not to suggest an eternal process, but **a process unstoppable until its end is reached.**]

What Does It Mean to "Die"?

Gen. 7:21–23 And all flesh **died** [*apéthane*] that moved on the earth: . . ."

John 11:26 "'And whoever lives and believes in Me shall **never die** [*apothánē*]. Do you believe this?'" [Logically, thus, those who **do not** believe **will** die at some time, becoming like those who died in the Flood. If they **die**, they are **dead**, and if they are **dead**, they are **not alive**, and if they are **not alive**, they **cannot experience eternal torment. Death does not mean life.**]

What Does "Devoured" Mean?

2 Kings 1:12 "And **fire of God came down from heaven and consumed** [*wattō'kal*[4]/*katéphagen*] him and his fifty." [καὶ κατέβη πῦρ ἐκ τοῦ οὐρανοῦ καὶ κατέφαγεν αὐτὸν]

Rev 20:9 "They went up on the breadth of the earth and surrounded the camp of the saints and the beloved city. And **fire came down from God out of heaven and devoured** [*katéphagen*] them." [καὶ κατέβη πῦρ ἐκ τοῦ οὐρανοῦ καὶ κατέφαγεν αὐτούς] [If in Elijah's day God literally kills the wicked with fire from heaven, and if John then quotes this phrase exactly to

---

God" and the "eternal Spirit" because of God's "eternal purpose." It is interesting that when it refers to God, "eternal" has no implied beginning or end, but "eternal life" begins when we begin sharing in God's own eternality, so for us it is eternal in only one direction. Similarly, the "eternal covenant" was not always in place. Sometimes an "eternal" event has a clear beginning and end, with only the effect being eternal.

[4] From *'ākal*, to "eat up" or "consume."

indicate what he has seen in vision about the fate of the wicked, how can we say they will not be **devoured to death?**]

Isa 24:6 "Therefore the curse has **devoured** [*édetai*, eaten] the earth, and those who dwell in it are desolate. Therefore the inhabitants of the earth are **burned**, and few men are left."

Isa 26:11 ". . . Yes, the fire of Your enemies [*hupenantíous*] shall **devour** [*édetai*, eat] them."

Heb 10:27 ". . . but a certain fearful expectation of **judgment**, and **fiery indignation** which will **devour** [*esthíein*, eat up]the adversaries [*hupenantíous*]." [**What has been devoured or eaten up exists no longer. What has been devoured by fire can no longer be alive.** *Esthio* and *edo* usually refer to eating food, and they are often used metaphorically, but they are **not** metaphors of something **never eaten** but remaining **eternally uneaten**, though **eternally chewed.**]

What Does "Perish" or "Destroyed" Mean?

Matt 22:7 "'But when the king heard about it, he was furious. And he sent out his armies, **destroyed** [*apólesen*] those murderers, and **burned up** their city.'" [Jesus is not revealing that the murderers were **tortured forever**, but that they were **killed. This is the primary meaning of the word.**]

Matt 26:52 "But Jesus said to him, 'Put your sword in its place, for all who take the sword will **perish** [*apolountai*] by the sword.'" ["**Perish**" here means **death**, not some never-ending flaying with a sword throughout eternity.]

Luke 11:51 "'from the blood of Abel to the blood of Zechariah who **perished** [*apoloménou*] between the altar and the temple. Yes, I say to you, it shall be required of this generation.'" [Was Zechariah **still perishing** in Jesus' day, or had he **completed** the process implied by the word and **perished**, as the text says?]

Luke 13:3, 5 "'I tell you, no; but unless you repent you will all likewise **perish** [*apoleísthe*].'" [If the process of perishing **cannot be completed**, then Jesus is wrong about this.]

John 3:16 "'For God so loved the world that He gave His only begotten Son, that whoever believes in Him should not **perish** [*apóletai*] but have everlasting life.'" [If **those who believe do not perish**, then **those who do not believe logically must perish.** But if the wicked suffer everlasting torment in Hell, then they **don't perish**, and they **also** receive **everlasting life.** Thus, both the righteous and the wicked receive **everlasting life**—the difference is only in the nature of that life. **If this were so, then Jesus would be wrong here.**]

2 Pet 3:6 "by which the world that then existed **perished** [*apóleto*], being flooded with water." [That world **died**, along with the people in it, except for Noah and family.]

2 Pet 3:9 "The Lord is not slack concerning His promise, as some count slackness, but is longsuffering toward us, not willing that any should **perish**

[*apolésthai*] but that all should come to repentance." **[Those do not repent perish. If they cannot die, they cannot perish.]**

Rom 6:23 "For the wages of sin is **death** [*thanatos*], but the free gift of God is **eternal life** in Christ Jesus our Lord." **[The wages are not eternal suffering, but death.** If we are not Humpty Dumpty, then **death means death, not life.]**

Luke 17:29 "'but on the day that Lot went out of Sodom it rained fire and brimstone from heaven and **destroyed** [*apōlesen*] them all.'"

Matt 10:29 "'And do not fear those who kill the body but cannot kill the soul. But rather fear Him who is able to **destroy** [*apolésai*] **both soul and body in hell.**'" **[If they live on in eternal torment, they have not been destroyed.]**

How Long Does "Stubble" Burn?

Exod 15:7 [Against Egypt] "'You sent forth Your wrath; It **consumed them like stubble.**'"

Obadiah 16, 18 [Against Edom] "'And **they shall be as though they had never been.** . . . The house of Jacob shall be a **fire,** and the house of Joseph a **flame;** but the house of Esau shall be **stubble;** they [Jacob and Joseph] shall kindle them and **devour** them, and **no survivor shall remain** of the house of Esau,' for the LORD has spoken." [This is metaphorical, but it points to a process leading to **swift and certain death.** It points not to a **never-ending process,** but to a **process that will reach a completion.**]

Isa 47:14 [Against Babylon] "'Behold, they shall be as **stubble,** the **fire shall burn them.**'" [Experience shows us that **stubble does not burn forever,** but **once burned, it cannot be restored,** so the **effect is permanent.** The usage here is metaphorical.]

Nahum 1:9–10 [Day of the Lord] "Affliction will not rise up a second time. For while tangled like thorns, and while drunken like drunkards, they shall be **devoured like stubble fully dried.**" [Whether metaphorical or literal, the **fire burns quickly.** Note that the Old Testament prophets do not distinguish, in their "Day of the Lord" language, between the death of the wicked at Christ's coming, as seen in Revelation, and the punishment of the wicked in Rev 20. They know only the latter, and they see the burning as swift, with the effect permanent.]

What Are "Ashes"?

Mal 4:1, 3 [Day of the Lord] "'For behold, the day is coming, Burning like an oven, And all the proud, yes, **all who do wickedly will be stubble.** And the day which is coming shall **burn them up,**" Says the LORD of hosts, "That will leave them neither root nor branch. . . . **You shall trample the wicked, for they shall be ashes under the soles of your feet** on the day that I do this,' Says the LORD of hosts." [If the wicked burn in eternal conscious torment for all time, **they cannot be ashes** under the soles of the feet of the righteous at any time, much less "on the day" their burning begins. Even if the language is metaphorical, the metaphor points to **death**, not to eternal life apart from God.]

Ezek. 28:18–19 "'By the multitude of your iniquities, in the unrighteousness of your trade you profaned your sanctuaries. Therefore I have brought **fire** from the midst of you; it has **consumed** you, and **I have turned you to ashes** on the earth in the eyes of all who see you. All who know you among the peoples are appalled at you; you have become terrified and **you will cease to be forever.**'" [Some think this is speaking covertly of Satan. Whoever it may be speaking of, **to "cease to be forever" cannot mean to be forever,** even metaphorically. **One cannot be "ashes" until one has "ceased to be." Ashes, formed during combustion, are what is left after something has been burned up.**]

What Does "Slay" Mean?

Isa 65:15 [Day of the Lord] "'For the Lord GOD will **slay** you.'"

Isa 66:15–16 [Day of the Lord] "'For behold, the LORD will come with fire and with His chariots, like a whirlwind, to render His anger with fury, and His rebuke with flames of fire. For by fire and by His sword the LORD will judge all flesh; and **the slain of the LORD shall be many.**'"

Isa 66:24 "'And they shall go forth and look upon the **corpses** of the men who have transgressed against Me. For their worm does not die, and their fire is not quenched. They shall be an abhorrence to all flesh.'" [**One is not slain until one is no longer alive.** If the wicked have been slain by the fire of God, **they cannot still be alive.** They are **corpses. To say that "slain" here does not really mean "slain" but "not slain" is again to imitate Humpty Dumpty.**]

What Does "End" Mean?

Zeph 1:18 [Day of the Lord] "'Neither their silver nor their gold shall be able to deliver them in the day of the LORD's wrath; but the whole land shall be **devoured by the fire** of His jealousy, for He will make **speedy riddance** [NIV, "a sudden end"] of all those who dwell in the land.'"

Matt 13:40 "'As the weeds are pulled up and burned in the fire, so it will be at the end of the age.'" [There can be no "sudden end" of people who suffer eternal conscious torment for all eternity. Either the doctrine is wrong, or the Bible is wrong.]

Any fair discussion of the fate of the wicked should include these verses. Base beliefs on the entire biblical witness, not a few proof texts. Establish the meaning of seemingly clear words by seeing how they are used elsewhere in Scripture. Do not twist the meanings of words so they fit beliefs. Let what is clear explain what is ambiguous. These are basic rules of sound interpretation, but they have been ignored too often in discussions of this topic.

BibleOnly Press

Quick Order Form

Fax orders: (407) 629-2922. Send this form.

Telephone orders: Call (407) 629-2922. Have your credit card ready.

e-mail orders: BOPress@bibleonly.org

Prices for additional copies of:
I WANT TO BE LEFT BEHIND

Copies	Price
1-3	$15.95
4-9	$14.00 each
10-24	$12.00 each
25-99	$10.00 each
100 or more	$8.00 each

Terms:
Check, Money Order, or approved credit card.
Shipping: $4.00 for the first book, and $2.00 for each additional book.

Number of books _____ @ _____   Total   _____._____

Florida residents add 6.5%   _____

Shipping   _____

Total Order   _____

Payment method:
Check
Money Order
Master Card/Visa   Number _____
              Name on Card _____ Expires _____
              Signature _____

BibleOnly Press
1404 Baldwin's Ct, Suite 2
Maitland, FL 32751
(407) 629-2922
http://www.bibleonly.org/press/